RELEASED

Rise Of The Vadim #1

Sydney Raine

For my beautiful daughters, who have spent the past few years becoming the three most amazing young women I've ever had the honor of knowing.

Tracy, Jordan, and Micayla: You Are My World And My Heart.

Released
Prologue

"Please," she begged. "Just leave me alone."

He shook his head, disapproving. His movements were so slow, so menacing. He circled her, but she refused to move a muscle.

"The thought of ever leaving you makes me..." He paused, finishing the round until he was nose to nose with her. "...I can't even imagine. I can't let you go. I won't. Ever."

Refusing to make eye contact with him, she held her ground but didn't respond. There wasn't any point in arguing when she knew he was right.

He wrapped his fingers around her throat, forcing her face upward to look at him. "Someday, you will come to me, and only me. We made a deal and you are mine. Keep that in mind Carina. I have no problem destroying any thing and every one that gets in my way."

Defeated, she brought her green eyes up to meet his harsh brown ones and nodded. Not in agreement, but in understanding. He was right. They made a deal and deals with the devil can't be broken.

"What do I have to do Zandros? I don't want to play games forever."

He smiled, his white teeth gleaming deliciously. His face moved away from hers as he began circling her body again, slowly inhaling, breathing in her innocent essence. "You begged me for freedom. You swore that you would do anything to be free from her."

"But I'm not free," she hesitantly reminded him.

Again, he smiled, facing her and drawing her in one more time. "A deal is a deal. You should've been more specific."

Released

A swift movement startled the girl, nearly knocking her to the ground.

"Back away fiend!" A powerful voice growled from the dark haired stranger. "You have no claim to her."

"But I do," Zandros insisted. "We are betrothed."

"She is not of age. The laws forbid binding a child." The dark haired man grinned, offering an unspoken challenge. "Do you need someone to remind you of our ways? I could easily summon Mother Aiyana?"

Zandros hissed at the mention of the woman's name. "Dear Aniketos, who ever thought it wise to let you out of your cage?" Without another word, he charged at his nemesis, wrapping snakelike arms around him.

Aniketos fought back, pounding against the man, matching each blow with equal force. They spun until the two figures blurred into one massive being.

The girl fell back against the cold wall and watched the melee, bile rising from her stomach. She loathed Zandros, but the thought of him being hurt was almost too much to bear. She could see blood pouring from a gash that ran the length of his cheekbone, a result of Aniketos' fingernails. Zandros howled in pain. The air seemed to vibrate as the bodies shimmered before disappearing.

All of the breath she had been holding came out at once. Carina was confused. The young girl cried out, lost without her constant tormentor.

The alarm woke me up long before I was ready for it. Another night spent tossing and turning had left me so tired, I might as well have not gone to bed at all. I groaned against my pillow and forced myself to get up. It was a big day after all, so I had to get ready and look my best. I barely had enough time to pull on a clean t-shirt and jeans when my bedroom door burst open and a huge bouquet of brightly colored helium balloons floated inside my bedroom.

"Happy birthday!" shouted Sarah, my stunningly gorgeous and perky blonde sister. Her twin brother Spencer followed in her footsteps as they both came in with big smiles. "You're officially a grown up!"

"Don't remind me," I objected playfully. I'd been living with the Matthews family for the past four years. My bio-mom died when I was ten and I'd bounced around the foster system for a while before landing here. It didn't take very long before their family made the huge decision to let me legally change my name from Carina Copeland to Cadi Matthews.

"Did you make your wish yet?" Spencer bounced on my bed like an excited three-year-old. "Like school being cancelled for a week?"

I couldn't help but laugh at him. "No wishes. I've got everything I could possibly want already."

"Well I guess I can take back my gift then?" Sarah grinned.

"No!"

Released

She handed me a very messily wrapped box. I was careful not to rip it to shreds regardless. Nestled inside the reused tissue paper was a handmade, bedazzled frame that held a photo of the three of us. The picture had been taken a few months earlier at our dad's birthday party. "Trio of Terror" had been scrawled across the bottom underneath our goofy faces.

"I love it." I placed it on the table right next to my bed. "Now get out so I can finish getting ready for school."

"You could've just made that wish you know." Spencer gave me a bear hug.

"Probably," I countered. "But think of all the great knowledge you'd miss out on if I did."

Sarah shook her head as she walked out of the door, muttering loud enough that I could hear. "What kind of eighteen-year-old actually likes school this much? It's sick!"

After the door was closed and I could hear their footsteps going down stairs, I sat on the edge of my bed and looked at the photo again. I wasn't lying when I'd said I had everything I could ever wish for. Eight years ago, I couldn't imagine being a part of a family, let alone one as great as the Matthews'.

Eight years ago, I was an only child being dragged from one state to the next, watching my mother destroy our lives one man at a time.

My mind wandered, recalling in perfect clarity the day that wound up changing my whole life.

The day of that freak accident on the expressway…

Released

I could tell you what shade of blue the sky was and how many white puffy clouds I could see.

I remembered the combination of smells that came from my mother's stale cigarettes, the discarded fast food garbage, and the old pine tree air freshener that dangled from the rear view mirror.

I could still feel the cracked leather against my bare leg, not sharp enough to cut my tender skin, but enough to make ugly red welts if I sat there too long.

My mother was yelling at me while driving down the road at a higher speed than was safe. It wasn't out of character for her to do things like that, but a kid never gets used to it. I eventually learned how to tune out the angry words and just listen for the silence that would eventually come.

When the brick hit the windshield, her shrieking was replaced by breaking glass and screams of agony.

Then I smelled spilled gasoline and blood.

I felt heat and fear.

I saw red and death.

I wanted to see the clouds again.

Unconsciousness took me away from the pain and before I woke up, I'd met Zandros for the first time. Of course he was just a dream, but it had seemed so real. Ever since, he'd been a regular visitor in my dreams, like an old friend come to comfort and terrorize me both at the same time.

I loathed my mother. Even now, I don't know that I felt any different. Other than the guilt I feel over hating my own mother. I mean, what kind of monster doesn't love the woman who gave her life? I try not to think about it, but it always seems to bug me on my birthday especially. I pushed her out of my head and reminded myself that I had a mom and a dad now that I adored who loved me right back.

With a smile on my face, I finished getting ready for the day. Brushing out my long auburn waves, I let my hair fall against my slender body. I'd never been a huge fan of the daily task of makeup so I dotted some mascara around my emerald green eyes and applied a light lip-gloss. After grabbing my jacket and backpack, I followed the smell of pancakes and bacon to join the rest of my family for breakfast.

"Cadi." My dad Steven greeted me with me kiss on the forehead. His scruffy stubble scratched my skin in a comforting way. "Do you feel a whole year older this morning?"

I smiled and sat down at the table. "Strangely enough, I only feel a day older than when I was seventeen."

"That means you've got eternal youth, dear." My mom played along with the old joke while piling fresh pancakes onto a plate. "Do you have plans tonight?"

I shook my head while drenching my breakfast with sticky butter maple syrup. "I thought maybe I could invite a few girls over this weekend. We could have a movie party or something."

"Or a pool party if Dad ever gets the dumb pool done," Sarah interjected with a pout.

Eight eyes trained themselves on the man at the same time. He threw his hands up in defense. "Hey! It's not my fault the liner isn't fitting right. I'll call the guy today, I promise."

Released

I smiled warmly at the man I'd grown to love. He was simple, but he'd do anything to give the world to his family. If that meant buying a used pool and fighting with the installation just so that we could have a few wet laughs over the summer, that's what he would do. I knew these were the memories that I'd hold onto forever.

After downing the remaining coffee from his favorite mug, Dad reached deep into his pants pocket. "Heads up." He tossed a shimmering metal object toward me with a sly wink. "Happy birthday, Princess."

"What?" I sat dumbstruck, as I held the up the shiny silver crown that held a single car key. He sauntered out of the house without a backwards glance, but Mom and the twins all grinned at me like they were Cheshire Cats. Unable to contain my excitement, I forgot all about my breakfast and ran outside.

Nestled between my mom's minivan and the car that I'd been sharing with the twins was an older, small-sized, blue SUV. It might have been used, but it looked like it was in pretty good shape. There wasn't a spot of rust on it, which was rare for vehicles around here. A bright red Christmas bow was stuck to the middle of the hood and temporary license plates were affixed to the back.

"It needs work," Mom called out from the back porch. "Dad says straight to school and back home only until he has a chance to get a tune up done on it."

"This is..." I was speechless. No more begging Sarah or Spencer for a turn with the car. No more borrowing the Mommy-Mobile when we all needed to be somewhere different at the same time. No more muffler rattling or loud backfiring when I had to use Dad's old pickup truck. "I don't know what to say!"

I opened the front door and slid into the driver's seat, checking out all of the instruments; sunroof, heated leather seats, and a Bose sound system. I didn't care that it was used. It was mine!

Sarah and Spencer reappeared from the inside of the house carrying their backpacks along with mine. They climbed in and we all waved goodbye to Mom before I pulled out of my parking space and eased down the gravel driveway. With every window open including the sunroof, we blasted the stereo as loud as we could stand it and laughed the entire fifteen-minute ride to school. I pulled onto a side street near the school and found an empty spot to park. Sarah grumbled about forgetting her parking lot pass during the entire two block walk.

Once inside, it took a minute for my eyes to adjust to the harsh artificial lights as I headed to the long hallway filled with lockers. When I opened mine, I found a small white box sitting on the top shelf.

Other than the usual crowd, no one seemed to be watching me as I looked around to find my gift-giver. I took the box down and hesitantly removed the lid to reveal a simple black leather string bracelet. It had two loops tied on each end, held together by a silver ring. Inscribed on the ring was the word *Aeternus*. I was pretty sure the word was Latin, but would have to look it up to be sure of its meaning. There was no note or anything to give me a clue where the gift had come from but I assumed it was from my friends. With a quiet smile, I slipped it onto my wrist and tugged the strings so that it wouldn't fall off.

Released

The bell rang out, warning students that we only had a few minutes to get to class. I quickly grabbed the books I'd need for my morning classes and slammed the locker shut. In a hurry, I ran right into someone as I rounded the corner.

I couldn't stop the blush no matter how badly I wanted to crawl under the floor. I looked up and was instantly drawn into the dark eyes of a guy I'd never seen before. At least, I was pretty sure I'd never seen him. There was no way a six-foot plus, dark haired dream with perfectly chiseled features could've been around this place without everyone in the school knowing.

"I'm so sorry," I gushed, instantly giving myself a mental kick. Could I sound more like a twelve-year-old?

"No problem." He flashed me a slight smile before stepping aside so that I could pass. I moved on to my class but not before making a determined mental note to find out who he was.

Monday mornings were always chaotic, but today seemed worse than normal for some reason. I didn't have one spare moment to think about anything but course work. Lunch break finally offered a much-needed reprieve. Once in the cafeteria, I slid into my usual table, surrounded by all of my friends.

"Happy birthday!" The group chorused in unison. Before I could react, one of the girls produced a chocolate cupcake with a candle in it. As she lit the flame, the group started singing. When I blew it out, a cheer filled the entire room. I didn't have time to properly thank anyone before an unwelcome announcement came bellowing out of the loudspeaker.

Released

"Cadi Matthews to Guidance. Cadi Matthews, please report to the Guidance Office."

Collective taunts rang out while I blushed. Again. Apparently, I was going to spend my eighteenth birthday with a steady red face. I grabbed my sack lunch in one hand, the dessert in my other, and made my way toward the cafeteria exit.

"What did you do?" chided Spencer when I passed his table. I answered by taking an exaggerated bite out of the cupcake before tossing the rest toward him.

Without real concern, I headed toward Dr. Robinson's office. I was involved in several activities at the school so it wasn't unheard of for me to spend extra time in the offices. When I opened the door, I'd expected to see a smile. Instead, a rather grim looking older woman sat behind her desk.

"Have a seat," Dr. Robinson offered.

I sat down nervously. "Is there a problem?" For some reason, my heart was racing; afraid in a way I hadn't been in a very long time.

"Not yet," she replied. "But there could be. I have your last Biology test here and frankly Cadi, you didn't do well. In fact, this is the lowest grade I've ever seen from you."

I swallowed an inward groan. I hated Biology. It wasn't surprising that I didn't ace the test but I was shocked to have done so poorly that Dr. Robinson felt the need to intervene. "How bad is it?"

"Fifty-four percent." She handed me the graded test and I glanced through it. It looked like there was more red ink on the page than black. "I'd hate to see you lose your spot at graduation because of one test score, but it's entirely possible."

Released

"Is there anything I can do?" I was hopeful. After all, I'd spent numerous hours volunteering for things at the school, including covering the guidance secretary's lunch period once a week. Maybe those good deeds could be cashed in for a better grade.

"I talked to Mr. Blackburn this morning and he agreed to allow you a chance to bring this grade up."

It wasn't that I didn't appreciate the help, but this could only mean extra Biology work. I waited with baited breath for my guidance counselor to tell me the details.

"First of all, you are to write an argumentative paper, a debate between Creation and Evolution." I nodded. The years I'd spent on the debate team made that assignment almost too easy. Besides that, composition was one of my strongest subjects. Dr. Robinson continued. "You have one week to retake the exam. Both scores will be taken into consideration when replacing this test score."

I couldn't help but groan out loud. "Thank you," I said despondently. Some birthday present this was. "I'll do my best."

"I know you Cadi. I doubt you would do anything less than your best on this test. What happened?"

"I did study; just not like I should have. I just don't get this stuff sometimes I guess." I wasn't about to mention the fact that my nightmares weren't just frequent, they were every single night. I hadn't slept a wink the night before the test, and barely more than a few hours that whole week.

Dr. Robinson smiled. "I figured as much," she said warmly. "I've arranged a tutor for you. If you'd like to work here after school,

that would be fine. You'll have until five o'clock each night this week.
Otherwise, you can arrange to meet off campus if you'd prefer."

I was not about to invite a stranger to my house. I'd seen
enough TV talk shows warning against such things. "Here will be fine.
Who is the tutor?"

"His name is Nick Vikenti. He's actually new to town and has
enough credits to already graduate. He just needs to put in the few
hours that are left in order to complete state requirements." She took
the test from me and placed it back in my folder. "His transcript from
his previous school speaks volumes. There hasn't been a single year
since fifth grade that he hasn't volunteered as a peer tutor and his GPA
is a 4.48. You can meet him right after school today in Mr. Blackburn's
room."

I nodded in agreement. I really wanted to go straight home
from school. I had homework and chores to finish so that I could
celebrate with my family.

In the long run, good grades were more important than cake.
If I was efficient with my time, I would be able to have both.

It wasn't until the day was almost over that I realized staying
after school meant that Sarah and Spencer didn't have a ride home. I
found my sister waiting by the front door and tossed my keys to her.

"Please be careful and pick me up at five?" I'd already
explained the tutor situation to her and made her promise not to let
Spencer drive.

She just laughed and saluted me as she twirled the key ring on
her finger. "See you at five."

I made my way to the third floor science room. There had never been a subject that I couldn't instantly grasp before, so my frustrations grew every day with Mr. Blackburn's biology class.

Biology is the study of life.

Who can't grasp the basic concept of human life?

Me.

When it came to the cold, clinical sense of it all, I never understood any of it.

Mr. Blackburn's room was open halfway when I finally reached my least favorite place in the building. The new boy that I'd literally run into by my locker this morning was sitting at one of the tables in the middle of the room. His feet were kicked up on the table, balancing on two chair legs. He was so engrossed in whatever book he was reading that he didn't seem to notice me until I reached the table.

"Cadi Matthews." He slowly looked up, his thick, dark hair hanging to his shoulders in soft waves. The deep brown of his eyes was breathtaking and that slight smile crossed his lips again. There was something warm and inviting about the way he looked at me as if we'd known each other our entire lives.

I smiled and offered my hand as I sat down. "Nick Vikenti, right?" I shook his calloused hand.

"The one and only," he laughed confidently. "So where do you want to start?"

I unpacked my backpack and laid out my books on the table in front of me. "I already know what I'm doing for my paper, so I guess I just need to study for the test."

"What topic did Blackburn assign for your paper?"

Released

"Creation versus Evolution." I rolled my eyes. "I'm going to write about Thomas Jefferson's statements regarding the separation of church and state. The United States Supreme Court has ruled that the teaching of creationism in government-funded public schools is unconstitutional. It should be a pretty cut and dry essay once I get all of the ruling cited properly."

Nick sat back into the chair, arms crossed in front of his chest. I didn't know what was the most distracting, the way the muscles and veins in his arms bulged in a seriously unintentionally sexy way or his precarious balancing act. "So you're anti-religion? You don't believe in the Story of Creation?"

I smiled. "I never said that. I'm not anti-anything other than being forced to do something that the law prohibits. Mr. Blackburn cannot legally assign a paper that involves religious theory as one of the base points. As for Creation versus Evolution, I wouldn't know. I wasn't there."

The balancing act was over. All four chair legs hit the floor but his arms remained tightly crossed in front of him. That half grin turned into a definite smirk. "Everyone has an opinion," he pressed. "What's yours?"

I noticed he'd pushed his biology textbook to the side. "I don't really know. What's yours?" I opened my notebook and took out the test study guide, not expecting a real answer from him.

He leaned onto the table, forearms pressing into the wood, fingers twined together. "Oh I definitely believe that there was once a great beginning filled with good and evil." He challenged me with a direct stare. His gaze drew me in, almost hypnotically. It took sheer willpower to break eye contact with him.

"Well, if there is an all-powerful God out there, watching over His sheep, I'm pretty sure He wants me to pass this test." I gave my book a pointed look and pushed it in front of him. "Shall we get started?"

Nick took the cue and instantly switched his focus to the study of genetic biology. By the time an hour had passed, my brain was swarming with RNA, DNA, mutations, and traits. It wasn't String Theory, but it might as well have been. It didn't take long before I realized there was only one solid course of action I could take in order to pass this test.

"I just need to steal a copy of the test so I can memorize the questions and answers." I sighed heavily, shutting my book and running my hands through my hair in frustration.

Nick smiled at me. "You'll get it. It will just take some extra work. What are you doing tonight?"

My heart skipped a beat. Or three. For the first time in my memory, I'd met a boy who actually stirred my interest. I stammered and blushed when I realized that he had actually only offered to study more, not date me. "It's my birthday, so I'm spending the evening with my family. Tomorrow though?"

"I look forward to it." Nick shoved his books into a satchel bag. "And happy birthday."

"Thanks." I blushed again.

Maybe it was his perfect white teeth or glimmering chocolate brown eyes that made my brain tremble nervously.

Released

It could've been his chiseled jawline or soft red lips.

Possibly it was his muscled torso, covered by a t-shirt tight enough to show off regular workout habits without looking like a second skin.

Whatever it was, Nick Vikenti definitely made an impression as I slung my backpack over my shoulder and followed him out of the room.

We walked together through the empty hallways, my footsteps falling silently as the heavy steps of his boots echoed off the walls. I finally broke the silence and thanked him for his help when we reached the front doors. A light spring rain had started while we were studying. I regretted leaving my jacket back in my locker, but Sarah was waving at me like a wild woman. I gave Nick a brief farewell before I ran to my car and jumped into the driver's seat.

Sarah's attention focused on the dark-haired tutor who casually walked through the rain to the student parking lot. "Who. Is. That?"

"Nick Vikenti," I answered nonchalantly. "He's new to town."

"He's freaking hot!" Sarah cheered as she turned to face me. "Is he your tutor? Man, I need to start failing biology!"

I laughed as I pulled away. "You'd have to take biology before you can fail it. He's quiet, but nice."

"Ohmygod, can you introduce me?" Sarah laughed but then suddenly got very serious. "Unless you've got dibs. Please tell me you don't have dibs."

As I turned onto the country road that led to our house, I wondered silently to myself. Did I have dibs? Of course I didn't. I'd just met the guy, but that didn't stop a jealous streak from creeping through my mind.

"I don't have dibs," I said quietly. "He's not the last candy bar or something. Besides, who calls dibs anymore?"

Sarah fell into a fit of giggles as the rain started coming down harder. My grip on the steering wheel turned white-knuckled and our conversation stopped, along with the car, at the next intersection. Before I had a chance to put my foot on the gas, the engine began to sputter. Through the rain, I saw wisps of white smoke come from underneath the hood, steaming up the windshield.

"Oh crap." Sarah looked frightened. "I didn't do anything, I swear."

My frustrations over biology paled in comparison to this. Could my day get any worse? I reached into my bag and pulled out my cell phone to call my dad. There was no answer, so I hung up and turned on the emergency signals. I began to dial Spencer's number only to see the low battery warning flashing. I dialed quickly, praying that the call would go through in time. The phone powered down before my brother could answer.

"Damn it!" I threw my phone back into my bag, angry at the world.

Sarah dug through her purse. "It's on my bed," she groaned after realizing she didn't have her phone with her. "Now what?"

"Now we walk." I shrugged and reached for the door handle.

"What? It's too far!" Sarah protested. "I can't walk that far in these shoes! In the rain!"

Released

"Fine," I replied with a dramatic roll of my eyes. "You wait here. I'll walk to the closest house and call Mom."

"Cadi, the closest house is almost a mile away." Sarah shrank back into her seat at the mere thought of walking in the freezing rain.

"Don't remind me." I grumbled when the cold rain hit my bare arms, making me catch my breath. I cursed myself for not going back to get my jacket, tucked my head down, and began walking in the direction of the nearest farmhouse.

By the time I made it half way there, I couldn't see my car anymore. I was soaked to the bone; my t-shirt and jeans clung to my body like a cold, wet, second skin. My hair literally dripped down my back while I reminded myself that I only had another half mile to go. Not a single car passed the whole time and by the time I finally saw the two-story house set back from the road, my spirit was nearly broken.I picked up my pace, kicking mud up the back of my jeans with every step. I hurried down the gravel driveway toward the front door. After silently begging someone to be home, I took a deep breath and knocked on the door. There was a large picture window that opened up to a large living area. All of the lights were turned off. I didn't see any indication that there was anyone home, but I knocked one more time and prayed someone would come to my rescue. If not, it was at least another mile before I'd get to another house.

Just as I'd turned to walk away, the sound of the door opening frightened me. I jumped back and nearly fell down the front steps.

"Hello?"

The man that stood in the doorway spoke with a soft voice. He looked like he was a few years older than me, but not many. His disheveled blonde hair that curled around his collar momentarily hypnotized me. He wore an unbuttoned flannel shirt, displaying his tall, athletic build, cut abdominal muscles, and deep v that disappeared into his blue jeans. He had the kindest blue eyes that I'd ever seen.

"Um, hi. I'm sorry to bother you." I stammered, struggling to form complete sentences, let alone complete thoughts. I pointed off in the distance. "My car broke down and..."

"You're soaking wet." He interrupted me mid-sentence, unable to ignore my drenched appearance I guessed. In two steps, he had pulled off his shirt and was by my side, wrapping the warm, dry fabric around me.

Dread filled the pit of my stomach when I realized that my shirt must've been completely see-through. I pulled the soft flannel around me tightly, probably turning the brightest shade of red ever found in nature. "Do you have a phone I can use?"

The man shook his head. "I don't, I'm sorry." He wrapped his arm around my shoulders and started to lead me inside his house. A sudden shock of electricity jumped between our arms and he took a step away from me, dropping his arm as he did so. "Let's get you warmed up before you catch your death. I don't have a phone but I can drive you to one."

Warning sirens went off in every part of my brain. No matter how polite his soft spoken, slight English accent sounded, no matter how gentle his ice blue eyes were, there was no way I could go into the house of a stranger. I stopped dead in my tracks, right in the threshold, feeling the warmth of his body leaving my side. He stopped and looked at me, confusion washing over his friendly expression.

"I'm sorry." He apologized again, probably realizing how awkward the situation was. "I can go inside and bring out a blanket if you'd like. Once you're dried a bit, I'll take you home or wherever it is you need to go, okay?"

I warmed at the thought of drying off but I wasn't so sure about getting into a car with him. That was just as dangerous as going into his house. The innocent sparkle in his eyes instantly banished all fears and I was drawn to him, to his hospitality.

"No, that's alright. I'll come in." I followed him into the room that was only lit by the scattered light filtering in through the windows.

"My name is Alexander Maxwell." He held his hand out for a proper greeting. "And you are?"

"Cadi," I replied with a smile and a confident grasp. The second electrical shock traveled up my arm. It was intense, like I'd shuffled my feet across carpet and then touched a doorknob. I watched his fluid, graceful movements as he went to the couch and grabbed a throw blanket.

"Here," he offered, wrapping it around me. "Would you like me to start a fire?" Alexander pointed toward a huge stone fireplace at the end of the room.

I looked over and longed to be in front of a crackling fire. The room was spacious with luxurious hardwood floors, antique furniture, and walls that were made of built-in mahogany shelves. Every nook and cranny was filled with books and relics. There was a lot of money in this room. I remembered things like this from my life before my mother died.

Back then, we lived in the lap of luxury, never wanting for a thing. It was a time I never talked about to anyone, especially my new family. Every time one of them complained about wanting more, I cringed. I'd once known money but not love. Now that I had the love of family, I knew that no amount of money or possessions would be worth giving that up. My thoughts ripped me back to reality.

"Sarah!"

"Excuse me?" Alexander looked at me quizzically.

I pulled the blanket around me even tighter. The thought of going back out into the rain so quickly wasn't a pleasurable one, but I had to get back to Sarah as soon as possible. "My sister is waiting at the car for me to call our mom."

"You have a sister named Sarah... and your name is Cadi?" He spoke aloud as if he were putting a mental puzzle together. "Is your father Steven Matthews?"

I was stunned. "How do you know my dad?"

Alexander looked pained. He went to the adjoining dining room and grabbed another shirt out of a laundry basket that was sitting on the table. "I'm so sorry," he apologized yet again.

"Why are you sorry?" I watched him slip his muscled arms into the shirtsleeves of another plaid flannel shirt. I couldn't help but watch how nimble his fingers were as he fastened each button in a hurry.

"I shouldn't have sold it to him this weekend. That thing never ran right when it got wet." He fished keys out of the front pocket of his jeans and twirled them on his finger. "Let's go save your sister."

I draped the blanket over the back of a chair and followed him. We walked through one of the nicest kitchen I'd ever seen. Stainless steel appliances and black marble countertops made the room look sleek and polished. Not a thing was out of place, not a dirty dish in the sink. I couldn't help but wonder who else lived here. I couldn't imagine a single guy living in a place so pristine.

Released

Alexander opened a door toward the back of the kitchen and led me into a dark room. I couldn't see a thing in front of me, but it sounded like he moved through the space with the same grace he had in the house. The click of a car door opening illuminated the garage. Alexander opened the passenger side door of a Land Rover for me. As I climbed in, he manually pulled open the garage door. After backing out, he had to pull the door back down. By the time he climbed back in, he was just as wet as I was.

"Where is Sarah waiting?"

"We broke down at the Banks intersection." I pointed to the right once we reached the end of his driveway lane.

"Your father said it was a birthday gift for his daughter. So tell me, which one of you is the birthday girl?"

"Me," I replied, leaning back into the leather seat.

"Well happy birthday, Miss Matthews." Alexander reached over and flipped on the seat warmers before pushing the wet hair back out of his face.

His incredible good looks made me self-conscious about my own appearance. Embarrassed, I pulled the borrowed flannel closed and tried to tame my own wet locks. "I appreciate your help Alexander."

"Please, call me Alex," he insisted. "I owe you. I should've known better than to sell it before I fixed it."

"It's okay, don't feel bad. My dad can fix it." It didn't take long before I spotted my disabled car in the distance and pointed. "There she is."

"I have a chain in the back. I'll just hook it up to you and tow you back to your home. At least that way I'll know you made it safely and you're not getting caught in this awful rain again."

I nodded as we pulled up alongside the car. Alex did a careful U-turn and backed up so that his rear bumper was as close to the front of mine as it could be. "You stay put and dry. I'll tell Sarah to come up and wait here with you while I hitch the chain up."

"No way," I insisted as I opened my door. "I can help."

Alex raised an eyebrow. "Then I suppose we'll get done twice as fast," he smiled.

I ran back to my car and opened the driver's door. Grabbing my backpack, I thumped my curious sister on the leg. "Come on, we're going home."

"Who? Is? That?"

"Alex." I looked up at the man as he pulled a heavyweight chain out of the back of his truck. "He's going to tow us home."

"Two hot guys in one day. How can you be so lucky?" Sarah stared at Alex who seemed unaffected by the rain as he untangled the links.

"Stop it," I scolded, hoping to hide my embarrassment. "Go get in his truck. It's warm and dry."

"Okay, but can I have this one and you get the tutor?" Sarah giggled, hopping out into the rain and hurrying to climb into the backseat of the Rover.

I tossed my bag into Alex's truck and headed around to the back to see what help I could offer. Alex was already lying on his back in a muddy puddle, hooking the chain to the frame of my car.

"Can I help?" I had to yell to be heard over the driving rain.

"Grab the end of this and pull it through!"

I saw the chain being pushed through the front and went down to my knees next to him so I could grab it. "Got it!" I hollered as I pulled on the chain.

Alex grabbed ahold of both ends as he slid out from underneath the vehicle. It took everything I had not to laugh at the mud dripping from the back of his head. Now it was my turn to apologize. "I am so sorry." I swiped away a clump of mud from his hair.

"It'll wash," Alex replied quietly, staring intently into my eyes. It felt like he was gazing directly into my soul. After a moment, he tore himself away and turned back to the task at hand; but for those few brief moments, I forgot all about how cold and wet I was. His eyes drew me in just as they had when I'd first seen them and my heart skipped a beat. Heck, maybe they skipped a few beats.

"Can you hold this for a minute please?" He handed me one end of the chain while he forced the other onto a tow hitch. Our hands touched when I passed the chain back to him and that unexplained shock travelled up my arm again. I didn't pull away this time and Alex seemed to ignore it as he continued to connect our vehicles.

When he finished, he straightened up and stood in front of me again. "Cadi Matthews," he laughed softly, stepping closer so that we shared the same space. He tucked a wild strand of hair behind my ear and glanced down at me. "You are soaked to the bone. I may be a gentleman, but I am still a man. Let's button up, shall we?" He reached forward and began buttoning the flannel that had fallen open in the rain; exposing my see-through, wet t-shirt again.

I stood silently, allowing him to touch me in the most intimate way I'd ever been touched by a man before. The fact that it was the exact opposite of sexual made the moment even more intense as he finished, one by one, never taking his eyes off of mine for a moment.

"Now I can take you home so you can get out of this weather."

"I don't mind the rain." I whispered, wishing the moment didn't have to end so soon. Before I'd come to my senses completely, I was back in the front seat of the Rover listening as Sarah gave him directions to our house.

"How come I've never seen you at school Alex?" Sarah was never shy.

"I've graduated," Alex answered matter-of-factly. "Why have I never seen you outside of school, hmm?" He raised a playful eyebrow and grinned at her through the rearview mirror.

"I don't know," Sarah giggled. She giggled. I couldn't believe she giggled. "We drive by your house every day but I never knew anyone lived there."

"I've only recently moved in and haven't had time to explore the area yet." Alex still held that friendly, inviting smile on his face.

My sister was *giggling* at him.

"Well we have a really big farm with lots of hills and trails if you like to go four-wheeling. I'm sure Dad won't mind." Sarah prattled on and on about the joys of country living while I leaned against the door, watching Alex out of the corner of my eye. I didn't want to be too obvious about the fact that I wished we were still out in the rain, far away from Sarah's annoying banter.

"You have a tutor?" Alex's direct question brought my thoughts back to the present.

I blushed, completely unaware that they were talking about me while I daydreamed. "Just some extra help for a test," I muttered, Nick's image dancing through my mind.

"Yeah, you'd think she wasn't even alive with all the troubles she has with basic biology." Sarah laughed.

I almost preferred the giggles.

No, I actually preferred silence.

"It's Advanced Genetics," I defended. "And it's just one chapter." I didn't know why I was being so short with my sister. It wasn't like me at all, so I took a deep breath and forced all of the tension out of my mind.

"No worries," Alex reassured me. "I've never been a fan of the sciences myself. Seems they spend all their time proving why something is improbable rather than opening their minds to the possible."

I softened while Sarah broke in again. "I love your accent. Where are you from?"

Alex glanced in the rear view mirror as he turned down our long farm lane. "Originally just east of Holyhead, Wales in the United Kingdom. I've traveled the world and have lived on nearly every continent since, so I'm afraid all of the accents have become somewhat blended. I can't say which one you're hearing."

"How exciting!" Sarah squealed. "Which place is your favorite?"

"I'd have to say where I am right now." I caught the quick glance he cast in my direction.

"I think Dad would want her car back by the shop." Sarah pointed at a big red barn near their two-story house.

"I'll drop it there then." He pulled to a stop in front of the house. "Here you are. It was lovely to meet you Sarah."

"You too! Thanks for the rescue!" She oozed flirtation as she climbed out of the truck into the rain.

"I'm going to help him get this unhooked," I explained to my sister when she waited for me to get out. Sarah shot me a quick glare before turning to run into the house.

I turned back to Alex. "If you can use my help, I mean."

"You really do like playing in the rain, don't you?" He grinned and put the Rover into gear, proceeding down to Dad's shop.

I searched my mind for a reasonable explanation other than the fact that I just wanted to spend more time with him. "It's just that it's my car, so I should help." I passed it off with a casual shrug.

Alex nodded, accepting my excuse without question. When we pulled in next to the building, I pointed to an area for him to park. Expertly, he pulled the Rover in and gently backed into my car, using the bumpers to push it into position before getting out. I joined him and we worked together, quickly getting the chains unhitched and back into his Rover.

He looked down at our muddied hands. "I don't suppose there is a wash sink in there?"

I nodded and led him into my father's workshop. It was dusty, cluttered, and smelled like years of old grease covered everything. We passed through the front part of the building that was filled with rickety metal shelves stuffed full of spare parts and various junk before entering a larger room where Dad worked on his trucks and tractors when they broke down. Toward the back corner was an old washbasin sitting under an antique pump well.

"It's not much, but it works." I pumped the ice-cold water out and it splashed into the basin.

Alex rubbed the orange scented soap on his hands and stuck them under the water, grabbing my hands in the process. This time when we touched, the shock was so mild I barely noticed it. Very gently, he began washing my hands off, making sure to remove every trace of mud before stopping.

"I'd like to see you again, if that would be possible," Alex said before releasing my hands.

I nodded. "I'd like that." I replied with a warm smile.

"You'd like what?" My dad's voice echoed through the barn as he walked into the room.

"Mr. Matthews." Alex greeted my dad with a firm handshake. "It is good to see you again. I was just asking your daughter if she would like to go to dinner with me sometime; with your permission of course."

Dad arched an eyebrow in my direction. "You were, huh? And would my daughter like it if I said yes?" He watched me nod before agreeing. "Fine, but not on a school night. So what happened to the car?"

"It's possible that the spark plug wires have gone bad," Alex answered. I groaned inwardly as the "shop talk" started. Other than how to drive them and put gas in them, I was clueless when it came to car repair or maintenance, so I excused myself as soon as the rain let up and went back to the house.

By the time Dad came in, I'd already showered and put on dry clothes. When I heard him introducing Alex to my mother, I was glad I'd put on a sundress instead of sweatpants. I heard him climbing the creaky old stairs and held my door open, smiling as he came in.

Alex glanced around the room quickly. "I shouldn't be in here," he said nervously. "I just wanted to say goodbye."

I nodded. "Thank you again."

"I meant it when I asked your father if I could take you to dinner sometime. Would you like to go?"

"I'm free this weekend," I nodded. "Wait, not Saturday. I'm having a little birthday party, if we get the pool installation done that is."

"Maybe I can help with that," Alex offered. "I can be a bit handy sometimes."

I couldn't help but grin at him. "You travel the world, fix cars, rescue damsels in distress and now you fix pools. Is there anything you don't do Alexander Maxwell?"

"I do a lot of things," he agreed. "But one thing I don't do is spend time in a young lady's private rooms without supervision."

My face turned red hot. Again. "Yeah, that's not exactly something I'm in the habit of doing either. Hanging out in young ladies' rooms I mean." I tried to laugh off my embarrassment. "Friday night then?"

Alex nodded and took my hand in his. Once again, the tingle traveled up my arm, now more of a thrill than a shock. He lightly brushed his lips across my knuckles, bid me farewell, and retreated down the stairs.

I watched out the window as the taillights of his Rover disappeared into the distance. Sighing deeply, I fell back onto my bed and began playing with the new bracelet wrapped around my wrist. The water from the rain and my shower had tightened the leather straps so that it was too snug to slip off. At least it wasn't too tight, I conceded, spinning it around as I wondered where it could have come from.

In a daydream, I played out a scenario where Alex presented me with the small white box. Just as I opened it, Alex's face morphed into Nick. Now the dark haired boy stood before my mind and I smiled longingly. My mother's call for dinner snapped me back to reality and I joined my noisy family in the dining room.

By the time the cake had been cut and all of the dishes were cleared, I was well past ready to go to sleep. It had been a very long and eventful day, capped off by my sister's relentless teasing about the two boys I'd met that day. Of course, that only led to jokes from Spencer and endless questions from my mother. Dad, on the other hand, stayed quiet, occasionally smirking at some of the jabs but never making fun at my expense.

Just as I was finally climbing into bed, Dad popped his head into my room. "So Alex, huh? Wanna tell me about him?"

I shrugged. "I would if I could. Other than the fact that he rescued me in the rain today, I don't really know much."

Dad nodded; keeping whatever opinion he had to himself while he stood in my doorway. "How old is he?"

"I don't know. I didn't think to ask?" Great, I thought. With my luck, Alex would end up being too old and Dad would change his mind about our date.

"Well," he hesitated. "Find out. I hope you had a good birthday. I just wish it would've happened a few years from now."

"What? Why?"

"Just wish I had a few more years before you were all grown up." His eyes were wetter than normal and there was a slight quiver to his stubbly chin when he spoke.

I climbed out of bed and went to hug him. "I'm never going to be too grown up to need you to be my Dad."

"Good." He patted me on the back a few times and pulled himself away before the moment could get too emotional. "Get some sleep."

I flipped off the light and closed the door behind him. I climbed back into bed and pulled my blankets up around me, wishing away the chill that suddenly washed through my room. Sleep came quickly, and for that, I was grateful.

By the time morning finally came, I was more annoyed than grateful for that sleep. Not a single hour passed that I didn't wake up either too hot to be covered up, or so cold I felt like I was freezing to death. The only thing that offered me any comfort was the fact that my nightly dream visit from Zandros didn't happen. By the time I'd sluggishly moved through the motions of getting ready for school, Sarah and Spencer were already out the door and waiting impatiently in their car.

So much for having my own transportation, I thought glumly from the backseat. At least the morning sun had burned away most of the mud puddles from yesterday's rain already.

Spencer and Sarah sang along to the music pumping loudly from the radio while I cowered in the backseat, trying to ignore the pounding headache that was beating along with the bass. Maybe I was sick from the rain. If so, it would be the first time I could remember being sick in a long time.

In fact, I couldn't think of a single time I'd ever suffered from the flu or even a cold in my whole life.

The headache got worse throughout the day. Several times, I thought I was going to throw up because of it. Right before last hour started, I found myself in the bathroom near my locker, emptying the contents of my stomach. After splashing water in my face, I shuffled into the hallway, determined to endure the rest of the day.

"We have a bad habit of running into each other, don't we?" Nick joked as I bounced right into his chest. He took a step back and looked at me from head to toe. I knew it was easy to see that I was in bad shape. My hair was frizzy and my clothes were wrinkled. Dark circles formed under my puffy eyes and my normally creamy skin was looking very sallow. "Are you okay?" he asked.

"I'm fine, I promise." I tried to conjure up a smile. I didn't really feel like being friendly, but that wasn't his fault. Besides, his presence actually made me perk up a little bit. "I think I might be coming down with something, so if you don't want to be around me, I won't blame you."

"Do you want to reschedule?"

There was so much concern in his tone, I felt bad for making him worry. His face was just so lovely to look at, I didn't want to reschedule at all, no matter how bad I felt. It was the only bright spot in my day. "It's up to you, really."

The corner of his mouth turned up in a playful smirk. "Good. Then I'll see you in an hour." He winked before heading down the hallway toward his last class.

I watched him walk away slowly. How could I have let him fall away from my mind so easily yesterday? Alex's face danced behind my eyes for a moment and I remembered instantly. Yes, Nick was lovely to look at, and even made me forget my other senses for a minute. But Alex was... I wasn't sure about Alex yet. I sure as hell couldn't wait to explore both mysteries.

What.

The.

Heck.

What was happening to me?

I went to bed a levelheaded seventeen year old that focused on my studies, family, and friends. I never paid attention to boys. Now, in just one day, I couldn't keep my mind off of them. Well, two of them specifically. I made my way down the long hallway to my last class, shaking my head at my inner dialogue.

On the way, I couldn't help but notice that several boys were watching me. Not like normal, just shooting casual glances or friendly looks my way. Today it seemed lecherous and gross. It must've just been my imagination though, because I knew I looked like complete crap.

There was no time to contemplate the strange new interests as my Composition teacher was discussing our final thesis themes. After class was over, Mr. Garrey stopped me before I could leave the room.

"Are you feeling alright, Miss Matthews?" he asked.

"I'm fine, just a little tired." I shifted my heavy book bag from one shoulder to the other.

"You seemed very distracted in class today. Is there anything I can help with?" He sat down on the edge of his desk right in front of me, his hand clasped in his lap.

"How about an automatic A on my paper and I don't have to write it?" I joked.

Mr. Garrey seemed nonplussed. "I'm sure that can be arranged." He replied with a weird tone in his voice. "After all, you've scored nothing less in my class all year."

I couldn't help but feel the creep factor wash over me. "In return for...?" I let the question dangle in the air unfinished. Plenty of rumors had flown through the school about inappropriate behaviors between students and teachers, but I'd never heard any mentioning my Comp teacher. While I waited for his reply, I almost threw up again.

Mr. Garrey looked completely lost. "I thought you weren't feeling well? It's safe to assume you'd get a good grade anyway, so why exhaust yourself further by writing an unnecessary paper?" He smiled brightly and stood up. With a light hand on my shoulder, he led me toward the door. "Besides, I'll never complain about one less paper to grade," he laughed.

I studied him carefully. He really wanted nothing in return. Weird. "Thanks," I muttered.

"My pleasure. If you ever need anything, you just let me know. Feel better!" His broad grin didn't falter as I left the room and made my way to the science lab.

Nick was reading his book again, his feet propped up on the table, when I walked in.

"Sorry I'm late." I took the seat across from him.

"Not a problem. Feeling better?" He kicked his feet to the floor and put his book away. "Doesn't look like it."

I managed a slight smile. "I'm fine, I told you already. Ready to quiz me?"

Nick grinned and leaned forward onto his elbows. "Depends. Did you study at all last night? Because you look like you celebrated that birthday a bit too much."

I had no defense. It wasn't that I'd celebrated too much, but by the time everything else happened, I actually didn't study at all. "My car broke down on the way home last night. It was a long walk in the rain to find help. I think I caught a cold or something. And no, I didn't study," I admitted. "It wasn't because of my birthday though. It was just a really long day."

Nick laughed and opened his satchel. "I brought you a belated birthday present." He pulled out a box that reminded me of my mom's recipe holder and handed it to me.

I opened it and found it filled with flashcards. Flipping through them, I saw every term and miniature chart I'd seen in my textbook this past semester. "This must've taken you hours! Thank you."

"All night actually." He grabbed the box and pulled out half of the cards. Without pause he began drilling me, making three piles as he went; answers I knew, ones I guessed correctly, and ones I was clueless about. By the time our hour was up, the clueless pile was still twice as tall as the other two combined.

"Don't worry," Nick smiled. "I'll try to come up with something more brilliant tonight. You take these and go through them again if you have time tonight."

I nodded as we gathered up our belongings and headed toward the door. "Thanks again. I really do appreciate your help," I said. Maybe instead of studying I should casually joke about another A from Mr. Blackburn just like my Comp teacher agreed to. I almost laughed out loud at my private joke, but kept it inside as we left the room together.

"I told your sister I could bring you home today instead of her having to drive back into town. I hope that's okay?" We'd reached the front door and I was looking for Sarah.

My stomach jumped in excitement.

Just as I was about to accept his offer, the familiar sight of a shiny black Rover pulled up in front of the building.

"It looks like I have a ride." I watched Alex hop out and come around to open the passenger door. He leaned against the truck and stuffed his hands in the front pockets of his jeans.

Nick's eyes focused on the new arrival and squinted into a glare. "Okay, no problem," he forced out. "What are you doing Friday night?"

I had a date Friday... "I'm having a birthday party on Saturday. Do you want to come?" I tried to sound casual, but I was silently praying he would say yes.

"Sure. What time?"

"Five-ish? Come whenever. Oh! We might be swimming, so bring trunks if you want. I'll see you tomorrow!"

I didn't wait to hear a goodbye before going outside to join Alex in his truck. Without a word, I climbed in and let him close the door for me. I noticed him flash an odd look toward Nick before getting in himself.

Triumph?

3

"I take it that's the tutor?" Alex asked as he pulled out of the parking lot.

I nodded. "Nick."

"He's very enamored with you." The friendly look on his face was still there, but the line of his mouth drew tighter as he spoke.

"Enamored? I don't think so." Suddenly embarrassed by my haggard appearance, I began to regret Alex's surprise ride home. "What are you doing here?"

"I figured it was my fault you were without transportation, so the least I could do was come and pick you up."

"Oh." I didn't know what to say. "Nick was going to bring me home. It's no big deal, but thanks."

"And now I'm even happier that I decided to come."

He didn't say anything else for the next fifteen minutes that it took for us to pull onto my farm lane. Finally, I took a deep breath and broke the silence. "Did I do something to make you mad?"

Alex looked startled. "No, have I done something to make you think so?"

"Why haven't you talked to me the whole ride home then?"

He slowed the truck down and looked me in the eye. "I don't like the company you keep."

My emotions riled. "You don't even really know me, so the subject of your approval is irrelevant."

Released

He stopped the truck in the middle of the gravel lane, tires suddenly halting. "Again, I apologize for my arrogance."

I nodded reluctant acceptance. Alex was strange. I was inexplicably drawn to him, but the same warning bells that screamed at me not to go into his house alone were sounding off again. "It's fine, just don't act like that."

"Agreed." He smiled and I relaxed again. "I have a birthday surprise waiting at your home for you."

I gave him a quizzical look. "Steven was telling me about the problems he's had with the pool installers and you'd mentioned wanting to have a party for your friends this weekend, so..." He put the truck into gear and drove the last eighth of a mile until we pulled up in front of my house. Taking up most of the side yard was a huge above ground pool, completely finished. "You did this?" I was shocked. My dad had been fighting with the installation guy for weeks and nothing had ever gotten done. Alex had less than a day and the pool was finished. "This is amazing!"

"Actually, I didn't. I thought I might need a phone, in case someone ever got stranded and needed to make a phone call, so I went and got one. After that, I used my new phone to call someone who knew how to get it done right away." He smiled proudly and pointed toward the blue monstrosity. "Looks like Sarah enjoys it as well."

I looked and saw my sister floating on a blow-up raft. If the sun was out and it wasn't freezing, that girl was always working on her tan. If it was too cold, then Sarah spent most of her babysitting money on a tanning package at the local salon. "This is too much! Thank you!" I quickly turned in my seat and wrapped my arms around him in an awkward hug. The electric shock was more intense today than before and I recoiled quickly, gasping for breath.

"I'm sorry," Alex reddened, getting out of the truck right away. I was still trying to catch my breath as he opened the door for me. "I should go."

"What just happened?" I couldn't even think about moving, the shock was so frightening.

"Maybe the air is really dry now that the storms have moved through," he offered feebly.

I shook my head, refusing to budge. I finally gathered my senses, grabbed my bag, and slid out so that I was standing face to face with him. "That's a load of crap, and you know it." I hushed my voice and quickly looked to make sure my sister wasn't within earshot. "Every time I touch you it happens. Why?"

Alex looked genuinely pained. "I'm sorry, I can't give you any answers." His words were hot on my face, so close to me that I could hear him breathe.

"I don't believe you," I whispered. Fear filled my gut.

"I have to go." Alex didn't wait for a reply before he pulled away from me and got back into his truck. I was still trying to calm my breath and make sense of things by the time he was halfway down the road.

I didn't even remember going into the house but found myself sitting at the dining room table thumbing through the flashcards. It didn't even register that Mom and Dad had come home and were now outside with Sarah and Spencer, excited about the new pool. I ignored the growl in my stomach and the ache that was pounding in my head.

I gave up studying for the night and headed to my room. Slipping into the shower, I leaned against the wall and let the hot water stream down my body until it started to cool. Only then did I quickly wash my hair and scrub myself clean. Wrapped in a huge towel, I shivered as I went back to my bedroom.

Odd.

The weather had become so warm that Dad had talked about turning on the air conditioner already even though it was only the middle of May. I pulled on a pair of warm sweats and a t-shirt before climbing into bed. Shivering, I pulled the blanket up over my body. My joints ached and I was stiff and uncomfortable. Throwing the blanket off, I climbed out of bed and padded back to the bathroom to find some Tylenol. I grabbed the bottle and a thermometer, went back to my room and flopped on the bed. It took every ounce of strength I had to open the bottle, but finally managed to swallow two pills before sticking the thermometer in my mouth. After a minute, the contraption beeped and I looked at the digital read out.

"Mom!" I yelled and started heading down the stairs. "Mom?"

"In the kitchen," she replied.

I could smell pasta sauce bubbling on the stove and it turned my stomach. "What's the matter?"

"Do you have another thermometer? This one is broken." I pouted and sat down at the breakfast bar.

"You look awful." Mom took one look at me and removed the pan off the burner. "What does that say?"

"It says one hundred five point three." I laid my head on the countertop. I felt like crap, but one hundred and five? I didn't feel that bad!

"Oh my goodness!" Mom rushed over to put her hands on my forehead. "You are burning up." She let go and hurried to the back door. "Steven! We need to take her to the emergency room."

"What's wrong?" Dad dashed inside, came over to me, and started to pick me up like a small child out of sheer panic.

"I can walk," I protested, insisting he put me down on my own feet. "It's not that bad. The thermometer is broken."

"It says over one oh five," Mom explained.

"Mom, if my temperature was that high I wouldn't be conscious." My protest seemed to make sense to Dad, but Mom wasn't convinced.

"Fine, I'll go get the one out of our bathroom and we'll check it again. If it's high, you're going. Deal?"

I agreed just to shut the woman up. In the few minutes that it took her to return, Dad had given me a glass of cold water, which he had me drink quickly. The thermometer read only one hundred two point six when she took my temperature again.

"No hospital, but no school either," Mom ordered. "Go to bed and I'll be up to check on you in a bit."

I padded back up the stairs to my room. Flopping on the bed, I didn't even bother to get under the covers. Sleep came quickly, taking the aches and pains away. When I woke up, the fever was gone and I was cold.

So cold.

"Here," Zandros offered me a silken shawl, wrapping it around my body that was covered in the sheerest silk gown. "I will warm you."

His breath was hot against my cool skin as his lips brushed across my collarbone ever so lightly. Chills ran down my spine. "You aren't real. I'm sick and hallucinating."

I leaned back against his strong chest, feeling his heartbeat, and prayed that I was right. I didn't have the strength to fight with him tonight.

"Does it feel like I'm not real?" He ran his fingertips down the length of my arms, stopping once he reached the bracelet on my wrist. "Are you still cold?"

I could feel the intense heat emanating from his body and couldn't deny that I was feeling better. He stepped away, catching me by the arms as I fell backward against the voided space.

Zandros moved to face me, cupped my chin in his hand, and forced my face up to look at him. "The time has come sweet Carina." He smiled seductively and bent down as if to kiss me.

"No." I turned away from him. "My name is Cadi now. Carina is gone, she's dead."

Zandros' face flashed with fury. "I won't be denied."

"Please Zandros, please." I begged, tears flowing down my face. "I can't..."

"You have no choice. You gave me your word long ago and you won't leave me now."

My body felt heavy and I slumped forward a bit. "I was too young to know. I don't want to leave you but I'm not ready yet. Please, not yet." Looking at him directly, my resolve waned a bit. The ice blue *coldness of his eyes pooled like rain in front of me. "Give me more time. I'm not done yet."*

"Not done with what? You are no longer a child in every regard but one." His fingers snaked down my throat, tracing the curve of my cleavage before retreating to my face. I shook with fear.

"Zandros, please." My fingertips wrapped around his hand, tears pooling in my eyes. "I'm not ready... for that... yet."

He took a deep breath and loosened his hold on my arm. "I am no monster Carina. Don't make me become one."

I took a deep breath and steadied my nerves. "Give me more time. One year, and then I'll go with you. I'll do whatever you want without resisting," I bargained.

Zandros released me completely, leaving me weak. I leaned against a wall that suddenly appeared out of nowhere. He paced in front of me, considering my offer. Finally, he stopped and grabbed me roughly. "One month, not one moment more. At that time, you will not hesitate to fulfill your end of our deal."

I would have agreed to anything if it meant I had more time. He moved so quickly that he was standing in front of me, shaking me as he spoke. "Do not forget. You belong to me." My stomach lurched and my body shook in fear as he peppered light kisses along my jawline. "Mine," he whispered before disappearing.

Left alone, I slid down the wall, wrapping my arms around my knees and sobbed.

The beams of sunlight warmed my skin as I stretched myself awake. Somehow, in the middle of the night, I'd stripped off my sweatpants and replaced them with a light sheet draped across my body. I glanced at the clock and saw that it was nearly ten in the morning. That meant no one else would be home.

Slowly crawling out of bed, I moaned as each of my joints popped and cracked. I still felt like I had a slight fever, but nothing a few more Tylenol couldn't take care of. After grabbing the bottle off of my nightstand, I made my way downstairs to get breakfast. My stomach was empty and growled a loud complaint.

I scanned the cabinets and the refrigerator, nothing catching my interest, so I decided on some crackers and a soda. Settling in on the couch, I turned on the TV and started flipping through the channels. There wasn't anything terribly fascinating, just old reruns of shows I never wanted to watch the first time they were on. Frustrated, I turned off the TV and looked outside at the pool.

Maybe I could swim for a bit and then study.

That sounded like the best idea ever. I jumped up and headed to my room to get my suit. I pulled on the light blue boy shorts and bikini top and noticed how much they had shrunk in the two months since we'd gone on vacation to Florida. The shorts were snug on me, as if I'd developed curves overnight. The top was at least a cup size too small. I would definitely have to go get a new suit before Saturday.

Climbing into the pool, I squinted against the bright sun. The water was cold, but felt good once I dove in and got completely wet. I swam back and forth a few times and flew through the water gracefully. Climbing out, I went back to the porch and shivered against the cool breeze on my skin. I pulled the lounge chair into the sun, settled back, and closed my eyes to soak in all the warmth the day had to offer.

Released

Footsteps woke me and I fought to focus my eyes as the shadow loomed over me, blocking out the sun. Alex stood at the end of the chair with a pained expression. A lazy smile spread across my face as I watched him unbutton his shirt. My thoughts were all jumbled, but they all centered on the same thing.

"Well this is a nice surprise," I cooed, stretching like a seductive kitten.

"Damn it Cadi," he scolded, pulling the shirt off. "Cover yourself!" He came to the top of the chair and roughly yanked me to a sitting position before wrapping it around my form.

"Wha...?" I couldn't even form the words to fit the confusion I was feeling. It was as if I was drunk and couldn't think clearly.

He sat down on the edge of the chair and began doing up the buttons for me. "Some things are a gift, not to be shared with the whole world."

I shook my head, clearing some of the haze. "I thought I was alone," I defended myself. "Why are you here?"

"I've been working on your car. Your father gave me permission to use his shop." He gently pulled my wet hair out of the collar of the shirt, letting it cascade down my back in thick, damp waves.

"That doesn't explain why you're here, on my front porch."

"I saw you..." He hesitated, standing up and leaning against the railing with his arms crossed against his bare chest. "You should go inside before your sunburn gets worse."

I looked down at the pink on my legs and arms. Great. Nothing like getting burnt the first hour I spent outside in forever.

Begrudgingly, I walked inside the house, leaving the door open behind me as a silent invitation for him to join me. Alex followed after a moment but stayed just inside the door. I went into the bathroom and found a bottle of aloe lotion. I quickly rubbed it on my arms and chest, then applied a thin layer to my legs and came back out of the bathroom. "Do you mind helping me with my back?"

I almost laughed at the expression on his face. I could tell he wasn't sure if he should run away or just melt into a puddle right there on the spot. "It's not like you haven't seen me in my bathing suit already. It won't kill you," I teased.

"Fine," he said gruffly, taking the bottle and squeezing lotion some into his hands.

I turned my back to him and unbuttoned just enough to slide the shirt down to expose my back. The aloe was cold, but was instantly heated by the shock that always came with his touch. I didn't pull away. Instead, I let the electricity course through my skin, warming every muscle as his soft but calloused hands applied the aloe lotion.

"That feels good," I said as I leaned into his touch. I could feel his body relax a bit as he moved his face closer to the nape of my neck, drawing in a deep breath.

"You are trying to bewitch me," he whispered, seemingly intoxicated by my very presence.

I slowly turned so that there was nothing between us but the thin fabric of my bathing suit top. His hands were still absently rubbing my bare shoulders. "Bewitch you? Would it take a witch's spell Alexander?"

Released

Remember your duties.

I heard the thought as clearly as if he'd spoken it.

My brow creased as I backed away from his grasp. The pained look returned, as if I'd just taken away his favorite toy. Pulling the shirt back up onto my shoulders, I went into the kitchen without another word. Opening the fridge again, I pulled out a bowl of pasta left over from dinner last night. "Are you hungry?" I called into the other room.

"No thank you," Alex replied politely. He'd moved into the doorway of the kitchen now and was leaning against the threshold, defensively positioned with his arms crossed in front of himself again.

What happened to the Cadi I met only two days ago?

"What do you mean?" I asked, heaping a huge pile of spaghetti onto a plate and put it in the microwave.

"Excuse me?"

"What happened to me? What did you mean by that?" I put the fork in my mouth, licking off the sauce remnants. The taste soured in my mouth and I fought back a gag.

Alex stared at me intensely. *She can hear my thoughts.* Panic ran through his mind making it impossible for me to follow along.

Had I answered a question he hadn't voiced aloud? I dropped the fork on the floor, stunned. "You should go."

Alex said nothing, just pushed away from the wall and walked quietly out the front door.

The microwave beeped, making me jump in the empty, quiet house. I ignored the food I'd prepared, ran up the stairs into my room, and slammed the door. Standing in front of the mirror, I let the shirt drop to the floor and began studying my appearance even closer.

My hips were rounder.

My breasts were larger.

My hair was thicker, shinier; lips redder and fuller than just yesterday.

My eyelashes had grown longer and more lush overnight, making it look like I had on mascara even though I didn't.

No longer did I have the slender body of an awkward teenage girl. Overnight, I had become a curvy woman.

For the first time in my life, I thought I was beautiful. I'd never felt ugly, but never more than ordinary. I could see the changes Alex had noticed. I changed out of my bikini and pulled on several outfits, discarding them all for being too snug, before settling on a pair of Spencer's sweatpants and Alex's button down shirt. They were baggy and too big, which suited me just fine. If only I had answers about what was happening.

He may not have said it out loud, but I'd heard his thoughts and hoped Alex would know something. Immediately, I regretted sending him away. I grabbed my tennis shoes and laced them up, determined to get some answers from him. After taking my bicycle down from the peg on the garage wall, I cursed at a flat tire before furiously tossing the bike to the side. It slammed against the wall, bending the tire rim with the force of impact.

What the hell...

I ignored it and angrily began running down the lane. Never before had I been able to make it all of the way to the road without having to stop and catch my breath. I was a running machine, faster than before, and with plenty of stamina. It seemed like no time had passed when I arrived at the front porch of Alex's house. I didn't bother knocking and went straight through the unlocked front door.

Alex looked up from the couch, startled, knocking over the stack of books that were on the coffee table.

"What's wrong with me?" I demanded to know.

Alex shook his head. "I'm sorry?" He moved some of the books off the couch and offered me a place to sit.

I paced through the living room instead of sitting down. It was like there was a ball of fire inside of me and it threatened to explode if I didn't keep moving. "You know something," I insisted. "I heard your thoughts. Why can I hear your thoughts?" I couldn't sit down. I wanted to scream, to release the energy inside of me.

The numerous books caught my attention and I marched over to scan the titles. Paranormal studies in all languages imaginable filled the shelves. Non-fiction and fiction alike were sitting side by side in no manner that seemed to make sense. Dan Brown's The Da Vinci Code sat next to the King James Version of The Bible which was nestled next to something called The Book of Enoch. The one thing I noticed above all was the numerous book titles that mentioned angels or demons.

"What is all of this?" I backed away from Alex, suddenly repulsed by the fears that formed in my mind.

"Cadi, sit down. Please." He had come to my side and tried to lead me by the arm back to the couch.

I pulled away quickly. "What are you?"

"I am nothing, Cadi. Nothing for you to fear, I swear." That pained look was back.

Please let me help you.

"Help me with what Alex?" I shouted angrily, again answering his unspoken thoughts. "Help me figure out what kind of freak I am?"

"No," he insisted. "I just want to help you calm down." He grabbed both of my arms and forced me to look him in the eye. "You need to calm down. Everything is fine."

His voice was so cool and collected I had no choice but to relax a little bit. This time, when he tried to lead me to the couch, I allowed it and sat next to him. Trembling, the nervous energy that had built inside of me was replaced by fear. "Who are you?" I asked, afraid of the answer. Alex drew in a deep breath.

"My name is Alexander Maxwell, you know that."

"*What* are you? And don't lie to me, obviously I can read your mind."

"I don't think you want to do that." Alex stared at me. "The real question is what is happening to you."

"Don't do this, Alex. I can tell you're different. I feel it every time I touch you, every time I think about you." I looked down at my hands, ashamed at the weakness I felt.

Alex reached over and took my hands in his. "Cadi, there are greater things out there than you can see."

"Tell me who you are." Tears built up in my eyes but didn't fall. The electricity that flowed through my arms was a welcome relief.

Alex sat back against the couch cushions. "Fine, but you listen until I'm finished. Agreed?" His warm blue eyes shifted to a colder color. Only the pain in his face marred the determination in his voice. I nodded, perched on the literal edge of my seat. He got up, went to a bookshelf and came back to sit next to me again. He put the book in front of me. Opened to a page that discussed various myths about demons, he pointed at the crude, awful drawing of a naked male demon hovering over a sleeping girl.

"Have you ever heard of these?"

I shook my head, even though it seemed frighteningly familiar to me.

"This is the Incubus; a demon who preys on human women in their sleep."

"You think one of these is coming for me?" Images of Zandros filled my mind. He was too beautiful for words and compelled me greatly. I never saw him except for in my dreams. I quickly scanned the text in front of me. Why would I remember him in waking hours? Everything here said the victims were completely unaware.

Alex shook his head and turned the page, showing more demons, only in female form. "A female demon can prey on men the same way, attacking them in their sleep." He studied my face for a flicker of recognition. When he got none, he continued. "These demons walk the earth if they choose, stealing the souls of their hapless suitors. The women mature overnight and have the ability to put men under their seductive spells."

I blinked hard; wishing all of the words would make sense even though I had no idea how it related to me.

Are you a demon?

I could feel the fear behind the silent question. I glared at him, resenting the fact that he would even think such a thing. "Why would you think that? I've never even thought about having sex, let alone seducing a man so I could steal his soul," I spat at him.

Grabbing the book, I began frantically flipping through the pages, not noticing that he had left the room again. When he returned, he held a sketchbook. "The Incubus and his female counterpart don't always attack with acts of sexuality. They can absorb life force just by their mere presence. Besides, those are just two examples of different types of demons. There are more than mankind has names for."

He sat down again and opened the book in my lap. "If anything looks familiar to you, whatever you do, don't say a name out loud."

My curiosity piqued as I slowly began turning pages. Face after face filled the book, each one drawn more beautifully than the one before. None of them were familiar until I turned to one of the final pages. The eyes looked out from their two dimensions and I could hear the voice yelling at me to be quiet. Whoever had drawn this captured the woman perfectly, as if it were a photograph instead of charcoal.

"How did you get this?" I whispered.

"Don't say her name," Alex reminded. "Who is she?"

"My mother..." I began crying, looking into the exquisite face of the first of my tormentors. I loved the woman, and at times regretted wishing her away. I adored Cynthia, but this woman was the one who gave me life.

"Where is she now?" Alex took the book from my limp hands.

"She's gone." I looked up at him, tears streaking my face. "She died eight years ago."

Alex looked at me with understanding and compassion. "Are you sure she's dead?"

I looked down again.

"What was her name?"

"Melantha. Melantha Copeland." It was the first time the words had left my lips in my life. I watched Alex write the name at the bottom of the page. It occurred to me that most of the pages had names written on them. "Why can't I say the names?"

"If they are alive, speaking their names invites them to come to you anytime they want. It opens the door for them, so to speak."

I drew the book back into my lap and began flipping the pages again. "All of these people, the ones who have their names written, they are dead?"

"Yes."

I marveled at each face, man and woman alike. They were all so beautiful and my heart ached at the unknown loss. "What about the ones without names?"

"I don't know, but it used to be my duty to find out."

"Your duty? What does that mean?" I didn't look back up at him. Instead, I finished looking at the pictures, each more stunning than the one before. My heart stopped on the last one, an image of Zandros watching me from the page.

Something was wrong though. It was missing something. I pulled the pencil out from the spiral binding, not waiting for permission before etching lead onto the cheekbone of the face in front of me. I smudged the lines with my finger and didn't stop until I'd represented the scar perfectly.

"You know him?"

My heart soared and crashed at the same time as I handed the book back to him.

"And he is alive?"

I sat stone-like.

Should I tell him about my nightly visits from Zandros?

Should I tell him about the dreams I've always had?

Suddenly, thirst overtook my mind and I got up to find some water in the kitchen. I swallowed the water in big gulps and felt Alex's light touch on my shoulder.

"Cadi, I need to know. Is he alive?"

I refused to answer. Squaring my shoulders, I turned and gave him a dazzling smile. Something in the pit of my stomach wanted to protect Zandros from whatever threat Alex offered. "He is none of your concern," I replied automatically.

"Cadi, I can assure you that he is not a man you want to mess with. I need to know if he's alive."

"Why?"

Alexander seemed confused. "So I can kill him."

"Like all of the other people in this book?"

"All but two. I did not end your mother's life, nor is the demon Zandros conquered."

My stomach lurched again as he took hold of my arm, but I wrestled away from him and ran out of the house.

Released

Taking to the fields and wooded areas that filled the five miles between our houses, I ran with the grace of a woodland animal. I'd passed my own property and found myself in the middle of an old park that was overgrown with years of neglect.

I fell to my knees and begged for the fire inside of me to go away. Questions swirled in my mind; ones that I didn't even know how to ask.

Even if I did, who would I ask?

"ZANDROS!"

4

I screamed to the heavens, holding my breath, waiting to see what would happen. No loud cracks of thunder rolled overhead. Dark clouds didn't appear, no fissures cracked into the earth beneath my feet. The birds stopped their summer calls for only a moment, startled by the sudden noise, but even they continued their noisy song.

Looking around, I saw nothing but plush green growth and a bright blue summer sky. Nothing in the world around me changed. There was no spark of electricity in the air, nothing like I'd seen in the movies. Instead, it was calm.

Too calm.

Spasms wracked my body, making me double over in pain. Writhing on the ground, it felt like the fire inside was spreading, exploding through each individual cell. "Oh God," I sobbed.

Why was this happening to me?

Who was Alex?

More importantly, *what* was Alex and what did he have to do with this change in me?

It couldn't be just a coincidence.

Everything turned upside down the day I met him. These thoughts flew through my mind, dominating everything around me and pushing the pain to the background.

"Shhh." A quiet whisper in my ear made me stop writhing. It was as though that one simple sound soothed every pain I was feeling.

"Zandros?" I looked around and saw the illuminated figure standing just inside of the tree line. Sitting up, I found myself too dizzy to stand. The pain was still there, I just didn't pay attention to it as much. "Zandros, help me. What's wrong with me?"

My hand reached out toward him, begging. I could see him tilt his head to the side as if he were studying a curious creature instead of the girl he swore was his.

In the blink of an eye, he was standing over me, a wicked smile spreading across his face. "Ah, my sweet Carina." He knelt down and grabbed a handful of my hair.

I yelped in surprise and pain, holding onto his hand as he pulled me to a standing position.

"I do believe you called for me? Such a delicious change in attitude." His face was so close to mine again, just as it always was when he was terrorizing me.

I could smell the sweetness of his strong body emanating through the field. "What is happening to me?" I begged again.

He pulled me closer, until my body was completely against his. "Your destiny," he breathed into my ear.

"What are you?" I dared to look him in the eye, challenging him to tell me the truth.

Zandros laughed heartily, releasing his hold on my hair, but not on my body. "What is it they say? I am the man of your dreams."

"Are you a demon?"

Again, he laughed. "Mortals love their silly myths and stupid titles. I am Zandros. There needs to be no more explanation."

Released

"What are you going to do with me?" My voice shook with fear. I knew the answer, but I wanted to hear it from him.

"You will help me reclaim my rightful place."

"Please, I don't understand. Tell me." My green eyes widened, begging him.

He released his hold and walked away from me, as if distance would make me stop pleading with him. "One month. You asked for one month and I was kind enough to give that to you. How patient do you expect me to be Carina?"

"Who is Alex?"

Zandros laughed again. "All of these questions. What happened to my frightened little doe that always cowered and never bother to question anything?" He was by my side again in a heartbeat. "I liked that scared, little pet," he said huskily, brushing his warm lips across my collarbone.

Pulling his face back suddenly, he grabbed the collar of my shirt and ripped it off of my body, shredding it in the process. "Where did this come from?" he spat.

I crossed my arms across my chest, trying to regain a bit of dignity.

Should I tell him about Alex? He didn't seem to react when I'd said his name earlier.

"It smells like a filthy dog! Who have you been with?" He grabbed my wrists again, pulling me toward him. I stumbled and fell to the ground. Zandros grabbed a handful of hair and yanked me back to my feet. "Answer. Me." Zandros was nose to nose with me now and I trembled in his arms.

"Al..." I couldn't finish the word before Zandros suddenly let go of me, dropping me to the ground.

Scared, I looked all around to see what had caught his attention. The dark haired man was there again. "Aniketos," Zandros sneered. "You're a bit out of your element, aren't you?"

"My element is anywhere you are," he pointed out. "Are you going to leave this child alone, or am I going to have to remind you of your limits once again?" He drew a thumbnail across his own cheekbone, tracing the path of Zandros' scar.

My tormentor hissed before swirling away into instant nothingness. It seemed as though the dark haired man was about to say something when the breaking and cracking of branches drew his attention to the woods behind him. Turning back toward me, he smiled warmly before disappearing himself.

Alex sprang into the clearing, out of breath and scratched up. Rushing to my side, he leaned down and checked to see if I was injured. "Are you okay?" He was angry, and concerned, and confused, all at once. I could read it in his eyes.

I nodded, holding the back of my head with one hand while trying to keep my naked chest covered with the other. "How did you find me?

Alex didn't answer. Instead, he scanned our surroundings intently. "We're not safe here. Come on."

He didn't give me time to stand on my own. Instead, he gathered me into his arms and began walking back into the woods.

"I can walk," I protested.

Released

The pain started again, and I balled up in his arms. Sobbing and screaming, I let him carry me for what seemed like hours before we arrived back at his house.

"You'll be safe. He can't find you here." Alex laid me down on top of an oversized feather bed.

"Why are you helping me?" I whimpered.

"Because it's my job." He cast a soft look at me and pulled a light blanket over my body.

"Who are you? Just tell me that."

"Go to sleep. Hopefully I'll have a few answers for you when you wake."

"I'm not tired," I mumbled, succumbing to the warm blankets.

When I woke up, the room was dark, illuminated only by a single candle burning on the bedside table. The door was cracked open just enough to see that the hallway outside was dark as well.

I got up as quietly as possible and tiptoed over to the light switch. Nothing happened. When I noticed footsteps coming up the stairs, I quickly retreated back to the bed. Since I was dressed in a light nightgown that I'd never seen before, I covered myself with the blanket.

"I thought I heard you get up," Alex said coming into the room. "Did you sleep well?"

I nodded. "What time is it? I need to get back before my parents get home from work."

Alex shook his head. "You've been asleep here for a while. You needn't worry about your parents. I've taken care of them."

My heart sunk. *What had he done?*

"They are fine," he assured me. "My sister came to help."

That explained the clean house. "Your sister?"

"Crevan is her name." He smiled softly and sat on the edge of the bed. "Are you hungry?"

"No." I lied, ignoring the growl in my stomach. "Tell me about your sister."

"She has special... talents so to speak. Your parents don't even know you're gone."

"What does that mean?" I turned to face him. "Why can't you ever give me a straight answer?"

"You'd like a straight answer?" He cocked his head to the side and arched an eyebrow. "Okay, if you think you can handle that without running away."

"No running," I agreed.

"You said that last time," he reminded.

"I promise," I insisted, exasperated.

Alex started picking at the fringe on one of the throw pillows, took a deep breath and sighed. "Crevan and I come from a long line of beings born to protect the world from the darker forces. Each of us has our own special talent. Crevan can change her physical form to mimic anyone she chooses. Currently, she has been playing the part of Cadi Matthews for the past day and a half." He turned and smiled softly at me. "You got a perfect score on your biology test, by the way."

Biology was the last thing that was on my mind.

"I've been asleep that long?"

He nodded. "You've gone through a lot."

Released

Instinctively, I reached up to the tender spot on my head. The knot was gone, but I could see the bruises on my arm were still there. I could only imagine what my face looked like. Lightly touching my cheekbones, I could feel the tenderness under one of my eyes. "I bet I look fabulous," I grumbled.

Alex didn't reply right away, but I caught his blush. "So out of what I've just told you, the thing you worry about the most is the bruise on your face?" He shook his head in dismay.

"No, that's just the easiest to absorb. Do you want me to freak out? Okay."

I hopped up onto my knees, facing him full on and ready to pounce.

"How about I freak out about the fact that I was asleep for a day and a half, replaced by some doppelganger and no one who cares about me has noticed? How about the fact that some demon asshole is hunting me down? How do you have a book with my mother's face drawn in it? Maybe you'd prefer if I just sit here quietly and just marvel at the fact that I can hear your thoughts and grew boobs overnight. Exactly which reaction were you hoping for?"

"All of the above, but without the vulgar language." I could tell he couldn't help but give me a sarcastic smile. "My sister is very good at what she does. There is no way to explain this to your parents unless you want to see someone panic. They would lock you up in an asylum if you went to them with this. It's only due to Crevan's considerable abilities that no one has noticed. I'm sure they would be missing you greatly if they had. You should certainly be upset about the man who is hunting you. I have the book because I draw demons.

That's my gift. I see the faces in my mind and draw them. Eventually, everyone I draw ends up being someone I have to find. It's a bit of foresight I suppose. I assume telepathy is a gift you bear. And," he looked at me pointedly. "I'm not going to address your final issue. That's between you and your mirror I suppose."

I flopped back against the pillows next to him. "Great. Now what?"

"Now you eat."

"I'm not hungry," I repeated. Again, my stomach growled in protest, but it wasn't like any other hunger pang I'd ever felt before.

"You may surprise yourself." He stood up and waited at the door for me to follow.

When I finally did, he led the way through the darkness to the pristine kitchen. A huge bowl of fruit sat in the middle of the table. Next to it were the makings for sandwiches and an assortment of fresh vegetables.

"I didn't know what you like, so I got a variety," he explained, pulling a plate out of the cupboard.

"Thanks," I said meekly. I wished I didn't have to admit how wrong I was about being hungry. My appetite became instantly voracious when I bit into an apple. Alex sat down at the table without comment. In a half hour's time, I'd eaten a dozen pieces of fruit, half a bag of fresh vegetables and the whole loaf of bread. At the height of it, I hadn't even bothered to peel the orange. Instead, I ate it, rind, seeds, and all. By the time I realized what I had done, my belly was so full I could barely move.

Released

When he saw that all of the color left my face, Alex quickly pulled a trash bin over. Without apology, I emptied the entire contents of my stomach. It took nearly as long to heave it all out, and by the time I was finally done, he was standing behind me, holding my hair out of the way with a glass of water at the ready.

"I'm sorry, I should have warned you but I've never personally witnessed the transformation cravings. I've just read about it." He handed me a cool cloth to wipe off my face, which I took gratefully.

"It's okay. I'm just sorry you had to see that." I placed the rag on my forehead and leaned forward, afraid there was more to come. When nothing happened, I straightened myself again. "Is it over now?"

Alex shrugged. "I'm not exactly sure, but from what I've read..." Violent spasms shook my body, once again making me double over. This time, it wasn't in pain. It felt like someone had injected my bones with ice water. The shivering made my teeth hurt. My body was so tense it made the ache even worse.

Alex muttered something unintelligible as he lifted me up into his arms. I wrapped myself around him, trying to absorb as much of his body heat as possible, appreciative of the electricity that passed between us. He carried me back upstairs to the bedroom and pulled back the covers. He laid me down, pulled the warm comforter up over my body, and sat next to me.

I drifted in and out of a fitful sleep, finally waking up lying against Alex's bare chest with his arms still wrapped around me. I stayed put, not wanting to wake his peaceful sleep. The last time I saw him, he looked so tired. Now was no different.

His face showed a few days' worth of stubble and there were dark circles under his eyes. While he slept, he looked ruggedly handsome instead of his usual awe-strikingly-beautiful. I was warmer now, no doubt only thanks to the care he'd been giving me, but I still wasn't completely comfortable here. There were still too many questions.

Questions.

The concept of uncertainty was the ruling factor in my life now. If only I could get some solid answers. Then again, what would I do with the information? Obviously, there was something wrong with me.

Seriously wrong.

Alex's breathing deepened and he slowly opened his eyes. If it weren't for the dim candlelight, I wouldn't have known he was waking up. "What's with the no lights thing?" I pushed myself off him.

He released his snug grip and let me move away. "I never had the electricity turned on. Never saw a reason to," he shrugged.

"So you live in the shadows all of the time?"

"I see sufficiently in the dark; probably not as well as some animals, but just as well as any human sees in the midday. After a while, you may find that's the case for you as well."

He laughed at the silly look I was making at him. "And I saw that too," he added climbing out of the bed. Sweat beads glistened on his torso, proof that the warmth of our joined body heat was for my benefit, not his. Obviously he wasn't cold in the least bit.

"What about winter? Is the fireplace enough for you?"

He shook his head again, walking toward the door. "You'll find that these horrid body temperature shifts will stop soon. You will not need a coat in the winter, nor will you feel the oppressive heat of the summer sun."

"Is there a working bathroom here?" I wanted to shower or at least clean up a little bit.

"I'm not that medieval." Alex laughed. "Down the hall, last door on the left. I'll ready the clothes Crevan thought may suit you."

I followed his directions after he'd disappeared somewhere downstairs. Upon entering the large bathroom, I found an ornate claw tub with numerous scented soaps and shampoos on the counter next to it. A large stack of fluffy towels sat in a pile next to the tub. Cranking the faucet on, it squeaked but flowed nicely and didn't take long for the water to heat up and fill the tub.

Soaking in a hot bubble bath, I let the aromas invade my senses, blocking out all of the confusion that had filled my mind over the past few days. For the first time in awhile, I felt completely relaxed. More than once, Nick's image came to mind, but I forced it away. There was no way I could have any kind of friendship with someone 'normal' anymore, so it wasn't smart to even entertain the idea. I allowed myself to remain lost in the nothingness that surrounded me until my fingers pruned. Only then did I scrub myself pink.

Back in the bedroom, I found a neatly folded pair of jeans and a light blue sweater. Grabbing the top, I discovered undergarments tucked modestly underneath it. After getting dressed, I tried to adjust my eyes to the dim light but found it impossible to see clearly like Alex had described.

Downstairs, I found him sitting at the dining room table, a stack of journals next to him. He chewed on his pen cap while flipping through one of the journals and scribbling in a notebook. I quietly watched for a second as he hurried to jot down some important information he'd just found.

"Figure anything out?" I asked, still standing in the doorway.

"Maybe." Alex muttered quickly, not looking up from his work. Suddenly, he stood up, nearly knocking the chair over behind him. He stalked into the living room and retrieved another book from the shelves.

I sat across the table from where he was and nervously waited for his return. When he came back, he remained silent, furiously scribbling notes in a language I couldn't read. After suffering in silence for what seemed like forever, I became too restless to just sit there and watch him.

I went into the living room, only to come face to face with my mirror image. Startled was an understatement. I took a step back, my mouth dropping open in astonishment.

The girl before me smiled broadly, just as I did in all of my yearbook photos. "Cadi! So nice to meet you all awake and stuff!" The girl laughed at her own joke just as I sometimes did when I thought something was funny.

"Crevan, stop," Alex admonished from his position in the other room. "Cadi, meet my sister. I told you she did a good job."

"I'd say," I muttered, backing away from my body double. It made me more than uncomfortable to look at myself like this. It was like a weird dream but in real life.

"I've got to tell you," Crevan said, hopping up to sit on the table where Alex was working. "It's kind of fun being you. I've never been more popular!" Again, she laughed and popped the gum she was chewing.

How gross and annoying. I never chewed gum like that, did I?

She was being so cavalier about taking over my life like it was the easiest thing in the world. I couldn't help but feel a little resentful. "How are my parents? Sarah and Spencer?"

"Fine, fine. They're all busy polishing off plans for your big birthday blowout tomorrow night." She grinned wickedly. "Don't worry; you have a date and a bathing suit that is to die for!"

A date?

"What have you done?" My heart raced with panic. I didn't date. There was no one I was interested in dating... Well... Maybe Nick or possibly Alex... I held my breath in an attempt to hide my frustrations.

"I've been you. Dance team member, star student, perfect daughter and wonderful sister. It's actually quite easy you know. You pick fun people to hang out with."

"Who do I have a date with?" I walked purposefully into the dining area and crossed my arms against my body sternly.

"Who do you think? Dreamy Bio-Boy. And let me tell you, he's very into you, if you know what I mean."

Released

It must've been Alex's turn to be irritated. He snapped his head away from his notebook and scolded his sister. "Crevan, I told you not to do anything stupid."

"Stupid would be ignoring a guy like that!" She stuck her tongue out like a four-year-old to make her point.

I ran my hands through my hair and my fingers tangled in the damp waves as I pulled in frustration. The pain helped me refocus my anger. "Why am I suddenly dating Nick?"

"You're the one who invited him in the first place!" Craven hopped off the table and pointed her finger at me. "It was you not me, so lay off. I'm helping you."

Alex turned to look at me accusingly as I wracked my memory for when this could have happened. Nick asked me out on Friday, but I'd already agreed to dinner with Alex so I refused. I never said I'd go out with him, but I did invite him to the party. I groaned in concession and dropped my arms.

He turned back to his studies, but I noticed he wasn't writing anymore. Instead, I could tell he was trying to listen in without being obvious about it. "It wasn't a date," I stammered. "It was just supposed to be a few friends getting together for the pool party."

"MmHmm..." Crevan taunted. "I can see why you'd want to see that body in as little as possible!" She giggled and swooned at the thought.

My mind swam with jealousy. The thought of Nick spending time alone with Crevan turned my thoughts into a shade of green I'd never known before.

"Crevan!" Alex snapped. "That's enough. Go change into your own self. This must be disturbing for Cadi to see."

"Whatever." Crevan rolled her eyes dramatically and skipped toward the stairs. "By the way," she shouted back at me. "I like your house better. They believe in electricity!"

"So what have you figured out?" I hoped to change the subject and went to look over his shoulder. I couldn't read the words, but there were little arrows and lines connecting different sections. "What language is that?"

"Glagolitic," he replied matter-of-factly, as though I should know what that meant. Sighing deeply, he explained. "It's the base of all Slavic languages, many of which are now considered dead. There are few who still read it and even fewer that can speak it."

"You speak an ancient, dead language?" Stunned, I sat in the chair next to him and braced myself for his answer to my next question. "How old are you?"

"I know it simply because my family has preserved its importance; not because I was born during the time of its use."

"That didn't answer my question." I saw Alex breathe deeply and could tell he was trying to choose the right words. "I could just read your mind you know."

"Be careful with that. You might find things you never wanted to know," he warned mysteriously. "To answer your question, I can't give you an exact number. Age is kind of a concept my family doesn't really adhere to. I've been around a long time. Let's just leave it at that, shall we?"

"Fine," I allowed, leaning back into my chair. "Tell me what all of this says."

"Well, I've spent the last few days looking into your mother's name."

I nodded and held my breath, anxious to hear about my biological mother.

Alex continued. "I've found the name Melantha in many places, all agreeing that she is a demon. Most often, she is classified as a Succubus."

My head spun. If my mother was a succubus, what did that make me? I kept silent, waiting for the bombshell.

"She was very good at what she did..." He hesitated, a bright shade of crimson creeping across his cheeks. "She was able to seduce one of the purest souls. But things get a little odd two decades ago."

"How so?" I couldn't hide my revulsion at the thought of what my mother did. Suddenly, images of all the different men that had come and gone in the first ten years of my life filled my mind.

"Well, all trace of her disappears for a while, after she took up with a man called Micah. I can only find two references to a Micah and that's where I'm hitting a block." He pulled out his books again and flipped the pages, revealing more words in the dead language. "It says here that the last soul that a demon called Zandros took was called Micah."

I let out my breath slowly. "And the other reference?"

"That's the confusing part. It says here that Micah is direct kin of one of our people. It's odd that I've never heard he had a brother before now."

73

"Who's the man?"

"His name is Aniketos. No one has seen or heard from him since around the same time it says Zandros killed Micah. He was once one of the greatest warriors of our people, descendants of Seth and children of the Nephilim. Our history books tell thousands of stories of his conquests, but only this one brief mention of a brother."

Alex didn't seem to notice all of the color had drained from my face, but I felt it. He also didn't notice the fact that I was about to faint and grabbed the edge of the table for support. "Why can you say his name?" I whispered.

"This house has a strong ward on it. So long as we're here, no one can hear me call to them."

"But you said not to say the names the other night," I reminded him, still stunned at the sound of Zandros and Aniketos' names.

"I said you couldn't. It only protects my people, but if you're here and don't speak of him, he can't find you."

"I know him," I said, pushing the chair back and standing up. Pacing the floor, I wasn't sure what I should say or not say.

Aniketos was the name of the man who'd come to my rescue twice, the dark haired man with the beautiful face that attacked Zandros.

"He hates him."

Alex turned in his chair and watched me for a moment. "What do you mean?"

"Zand... I've been dreaming about him almost every night since my mother died. The night before my birthday, he came just like always. Only this time, Anik... the other guy, he came and attacked him."

"Are you sure it's the same man? Aniketos disappeared almost twenty years ago."

I nodded emphatically. "Yes, Zand... He called him by name and asked who let him out of his cage, whatever that means. He was there in the field the other day, too. I think he's the one who gave Zan... He gave him the scar on his face." I went back over to the table and grabbed the book that talked about Melantha. "What else does it say about my mother? Am I in this?"

Alex shook his head slowly. "Only that she had become with child. There was a great debate as to whether or not Micah fathered her child or if it was another of her many lovers. All traces of her disappeared before she gave birth."

My heart sank. I'd always wondered who my father was, if he was out there looking for me. Maybe he still was.

"Well I can tell you all about her life after that, at least for the next ten years before she died." I leaned against the wall and sank down to sit on the floor.

Alex came over and tried to comfort me. He crouched down and laid a gentle hand on my shoulder. "We don't know that it's the same woman," he offered. His mind spoke differently. I could hear that he was struggling to accept the fact that the child of a demon was in his home.

I glared at him and pushed away suddenly. "We both know it's the same woman!" I shouted, stood up, and resumed my pacing. "I shouldn't be here."

Alex stood suddenly and grabbed me around the waist. "You promised no running."

"Look at me!" I pushed him away and moved to stand in front of the full-length hall mirror. Even in the shadows, I could see the change in myself: the fuller hair, the pronounced lips, and the rounder chest. It was as if I'd entered a second phase of puberty and shed every ounce of child left in me overnight. "Is this the same girl you met five days ago?" I demanded.

"Yes," Alex said, exasperation filling his tone. He stood behind me, watching my face crumple in the mirror before us. "Yes you are. You may be softer. You may have some subtle changes, but you are still Cadi Matthews, the girl who doesn't mind rain and mud, the girl who loves her family and will do everything she has to in order to protect them."

"I don't want to be a monster, Alex."

He shook his head sadly. "You are not a monster. We just have to figure out what Zandros wants from you, that's all."

"I want to go home," I decided suddenly. It had been days since I'd heard the laughter of my family. I missed my friends and ached to have a normal life.

"He can find you there," Alex pointed out.

"He won't hurt me." I was certain of it, although I couldn't say why. "He promised me another month. That gives me twenty seven days left to be normal."

"But you aren't normal," Alex begged. "People will notice the differences in you. He may not take you, but he won't let go. Zandros will still come every night."

I moved away from the mirror, disgusted by my own appearance. I sat on the couch, pulled my knees up, and sank into deep thought. Alex took it as resignation and went back to his books. Actually, I was busy trying to solve the biggest problem I had at that very moment.

I suddenly ran up the stairs, knowing Crevan might be my only hope. Music poured from behind one of the closed bedroom doors. Knocking lightly, I waited a minute for the door to open.

Inside, I found a beautiful young blonde girl, wearing a flowing pink sundress. "Crevan?"

The girl smiled broadly. "Ah, you've caught me in my real skin," she joked.

I assessed her carefully. She had the same smile as Alex, the same strong features and blonde hair, but her body was small and lithe. Her eyes were big and bright, one the same blue as her brother's and the other a brilliant shade of green. She was at least three inches shorter than me and looked a few years younger.

"I wanted to ask you for your help."

"Name it!" The girl patted her bed, inviting me to sit next to her and talk. By the time we'd formulated the plan and spent an hour in the bathroom, we were ready to test our experiment on Alex.

He looked up from his place at the table, still working away, and his jaw dropped. Crevan grinned like a fool while I thrust my hands into my pockets nervously.

"Well?" I finally said.

"Uhhh..." was all he could say.

I caught a glimpse of myself in the mirror and felt like we did a good job. Crevan had pulled my hair back in a tight ponytail braid, hiding the new fullness of it. She also applied makeup to give me a less striking complexion, slight shadows under my eyes to offset the brightness of them. She'd wrapped my chest tightly and pulled a tank and blouse over it to hide the binding. The shirt was loose enough to hang at my waist, hiding my new curves.

"Now she can go home!" Crevan announced gleefully.

Alex shook his head. "No. He can find her if she's not here." He was adamant about it.

"But she misses her friends," Crevan whined. "And it's her birthday party tomorrow."

I stood up for myself. "I'll be fine. He won't come to me if there are people around so I'll make sure I'm never alone. The only real threat is when I'm asleep."

"Which is why her new bedroom is upstairs here and I'll be sleeping in the lap of air conditioned luxury every night." Crevan seemed more than pleased with the plan.

"It's only for a while," I assured him. "Until I can figure a way out of this."

"How will you get here every night? By yourself?" Alex was voicing all of the reasons why this plan would fail.

"You can pick her up if it makes you feel better." Crevan offered.

"I run faster than you can drive," I pointed out with a laugh.

"And school? You're willing to put your friends in danger? When he can't find your dreams, he will come for you. He may not hurt you, but he'll be there. If nothing else, just to remind you."

My resolve faltered, but only a bit. "I'll be fine, so will they. I've been playing his game for eight years. I think I know him better than you. I need to live my life. While I still have one to live," I added.

Alex's shoulders slumped in defeat. "Fine," he mumbled, turning back to his books.

Crevan clapped her hands. "So what fabulous plans do you have for this fine Friday night?" she grinned.

"Well, if memory serves me correctly, I think I have a date to get ready for." I looked directly at Alex, hoping he remembered his offer. "I could use a little fun." I picked my car keys up off the table and set out for the front door.

"Ooooh, with Nick?" Crevan asked excitedly.

"Nope," was all I said as the door closed behind me.

5

Sadness welled up inside me as I pulled into the parking spot behind my house. It had only been a few days since things began to get weird, but it felt like a lifetime had passed since the last time I was home. Sarah and Spencer were splashing in the pool, but Mom and Dad weren't home from work yet.

After heading inside, I got out the meat Mom had thawed and started cooking dinner. Even if I wasn't going to eat, or be here when my family did, it was the least I could do. The table was covered with junk food and soda pop in preparation for tomorrow's party. It didn't take long for me to clear it so that my family could sit down and eat.

I'd just finished chopping the vegetables and turned off the meat when Mom walked in the door. "Well this is a nice surprise," she said when she noticed that dinner was already prepared.

"It's the least I could do," I smiled. "Hope you wanted to have tacos tonight?"

She inhaled the aroma and smiled as she gave me a quick kiss on the side of the head. "That's exactly what I was planning. You must be a mind reader. I've got to get these shoes off."

I watched as she eased into the living room and kicked her shoes off. She worked at a hospital as a labor and delivery nurse and most of the time she came home exhausted. No matter how tired she was she always made sure she had time for us.

Released

My hand rested on my aching chest. It broke my heart to think that I might not ever see her again, that someday I might not see any of them again.

"Don't forget, I've got a date tonight," I reminded her.

"Which one are you going out with?" She snickered and grabbed the TV remote.

What had Crevan done?

At least now I'd be in control of my life. If the plan worked, that is. "Alex, the guy Dad bought the car from?"

"Ah, I see." Mom looked away from the TV and winked at me. "Steven really liked him. I'm glad to hear this Nick kid isn't the only one who's caught your eye."

I blushed. "I have to go get ready," I said, excusing myself from the room.

Once upstairs, I pulled my shirt off, released the binding, and took a deep breath. Pulling the tank top back on, I sat in front of my dresser and contemplated how I should wear my hair. I didn't want to have it tied back so extremely, but it still needed to look a little tamed. Tomorrow, I would go to the beauty supply store and buy some hair extensions. I wouldn't put them in, but I could tell people I had.

Finally deciding on a messy bun at the back of my head, I went to the bathroom to scrub off all of the makeup Crevan had applied. Back in my room, I added just the lightest touch of mascara and a shiny coat of lip-gloss. It was amazing how little effort it took for me to look almost glamorous, I thought vainly. A slow smile crept over my lips, enjoying the prospects of the new look.

Pulling a new blouse out of my closet, I added a tank top that was two sizes too small before buttoning it up almost all of the way. Once I put a light suede jacket on, it was hard to tell I'd removed the binding. This was definitely a better and more comfortable option.

A knock on the door startled me. I hadn't even heard anyone come up the stairs.

So much for being able to take care of myself.

Dad waited for an invitation before coming in. He had grease stained hands and dust covering his face. I smiled warmly, knowing how hard he must've worked today. "You're seeing Alex tonight?"

I nodded. "He's almost twenty, graduated last year." I remembered his instructions the other night and was shocked at how easily the lie came out.

"Where are you going?"

That was one thing I hadn't thought of yet. "I don't know," I admitted uneasily. "But I'll be sure to be home for curfew." I knew about the inquisition he always gave Sarah before and after every time she went out with a boy. Since this was my first real date, I had never been on the receiving end of it and waited for the rest to come.

Instead, he just nodded, looked like he had more to add, and then shrugged. "Well, okay then. Be careful."

That was easy.

Through my bedroom window, I could see the dust cloud that always surrounded a vehicle as it drove down our lane. By the time I'd checked myself in the mirror again and made it downstairs, Alex was already knocking on the door.

Dad answered it, stepping back and inviting him in. Alex held a beautiful bouquet of fresh wild flowers. I held my breath for a minute, admiring how handsome he was dressed in a white button up shirt and jeans.

"It's nice to see you again, Mr. Matthews." He greeted my dad with a firm handshake.

Mom had come over to the pair and stood next to her husband, enthralled with the handsome suitor standing in front of her.

"These are for you," Alex smiled, handing the flowers to her.

"Well thank you. I'll go put them in water." Mom blushed and gave Dad a raised eyebrow look of approval.

"Where are you two going?" Dad asked.

I caught Alex's eye and he smiled softly before turning his full attention back to my father. "I planned on taking her to St. Laurent's for dinner and if there is time, the Metro Theater is playing High Noon. I'd like to take her to see it."

Dad scratched his stubble. "Westerns, huh? I didn't take you for the type."

Alex nodded lightly. "I actually enjoy most cinema. Classical theater is my preference however. I hate to admit it's hard for me to stomach most of the so-called mainstream movies. It's a little too much... of everything I suppose."

"Well then," Dad didn't even try to hide the fact that he was clearly impressed by the boy. "You two have fun, be safe, and... all that jazz."

"I'll have her home by ten," Alex assured him.

"Eleven will be fine," he muttered before leaving us alone.

"You look lovely," Alex said, taking my hand and lightly brushing his lips across my knuckles. "Ready?"

I nodded.

As he led me to the Rover, I could see Sarah and Spencer were still horsing around in the pool. They stopped just long enough to wave goodbye to us before resuming their antics.

"My father likes you," I said after we were on our way. "And I think my mother has a crush on you now," I laughed.

"Your parents are good people." He kept his eyes on the road, gripping the steering wheel tighter than normal.

"Dad trusts you," I added.

Alex nodded. "I would never give him a reason not to."

I slumped in my seat. His behavior was even stranger than normal. I didn't know what to make of it. "Is something wrong?"

"Would you like me to lie?"

"If you feel the need," I countered.

"Then nothing is wrong. Let's enjoy the evening." His fingers drummed against the back of the leather wheel.

The sound irritated me. "Let's just forget this," I sighed. "You can just take me home and Crevan can come take my place later."

"No," he said quickly. Rolling his head, he forced himself to relax. "No," he repeated, this time softer. "I want to be here, I just have a lot on my mind."

I fought the temptation to scan his thoughts; heeding the warning he'd given me earlier. "Did you find out more?"

"Nothing of value." He looked frustrated as he sped down the highway toward town. "Do you like western movies?"

I suppressed a laugh. "I don't think I've ever watched one. But I like cowboys. Does that count?"

This seemed to lighten his spirits a little. "I love the stories of the American old west. Everyone had their priorities straight. No one had lost their morals yet."

"Well," I challenged. "If that were true, how come there were so many brothels?"

"Well a man knew how to be a gentleman and women knew the meaning of modesty."

This time I laughed aloud. "Are you serious? People killed each other over livestock. Sex was rampant in the whorehouses. Have you never heard of the lawless frontier? Things aren't that much different, people just don't hide it as much as they used to."

"It was only lawless because man hadn't written their silly rules down yet. People have always wanted what they cannot have. It's been that way since the Great Beginning. The only difference now is how freely they take what isn't theirs. This whole thing, what I have been fighting all of my life..." He ran his hand through his hair, returning it to the usual disheveled state. "It's all because of selfishness, greed. Creatures like Zandros, wanting what he should not have; taking what isn't his to take."

I wasn't about to question his monologue. "How many times have you had to rescue a girl like me from someone like him?"

"Never." Alex pulled into the parking lot of a dimly lit restaurant. It surprised me that we'd arrived so quickly. It seemed impossible that the necessary half hour of travel time had passed. "I actually retired some time ago. I'd hoped to leave that whole world behind me."

"What changed that?" I unbuckled my seatbelt.

"You knocked on my door," Alex replied, coming around to open the door for me.

He led me into the quaint restaurant and stopped to whisper something to the maître d'. The older balding man led us to a small table toward the back of the room. Alex stood behind my chair and waited for me to sit before gently pushing me in and taking his own seat.

"So what are your plans for tomorrow?" Alex asked after the man walked away.

I didn't have time to answer before the waiter came over.

"Hello," he smiled broadly at me. "My name is David and I'll be taking care of you tonight. Can I start you with something to drink?"

I returned his friendly smile and asked for an ice water.

"I'd like to see the wine list," Alex injected with a frown.

"Very well." David was still grinning like a fool at me. "May I suggest the Pinot Grigio?" He handed the wine list to Alex.

"No, you may not." Alex replied sharply. Glancing at the list, he handed it back to the waiter. "I'll take the 1961 Chateau La Mission Haut Brion Pessac Leognane. And we will both have the Beef Carpaccio, thank you." He spoke with a perfect French accent, his face glowing with arrogance.

David took the list back, a stunned look on his face. "I'm sorry sir, but I need to see your ID if you are ordering alcohol."

Alex rolled his eyes and pulled his wallet of the inner breast pocket of his jacket. He flipped it open and withdrew his driver's license and a black credit card.

David looked carefully at the ID before handing it back to him. "I'll have to run your credit card. All bottles in our exclusive collection have to be prepaid."

"Fine," Alex said, tucking the license back in his wallet.

David gave me one more flirtatious grin before leaving.

"Wow, whose benefit was that little macho show for?" I teased Alex.

"His. He was rude, and if you doubt me, read his mind when he comes back and you'll know his true intentions." Alex shifted in his seat uncomfortably.

"So do I get to look forward to the jealous little peacock displaying his feathers every time we go out in public together?" I placed my elbows on the table and rested my chin against my intertwined fingers.

"I'm sorry," he apologized. "It seems that I am being very rude. Again. Crevan always said I lack social graces. I hate to admit how correct she is. Don't tell her I said that."

My smile promised to keep his secret. "Well if it eases your mind at all, I have no intention of reading his mind because I don't care what he thinks." I blushed a bit and absently played with my napkin.

The waiter reappeared with the bottle of wine and poured a small amount of wine in a glass for Alex to sample. Once he approved it, David poured a glass for each of us. I took a small sip before placing the glass away from me and reaching for my water. "Am I going to get sick again if I eat?"

"Only if you eat too much or too quickly. It is desire you will have to learn to control. It is the same with all you enjoy; food, drink, everything. Once you have a taste of it, so to speak, you won't be able to satisfy the hunger."

"How is it that you know so much about all of this?" I sipped my water slowly, wanting to show myself that I could control the urge to gulp it down in two swallows.

"I've studied a lot. Sometimes it feels like too much, other times not enough." He drank the wine in front of him. "Right now, it feels like the latter." Changing subjects, he repeated his earlier question. "What are your plans for tomorrow?"

"I guess that depends on what plans your sister made for me. As far as I knew, a few friends were coming over to swim and maybe watch movies. We'll stay up too late, eat too much junk food, and gossip about boys. That pretty much sums up a party at the Matthews house."

David cleared his throat quietly, interrupting our conversation again to place our plates in front of us. "Enjoy," he muttered before backing away.

I reveled in the smells coming from my plate. The mustard sauce was intoxicating. The meat was paper thin and tender. I was amazed at how it melted in my mouth. I really wanted to discard the fork and dig in with my hands, but I took a deep breath and forced myself to take petite bites.

Released

"Is this too hard for you?" Alex asked, seeing the desire flash in my eyes.

"It's not easy, that's for sure." I put another bite of food in my mouth and savored it before swallowing. "This is amazing!"

"Do all of your friends sleep at your house after your party?"

"Probably," I said, only halfway paying attention to his words.

"So Nick will be spending the night as well?"

I looked away from my food and noticed he was sitting like a statue. His food remained untouched. "No, he won't. I mean..." I didn't know what I meant. "No boys sleep over. I've never had a boy-girl party before but that wouldn't happen. I mean, would you want to spend the night at my house with my father and his shotgun collection there?"

Alex smiled, taking a small bite of his meal. "Have I mentioned that I like your father?"

I couldn't help but laugh. "Don't worry, Sir Maxwell. My virtue shall stay intact."

"So what do you do for fun?" Alex asked between bites. "Surely there's more to you than school and bad dreams."

I began telling him all about myself, about how I loved to dance and laugh. I told him I liked going to the movies and that comedies were the best, but I enjoyed mindless romances too. I'd read more books than most of my classmates and got straight A's. I hated biology but loved PE. I enjoyed art class, though there wasn't a creative bone in my body. It only took me a week to discover I had no musical talent whatsoever and drop out of band. I went to church every Sunday with my family and nothing meant more to me than the fact that we all sat around the dinner table together every night to talk about our day. He was easy to talk to and everything about my life spilled out easily.

"I'm sorry," Alex sounded sad.

I frowned; my confusion must have shown on my face.

"I'm sorry that your wonderful life has been interrupted like this." He put his fork down and idly ran his finger down the dew of his water glass.

I reached over and grabbed his hand, this time enjoying the shock. "Don't be. I'm not. It isn't the worst thing that could've happened to me. What if I'd never met you and didn't know a life other than what Zand... What he had in store for me?"

"You like dancing?" He asked, his face lighting up again.

"Love it. Why?"

He pulled the napkin off his lap and set it on the empty plate. "I think I should take you to a movie another time."

David appeared instantly with the check when Alex motioned for him. Without even looking at the total, he scribbled a signature at the bottom of the slip and stood up. Coming around to my side of the table, he pulled my chair out for me. There was a little more energy in his motions, causing my curiosity to increase.

"Where are we going?" I asked as he grabbed my hand and pulled me toward the truck.

"Down the street," he said, beaming like a lunatic.

If I didn't know better, I would've sworn there was a skip to his step.

Two blocks away, bright lights illuminated the front of an old building that had been marked a historical sight. "What is this?"

Alex shrugged. "One of your presidents probably spent the night here once or something," he joked, leading me into the building.

Music was playing upstairs and we could hear people laughing. It felt like we were walking through a museum. Remnants of the Civil War era lined the walls and filled glass fronted cabinets. It was interesting, or it would have been if he'd slowed down enough to let me look. Instead, he pulled me along, leading me up the stairs with quick footsteps.

The entire upper floor was one big room, an old dance hall. There were a dozen couples, all dressed in period costumes. The youngest person in the room looked old enough to be my grandfather. Alex led me over to a row of wooden chairs at the perimeter of the room. We watched the couples go through two traditional dances before anyone paid attention to us.

Alex sat perched with his elbows on his knees, watching the dancers with glee. His eyes sparkled with delight when a grey bearded old man dressed in the dark blue uniform of a Civil War Union soldier approached us.

"May I have the pleasure?" He held his gloved hand out toward me.

I blushed and laughed, shaking my head no. Alex nudged me. "Go ahead! You said you liked dancing."

"T'would be my honor," the man said with a ridiculously fake accent. He bowed deeply as I stood and took his hand. Alex laughed and stopped just short of clapping his hands.

The energy of the room was quickly contagious. Everyone was having such a good time, following the polite protocols of the outdated dance. Eventually Alex joined in, expertly twirling the evening away with my partner's wife. We ended the night with a round robin dance and everyone took turns with each other's partners.

For the first time that night, I ended up in the arms of my date. He followed the steps perfectly light on his feet, leading me along like a professional dancer. By the time the music stopped, I was out of breath. It was hard to concentrate, but I hated to have it end.

Caught in Alex's strong embrace, I could feel the heat pouring from his body and his heartbeat pounding so strong that I could hear it. He smiled down at me softly, baring perfectly white teeth. "You must admit how much fun it might have been to live a hundred and fifty years ago."

"Admitted." My whole body tingled with excitement and electricity.

Alex led me back out into the cool night after refusing numerous offers to stay and have cookies and punch. Once back in his truck, he checked his watch and saw that it was nearly ten. "It is time to return you to your father." He started the engine with a roar, the happy smile still plastered to his face.

"You're quite the Fred Astaire, Mr. Maxwell. I take it you've spent a fair share of time in old dance halls?" I buckled my seatbelt and leaned into the warm leather.

"I wouldn't say a lot, but some, yes. Did you have a good time?" He looked over at my face, illuminated by the soft glow of the dashboard. "I did too."

It was amazing that I had forgotten all about the mess my life was becoming for the past three hours. I'd enjoyed dinner and had a normal conversation with someone. It was something I couldn't imagine happening less than twelve hours earlier. Alex turned on soft music for us to listen to while we enjoyed the quiet ride home. Through the open sunroof, the stars shone brightly once we were outside of the city. It was easy to get lost in the tranquility of it all.

Again, it seemed impossible that we'd been driving long enough to get home. When Alex pulled up behind my house, I realized that more than a half hour had passed in silence.

He took my hand in his and led me to the back door of my house. "Are you sure you had a good time?" he asked.

"A very good time," I smiled. "Very."

"Good enough to want to do it again sometime?" He looked hopeful, but guarded.

I nodded. "I heard them say they do it every Friday night."

"In that case," he said. "May I have the pleasure of your company in one week's time?"

I grinned. "Absolutely. However, I don't think I should take my eyes off you and Louise next time. She may steal you away."

Alex threw back his head in laughter. "I don't think her beauty will ever compare."

He leaned over so close to me that I thought he was going to kiss me. I turned my face to meet his, my heart beating so hard I thought it would burst, and closed my eyes. His warm lips brushed lightly across my cheek and he gently squeezed my hands.

"Thank you for a lovely evening." He whispered into my ear, his face against mine.

Released

Shivers ran down my spine as I opened my eyes to meet his. Biting my lower lip, I resisted the temptation to run my fingers through his hair. Instead of kissing me the way I wanted him to, Alex reached for the doorknob and slowly turned it. Releasing my other hand, he pressed his forehead against mine, both pain and desire covering his face. Pulling away from me slowly, he backed down off the porch, only breaking eye contact when his feet hit the driveway and he turned away to leave.

My heart dropped but the butterflies didn't stop swarming in my belly. I practically floated into the house and up the stairs, ignoring my sister who was following closely behind me. Falling face first onto the bed, I prayed Sarah would go away. When that didn't happen, I rolled over to see her sitting on the edge of my bed, and expectant look in her eyes.

"Dirt!" Sarah demanded. "He's such a dream! And that goodnight kiss? Wow."

I blushed but couldn't erase the smile on my face. "I need a shower," was all I said.

"I bet you do!" Sarah laughed. "A nice cold one at that!"

I rolled my eyes and dragged myself to my feet. Grabbing a fluffy robe, I winked at Sarah before walking down the hall to the bathroom.

Once the door closed, I grabbed my toothbrush and scrubbed my teeth clean. The flavors of dinner lingered in my mouth, making me wish I had more to eat. I'd have to learn to be happy with what I had. I smiled to myself, remembering Alex's lamentations about the selfishness of people. Maybe he meant exquisite food too.

Released

I had just turned the water on when I heard the rap on the window. I nearly had a heart attack when I saw my own face looking in from the outside.

Quickly, I pulled the window open and Crevan crawled inside. "I didn't expect you home so soon," she said in a hushed whisper. "I would have been here earlier. Anything I need to know?"

I shook my head. "Sarah is waiting for dirt, but I told her I have to take a shower."

Crevan looked at the steam pouring out of the tub. "Mmmm, a hot shower. I love those! What dirt do I give her?"

"None. Just tell her you had a lovely time, that he was a perfect gentleman, and that's all."

Crevan grinned. It was like I was beaming into a mirror. "Good thing. The thought of talking about making out with my brother makes me want to puke!"

"I didn't..."

Crevan held up her hand to silence me. "Good. Now go. He's waiting up the lane."

"How?" I panicked. *How was I going to get out of the house without being caught?*

Crevan stifled her laughter. "Go out the window. Damn, have you never broken a rule or two?"

I went over and looked down. It looked like a big drop. "I'll break my leg!" I protested.

Crevan rolled her eyes. "As if. And if you do, you'll heal in an hour if that."

"I will?" This wasn't something I'd considered yet.

Just how big are the changes going to be in me?

Was I invincible?

What else was going to change now?

"Just shut up and jump before we have to explain your physically split personality in here."

A loud knock on the door made us both jump. Sarah's voice called from the other side. "I have to pee. Can I come in?"

"Just a minute," Crevan sang out with my voice, pointing firmly at the window.

I groaned and steeled my nerves. Climbing up onto the ledge, I looked down again and held my breath before dropping the twelve feet to the ground.

My feet hit the grass with little more than a light thud. I stood up slowly, expecting to feel sharp pains shoot up my legs, but nothing happened. I took one last look at the window in time to see Crevan closing it.

The tree frogs sang louder than usual under the star lit sky as I took off at a dead run. Alex's Rover sat with its lights off at the end of the lane. I climbed in before he had a chance to come around and open my door.

Awkward silence filled the truck as he slowly drove down the road with his headlights still off. Once we came to the main drag, he turned them on and sped up.

"Why take me home if I was just going to leave right away?" I asked, breaking the silence once we were almost to his house.

Released

"It's only proper to return a young lady to her father after a night out." It sounded like he thought that was the most obvious answer in the world.

I laughed. "We need to figure out a compromise of sorts here," I suggested. "I agree with you that my generation is a little too free about some things, but you have to loosen up a little bit and realize this is the twenty first century."

He pulled into the garage, carefully wording his response. "It doesn't matter what century it is. Respect is a thing I hold sacred, and I will always do my best to show proper respect to you, your father, and your family. The rules of courtship make it easier for me."

"How so?" I turned to face him.

Alex took a deep breath and sighed. "If I adhere to the rules, it helps me resist the temptations you offer."

I leaned over to him so that my face was right next to his, my lips only an inch away from his. "Would it be so bad to let go, just a little bit?" I whispered seductively. It must've been that the sleeping demon inside of me was waking up because the only thing on my mind was the goodnight kiss I really wanted.

Good looking, knight in shining armor, angelic Alex was sitting right next to me...

Alex didn't pull away, but stiffened against my contact. I saw his eyes tighten, the ache returning to his face, but he said nothing. Scanning his mind, his thoughts shocked me.

Don't let her do this to you... It's not really Cadi doing this...

Angrily, I pushed myself away and jumped out of the truck. He followed behind, but I was faster. Finally, he grabbed my arm just inside the doorway.

"Cadi, wait..."

I spun on my heels and glared at him. "I don't know what's worse," I spat. "The fact that you have no faith in me or the fact that you think I'm nothing more than some demonic whore."

I didn't wait to hear a reply. Instead, I tore myself away from him and ran up the stairs. Only after I'd slammed the door shut did I let the sting of tears fill my eyes. It was easier to cry than admit how true his thoughts were. I had no idea what was happening inside my body or mind anymore.

6

When I woke up the next morning, the house was quiet. I was still stinging from Alex's thoughts last night, and angrily pulled out my cell phone to text Crevan. It took a few minutes for Crevan to reply, but when she did, she complained about how early it was and then said she'd be there within the hour. I sat back in the bed and fumed, waiting for her so that I could go home.

I didn't dare leave the confines of the room until I heard the front door open. I didn't want to see Alex and risk smacking his face. Briskly walking through the living room, I noticed he was sitting at the table, still dressed in the clothes he'd had on last night. Dark circles framed his tired eyes and the stubble had returned to his chin.

"Good morning!" Crevan cooed. "How was last night?"

"Great," I muttered.

"No one is awake, so no need to switch clothes today." Crevan stepped back and looked back and forth between her brother and me. "What happened? You were all smiles last time I saw you."

"Nothing," I growled.

Alex barely acknowledged our presence. Still hovering over his books, he yelled out just as I was leaving the house. "What was your birth name?"

I ignored him. I wouldn't give him a single bit of information more about my life than I had to. My real name was Cadi Matthews, and to me, that's all that mattered.

Home was becoming a foreign concept to me. How long would I be able to call this my home? Well, at least for the next twenty-six days I could and I'd just have to deal with whatever Zandros had in mind for me when it happened. In the meantime, I only had one week left of high school life to enjoy before graduation, then two weeks of being 'alive' after that.

How do people move on knowing the exact date their life will end? I tried to push the thoughts from my mind since they weren't helping. There was a good reason death was so anonymous. It was a blessing not knowing the truth. I had to focus on the here and now, on what I had, and not worry about what I didn't. I couldn't wish my future away, no matter how much I wanted a different outcome. That would be selfish. Alex's voice played in my mind. Selfish indeed, I thought, the anger returning.

Well if I only had three weeks left to live, I was going to do it as best as I could.

Dad was mowing the grass when I got to the house. Mom and Spencer were busy setting up a pop up canopy in the yard so that they could pull the picnic table under the shade. Sarah looked grumpy, skimming the pool, still in her pajamas. Dad waved and my sour mood disappeared completely.

Running over to my mom, I took the clumsy contraption from her. "Let me help," I offered.

"By all means!" She happily stepped out of the way. "I'll go get the food started."

"This thing is ridiculous," Spencer complained, yanking on one leg with no results.

I laughed. "You have to pull out the pin first." I twirled the link pin around on my fingertip and grinned triumphantly. Suddenly, the legs pulled apart easily and the tent was up. Spencer pulled the grill over, positioning it so that it was just outside of the tent while I moved the table into place. After I decided it was just right, I left my brother to grab a rake. It took over an hour for all of the clippings to be swept from the yard and by the time I was done, I had blisters on the inside of both hands.

Joining Mom in the kitchen, we stood side by side and cut vegetables. When that was finished, we moved on to a huge fresh fruit salad. My stomach turned with hunger. I knew that if I took a bite, I wouldn't stop until the whole bowl was empty and I was throwing up.

Luckily, Mom was distracted by Spencer's rather loud announcement that he was taking off to go play ball with his friends. "Be home by four, dear. We may need some help at the last minute!" She didn't notice that I had grabbed a loaf of bread and started up the stairs with it.

Sitting crossed legged on my bed I tore into the food, wishing I had something else to go with it; meat, cheese, maybe a big plate of the beef I had last night. When I had finished the last piece, my hunger was sated, but not satisfied. The smell of barbeque wafted up the stairs, making it nearly impossible to ignore. Groaning, I looked around and tried to find something to occupy my mind instead of the food. Spying the shopping bag that sat on my chair, I went over and emptied its contents.

I found a baby blue one-piece bathing suit mixed in the pile of new shorts and tank tops. I held it up to myself and saw that it would fit, but barely. Excitedly, I changed out of my clothes to try it on. It was kind of impressive, how long my legs looked in the high thigh cut. The neckline didn't plunge, but showed off just a bit of cleavage. It was snug, but not uncomfortable. Pulling on the shorts, I tied a halter-top around my neck and slipped on a pair of sandals.

If people noticed the physical change in me, they would most likely keep it to themselves. What would they think, that I'd had plastic surgery and healed overnight? The thought made me smile as I skipped down the stairs. No longer did the smell of food tempt me.

I was on a mission.

"I'm going to run into town to get a few things, is that okay?"

Mom stirred the large pan and nodded. "Go ahead honey. We've got everything under control."

I smiled and kissed her on the cheek before bouncing outside toward my car. "I'm running to the beauty supply store," I called to Sarah. "Need anything?"

Sarah came over to me, the grouchy look still there. "How about new parents?" she lamented.

I stood stock-still. "What's wrong?" None of us had ever had any major issues with our parents before. What could I have missed?

"Mom caught me sneaking out last night and grounded me for a month." Sarah obviously felt it was cruel and unusual punishment.

"What?" I grinned and hushed my voice. "Why were you sneaking out?" This was the first scandal to hit our family in the years I'd been a part of it.

"Blain texted me. There was a party at the bay. Everyone was there. Everyone." She looked like it was the most important event in the world and she'd missed out. "Dad decided I was grounded forever, but Mom talked him down. It's totally bogus! I didn't even go!"

"How far did you get?" It was getting harder and harder to stop myself from laughing at Sarah.

"The front porch. Mom heard his car." She stuck her lip out and pouted like a three-year-old.

This time, I did laugh. I could easily imagine the shades of red Dad must've turned. I looked at him, covered in dirt, while he threw big logs out of the back of his pickup for a bonfire. "I'm sorry," I said to my sister. "I'll be back in a bit."

"I'll be here..." Sarah grumbled. "Cleaning the bathroom..."

"Hey," I caught her attention as I climbed behind the wheel of my car. "I'll bring back something to cheer you up, okay?"

Sarah waved me off, stomping into the house where more chores waited for her.

I shook my head slowly, gave Dad a friendly wave, and left. Turning the music up loud, I opened all of the windows so I could feel the wind wash over me. What was it that the song said?

We are the youth gone wild...

That's exactly how I felt just then. Throwing my head back in laughter, I pressed the accelerator and drove as fast as the poor car would go.

About a mile before entering the city limits, the flashing blue and red lights brought my mind down out of the sky.

Shit.

I glanced at the speedometer and saw that I was going over ninety miles an hour. I pulled over to the side of the road, turned the music off, and waited. Taking a deep breath, I steeled my nerves and watched in the rear view mirror as the deputy ambled toward my car.

"License and insurance," he said, scribbling on his ticket book.

My mind raced. Leaning over, I pulled the requested cards out of my purse and handed them to him with a sly smile. "I'm sorry officer. I guess I wasn't paying attention."

He caught my eye as he took the cards from me. I bit my bottom lip and pouted just a bit. Maybe if I looked pitiful or flirted just a little bit...

"I shouldn't have been going so fast, making you have to chase after me in this heat," I cooed. I could see the man swallow hard, sweat beads forming on his forehead.

"Well," he stammered. "I clocked you going ninety-three in a fifty-five. That's extremely dangerous."

"I know I should've been more careful." I gave him another pitiful pout and practically whimpered. "How bad is the ticket going to be? I don't want my dad to kill me."

The deputy couldn't take his eyes off me, letting his gaze leave my face only to travel down the front of my body. He seemed mesmerized and licked his bottom lip. "I'd hate for that to happen too, miss. Just slow down and take better care. I'd hate to see you get hurt." He handed the cards back to me and leaned in the window just a bit, breathing deeply.

I was repulsed by the salty smell of sweat mixed with musky aftershave but held it in. "You," I flirted, tapping him lightly on the nose with my fingertip. "Are a prince among men." I let the smile fade and the poor schmuck looked confused as he straightened himself.

I waited until he'd backed away a step before pulling away. The laughter returned, along with the loud music and wind in my hair, as I forgot all about the ticket I almost got. There were definitely some perks to this newfound self I was becoming.

By the time I returned home, there was less than two hours before people would start showing up, and based on the amount of food my mother had set out, Crevan had invited the entire senior class. I asked Dad if he needed help with anything. After getting the all clear, I ran upstairs to my bedroom and began emptying bags.

Grabbing the blonde hair extensions, I went to Sarah's room. "I got you something," I grinned.

Sarah was sitting in front of her vanity, preparing her face for the night's events. Her eyes lit up when I held up a handful of long blonde tresses, the color matching my sister's bottle blonde perfectly. "Oooh! That's awesome!" Sarah took them and looked at my hair. She must've noticed the fullness now that my hair was down and windblown. "Did you get yours done?

I nodded. "They put in a few highlights and a clear gloss on it. Do you like it?"

Sarah whistled. "It looks great. How much did it cost you?" She had a guilty look on her face when she looked down at her gift. "These are expensive Cad."

"Don't worry about it. They were on sale. I had enough saved up."

Sarah accepted the gift with a hug and sat back down, holding the strands up next to her head. "Can you help me put them in?"

I started parting and clipping the fake hair onto my sister's head. "Wait until you see my new suit," I told her.

"I saw it the night you got it," Sarah reminded me.

I shook my head and motioned for Sarah to follow me to my bedroom. Pulling the skimpy blue fabric from the bag, I held up a bikini top that left little the imagination. The cups were padded with a gel pocket. "Guaranteed to make my B's at least a C!" I laughed.

Sarah grabbed it from me. "This is awesome! They feel so real!" She poked at the inserts with a grin. "Look who discovered she's a girl."

I chuckled. Now all I had to do was get the inserts out and I wouldn't have to spend the entire pool party in a bathing suit that was too tight. "Get out so I can change," I laughed. "Your hair looks really good, by the way."

Sarah flipped her hair dramatically. "Why thank you. I am fabulous, aren't I?" She giggled and walked out of my room.

After changing again, I admired myself in the mirror. The bright blue bathing suit looked great against my creamy skin. Unless she looked closely, I didn't think Sarah would notice I'd swapped the gel for the real thing.

Satisfied that I didn't look too freakishly different, I tied the halter back on and went downstairs. Before I could even make it outside, people began pulling up by the carload. In the two days that Crevan had taken over my life, she'd made a lot of new friends. People I knew by face but not by name greeted me the same way as my closest friends did.

Loudly.

Mom had to set up another table for the gift bags that were piling up. I had clearly told my friends not to bring presents. Apparently, Crevan felt differently. As the hour passed, parked cars filled the entire lane. There were so many bodies in the pool; it was hard to tell how many people were there. Some of the guys were helping Dad build up the bonfire, sparks crackling into the twilight sky.

The grill was on and Spencer took charge, tossing hot dogs through the air at his rowdy friends. Sarah was belle of the ball, horsing around in the pool. I couldn't wipe the smile off my face as I made my way through the crowd that had gathered.

In my honor.

Someone came up behind me and dangled a cold plastic cup in front of my face. Turning around, I found a lovely dark-haired boy grinning back at me.

"Happy birthday Cadi," Nick said. "I brought you a gift, but didn't want it to get lost in the pile." He reached into the pocket of his jeans and pulled out a clenched fist.

Holding it over my opened hand, he dropped a teardrop cut diamond pendant into my palm.

"I thought it would look nice on the bracelet you always wear." He took it from me and clipped it onto the Aeternus ring that held the leather strap around my wrist. "When I saw it, it reminded me of that sparkle you get in your eyes sometimes."

"This is too much," I protested, gazing at the stone in awe.

"Never," he smiled again, taking my hand. Someone had turned up the music and people had started to dance. Without hesitation, he pulled me over to the impromptu dance area and began dancing with me.

After four songs, I couldn't stop laughing. I was having such a good time.

No homework.

No school.

No demons.

No self-righteous-always-in-control Alex.

This was what it meant to have fun.

Without another thought, I abruptly left Nick's arms, stripped down to my bikini, and jumped into the pool.

The water was cold, but refreshing. Surfacing, I found myself in the middle of a game of chicken. I squealed as a member of the football team swam under me and came up with my body perched on his shoulders. The other girls splashed around on the backs of boys, while everyone tried to dunk each other.

After the sun went down, the air around the water got cool. I climbed out of the pool and shivered. Nick was standing at the bottom of the ladder and handed me a big towel. I wrapped it around my shoulders and thanked him.

He handed me another cup. "This will warm you up better," he said, encouraging me to drink.

I took a sip and the bitter liquid burned my throat as it went down. I fought back a sputter. "What is it?" It looked like cola.

"It's got a little whiskey in it." He stepped back. "I'm sorry. You don't drink?" He looked like the mere thought was incredulous.

I shrugged and took another big gulp. Wasn't getting wasted a rite of teenagers everywhere? I might be a demonic whore, but I was a teenager too. "More," I gasped, handing the cup back to Nick.

He laughed and went to refill it for me. It looked like we weren't the only ones partaking in the illegal beverages. Even Spencer was acting intoxicated. By the time I had downed two more cups of Nick's warm concoction, I was ready to dance again.

I didn't even care that I was almost naked. I let the towel fall to ground and wrapped my arms around Nick's neck. I nuzzled against his chest, deeply inhaling the clean scent of him. There was a trace of something bitter there too. "Do you smoke?" Only the kids with a bad reputation smoked cigarettes, not science geeks.

Nick grinned down at me. "You only live once, right?" He shifted and turned our bodies so the porch lights shined on my face. "I won't ever do it around you if it bothers you. Maybe you can convince me to quit."

I shrugged before returning to my lazy position, lying against his chest. "It doesn't matter." I mumbled against his chest. Lost in the haze of booze and music, I wasn't aware of how much time had passed.

A loud boom scared me to death, making me jump and gasp. From high above, bright golden lights rained down over the fields. Soon, another boom followed, this time raining red and blue sparkles. I grinned, seeing my dad at the edge of the field, lighting the fireworks. Leaning against Nick's chest, I watched as the sky filled with amazing colors.

It was as if Dad had brought the stars down to me since I couldn't get to them.

Nick held me tightly, gently kissing the top of my head. My whole body shivered when his hands lazily stroked my bare arms. When the show was over, everyone cheered loudly.

Dad paused on the porch to take an exaggerated bow before disappearing back into the house where he and Mom had remained hidden all night.

The buzz of alcohol was wearing off quickly and I found myself sobering up. It was then that I realized how exposed I was. Pulling away from Nick, I excused myself to find my clothes. Someone thought it would be funny to throw my top and shorts in the pool.

Spencer was in the middle of the water and called out to me. "Hey Cadi! Looking for this?" He laughed hysterically as he threw the balled up, wet halter-top toward me.

It hit me in the shoulder, but I caught it quickly. It was a good thing the party was at my own house. I had plenty of dry clothes inside.

I hadn't even closed my bedroom door when the blonde girl appeared. "Crevan," I gasped. "You scared me."

The usual giddy look was gone from her face. "Alex wanted to bring you a birthday gift," she said quietly.

I saw the wrapped package in her hand. "But he wouldn't come himself," I sighed. "It figures he doesn't want to be around the devil's spawn."

"He was here," Crevan quickly corrected and then paused. "But he couldn't stay, so he asked me to give this to you."

A mental image of Alex watching me with Nick from the shadows played in my mind. Guilt threatened to creep into my gut, but I refused to admit it.

Crevan handed the present to me and I took it hesitantly.

Sitting on my bed, I carefully opened it, revealing a pencil sketch surrounded by an ornate silver frame. It was a portrait of me, soaking wet but wrapped in his flannel shirt, standing on his front porch; a perfect representation of the moment we met. A small card fell out of the wrapping onto my lap.

Forever Your Friend. ~Alexander

"I don't know what to say." I looked up at my new friend, a tear in my eye. Was it a tear of sadness or of anger? "He thinks I'm a demon, the exact thing he hunts down and kills," I bemoaned.

Crevan shook her head slowly. "There's so much more to it, Cadi. It would take you forever to understand."

I set the frame on the bed next to me. "Then why didn't he stay tonight?" I knew the answer before I finished asking the question.

Nick.

The girl looked at me pointedly. "This whole situation is new for him, and he's not quite sure what to do about it."

"You're right, I don't understand." I pouted.

Crevan drew in a deep breath and exhaled, sitting next to me. "We come from a clan of people very deeply bound by traditions called Veduny. We've been around for a long time and some of us don't adjust to the culture changes that the passage of time brings. My brother is kind of stuck in some weird, chivalrous stand still of time."

I rolled my eyes. I appreciated the manners and understood his take on morality, but he called me a whore. Okay, he didn't use the word, but the intent was there.

"There is a very real issue of your bloodline. The Veduny way of life prohibits any relationship other than the ones most pure. Not everyone follows the rules, but Alexander always has without question. Our laws forbid all types of relationships, even basic friendship with someone who isn't one of us."

I started to defend myself, but Crevan held her hand up and wouldn't allow it. "I'm not saying you are unworthy. I'm saying that you just aren't one of us. Can't you see how this could be hard for him?"

"You don't understand." I didn't want to admit aloud how stupid it all sounded.

"Oh, I do. You think I've never been under the spell of a demon? It's not a common thing with our job, but it happens. Sometimes you can't help but be drawn to them. It's true the other way too. We both have powerful blood. It draws people to us. That's why we work together, so we can keep each other's souls a little safer. People want to be with us too, just because of what we are."

"And Alex thinks that..." I began to put the puzzle together.

"...That it's possible you may be drawn to each other because of your respective DNA and nothing more? Yep, that pretty much sums it up." Crevan gave me an apologetic look.

"Great." I rolled my eyes again. I had been stupid to think it was anything more than that, no matter how much I wondered if there was something between Alex and me. "What exactly are Veduny? I mean, I know what my mother was and what that makes me, but what are you?"

Crevan smiled softly. "We are tough to explain sometimes, so I'll use one of the more common myths. We are the result of the sons of God mating with the daughters of men. It even mentions us briefly in your Bible."

"You're Nephilim?" I was awe struck. It was written that angels came to Earth and married human women. Their offspring were called many things over the years, and most cultures had a similar myth, even if they were called other names.

Crevan nodded and grinned. "The offspring, that you call Nephilim, had the God given power of the angels as well as the downfalls of being human. Most of them took great advantage of that and angered the Creator. God brought the Great Flood to teach mankind a lesson as well as to destroy the Nephilim. When the Veduny survived, He granted us life on Earth so long as we do His work. It became our job to destroy the demons in the world in order to stop the Dark One's influences over mankind."

I looked back at the card that I still held. "This is Alex's promise to never come after me?"

Crevan nodded. "He would never hurt you, and neither will I." She hopped up. "Now, how about this party?"

The gleeful childish Crevan returned. My mood instantly lightened, whether I wanted it to or not. "You outdid yourself in two whole days. I don't think I've ever been this popular."

"What can I say? I attract people, even when I'm wearing your dowdy clothes." She giggled while I got up and grabbed some dry clothes to put on.

"I just wanted to thank you. No matter what your people think about me, you two are good friends to me."

"If you really want to thank me," she grinned like a cat again and popped her bubblegum. "You'll let me be you and finish out this party. Heck, you've got my Bio-Boy all warmed up!" She winked as I blushed.

"Don't lead him on, okay?" I pulled another halter top on that hung loosely over my body and changed my mind. Pulling out a more modest blouse, I pulled my arms through the sleeves and buttoned it up. "I don't want to be engaged when you and Alex decide it's time to take off and leave him to me."

Crevan snickered while I pulled on a pair of jeans. "You don't have to worry about that. He's not the marrying kind. We already covered that."

I groaned. I could only imagine what else she'd covered with Nick. I held up my arm and pulled the diamond charm off of my bracelet. "Put this on if you're going out there. He'll notice if it's not there."

Crevan took the charm and clipped it to the facsimile band she wore around her own wrist. "You sneak out the back. I'll go out the front and say hi to the parents."

I nodded, turning to the door. At the last minute, I stopped and grabbed Crevan in a tight hug. "Thank you. I mean it."

"Don't forget, Alex is human, too. Our people constantly have a battle waging inside of us. Don't make his any harder to fight than it has to be." The girl smiled and shooed me out the door.

Sneaking down the stairs, I froze in place when the step creaked. When I was sure neither of my parents had left their position on the couch, I continued out the back door.

Released

Skirting the party, I stayed to the edge of the field, out of the line of vision of any of the revelers. Crevan bounced out of the house and went directly to Nick, who greeted her with a warm embrace while I headed straight toward the man who would never be more than a friend to me.

7

The living room was darker than normal when I walked in and Alex wasn't at his usual post at the dining room table. It looked like most of the books were back on the shelves. Everything was silent, sending a shiver up my spine. It was as if I was in a haunted house, except there was no dust and no ghosts.

That I knew of...

Upstairs, my bedroom door was open. Other than the bed being made, nothing else had changed. My discarded clothes from the night before still sat in the middle of the floor. My empty water glass was still on the nightstand next to the half-burnt taper candle.

From the window, I could see Alex sitting in the backyard. The full moon lit up the sky brilliantly, but the small fire in front of him cast a warm glow across everything close to it. I watched him for a few minutes, marveling at the stillness of his body. Not once did he twitch a muscle. I wasn't sure if I should interrupt him or not, and decided it was best not to. Instead, I went to the living room and grabbed a book from the shelf. Curling up on the end of the couch, I began reading; or pretending to read. It was all about mythical and biblical creatures, but I couldn't focus on the words. Rather, I flipped the pages absently.

He still hadn't come inside by the time I'd turned the last page. I was just about to give up and go to bed when I heard the back door open. Holding my breath, I wondered what he would say to me. Would he scold me for yelling at him? Would he not say a word to me, too disgusted by what he saw at my party? I didn't have to wonder long when I heard his heavy footsteps going up the back stairs. Maybe he didn't even know I was there.

After flipping through the pages again and suffering in the silence, Alex appeared in the doorway. He was fresh out of a shower, dressed only in loose pajama bottoms. He was rubbing his wet hair with a towel when he first seemed to notice me sitting there. A normal person would have jumped or been startled, or even said hello, but not Alex.

He simply lowered the towel and looked at the floor.

"Are you not speaking to me?" I asked quietly.

He shrugged. Scanning the couch, he locked eyes on the book I'd been reading. Going over to the shelf, he pulled a different one down and handed it to me. "This may suit your needs better," he said cruelly.

I looked at it.

The Exorcist.

Cute.

He said nothing else, but his face spoke volumes. He was angry, so angry he was about to explode.

"If you don't want to help me anymore, just say the word and I'll leave. I'm sure Crevan will hate to leave the party early, but whatever." I threw the book across the room. "I never asked for your help you know! I'd rather he kills me now than have to deal with your mood swings another minute!"

"Damn it Cadi!" He went over to the discarded book and replaced it on the shelf with a careful shove. "Whatever you think of me and my repressed way of living, do you have to flaunt your lack of control? Was it really necessary to get drunk tonight?"

"You drank wine last night! What's the difference?"

He stalked over to me so that he was right in my face and replied. "I wasn't practically naked, hanging all over some hapless man who has no idea what he's getting into."

No words could express how I felt hearing the words. A cold hard slap to the face would have to suffice.

He placed his hand over the stinging welt that I'd left and raised an eyebrow at me, sneering.

"You have art all over this house; Da Vinci, Donatello, Botticelli, Raphael... There are naked people on every wall in this house, yet in real life, it's not okay? Is it that I'm not two thousand years old posing for a statue? Was Venus di Milo a whore?"

He tried to speak, but I wasn't done with my tirade just yet.

"It's just skin Alex!" I ripped the fabric of my shirt away from my body and stood before him bare from the waist up, except for the bikini top. "You're not going to hell because you saw it and I'm not going to steal your soul by showing it to you."

The square of his jaw tightened as he stood there, refusing to look at me. I reached out and gently rested my hand on his chest, feeling his strong heartbeat under my fingertips. "It's okay..."

"What name did your mother give you?" His breath quickened; his words faltered.

"Carina," I replied quietly. It felt strange to hear the name, even stranger to be the one who said it.

Alex turned away. "Cadi, I can't..."

"I know," I reassured him. "Crevan told me. Maybe someday we will figure out how we can be friends. But right now, I should go to my room."

Alex nodded and watched me as I silently walked up the stairs.

Sitting against the pillows, the silence in the house gave me time to reflect on my situation. Crevan was right about the attraction I felt for Alexander. It most certainly was there, but when I really thought about it, I wasn't sure how I truly felt about him. If it was 'the real thing', then why did I also feel the butterflies in my belly when I danced with Nick? I couldn't deny that I was drawn to Alex in a way that couldn't be explained. It was almost as if fate was involved in our meeting. As I succumbed to sleep, I knew one thing. Alexander Maxwell was meant to be in my life, and I would always think of him as my true friend. No matter what the Veduny had to say about it.

A dreamless night followed, interrupted by my cell phone vibrating on the nightstand. Checking the message, I saw that Crevan had texted me a half hour ago to let me know she was on her way.

"Honey! I'm hooooome!" Crevan yelled from downstairs.

I jumped out of the bed, tripping over the sheets that had tangled themselves up around my ankles. I was just regaining my footing when Crevan came into the room.

"Over sleep much?" she smiled cheerfully.

I nodded, rolling my eyes. "I'm sorry," I said. "It was a rough night."

Crevan looked suspicious, eyeing every corner of the room. "A rough night... Alone?"

I blushed and turned away from her. "Don't start," I insisted. Crevan pulled off the t-shirt and shorts she'd shown up wearing. I took them and pulled them on, completing our switch off in minutes.

"Okay," Crevan said after a moment of consideration. "But if you hurt him, you'll have me to deal with."

I stopped dead in my tracks. "Nothing happened. Don't…"

"I'm not. I'm just saying…" She got dressed in her own clothes. "Hurry up. Your mom is on the warpath because Spence is hung over. She's worried about being late for church."

I froze.

Church.

I hadn't considered that yet. Would I still be able to go? "What's going to happen if I walk into a church now?"

Crevan looked like she was seriously contemplating the situation. "I imagine lightning will strike and Lucifer will regain his hold on the entire world. Other than that, I think the only thing you have to worry about is an hour long nap and maybe some coffee and doughnuts."

I laughed at the absurdity of my worries. Of course, I could go to church. It's not as if I was really a demon, right? If I were all that bad, Crevan and Alex wouldn't want to be near me. After all, they were angels.

Sort of.

I made it home in time to shower and get ready for church before Mom had calmed down enough to notice I was there.

"Honestly, I don't know what's wrong with kids these days," she lamented. "Between Sarah sneaking out to meet a boy and Spencer getting drunk... I'm just glad one of you isn't in any trouble." She smiled warmly at me.

If only she knew...

The Matthews family sat in the middle of the chairs that had been set up for the weekly worship service. The church we attended met at the American Legion Hall every week, sometimes going to the preacher's farm for a potluck dinner or other fun activities. The congregation was somewhat small, but everyone was like family to each other.

"Easter Revisited" was the sermon theme for the week. The preacher spoke about the fact that people seemed to forget all about the sacrifice Jesus Christ made for them unless it was the holiday weekend. He reminded us all that it was important to remember, no matter what day of the year it was.

Mom and Dad nodded along with many other parishioners. Spencer looked like he wanted to throw up. Sarah was doodling in the margins of her opened Bible. By the time he'd finished speaking and the preacher invited everyone to stay for fellowship hour, I had begun to consider, for the first time, the meaning behind his words.

Was the sacrifice meant for all people, or was I just damned?

"Oh my dear," the sultry voice whispered into my ear. "You are most certainly damned. And you've tried to disappear from me."

My heart raced as I spun around and found Zandros.

"How are you here?" Frantically, I saw all of the people around me milling about, minding their own business.

My parents were deep in conversation with another couple. Sarah was flirting and Spencer was sitting quietly at a table alone, nursing a cup of coffee and his headache. He looked up at me, but didn't seem to notice the danger that was surrounding all of them.

Zandros laughed heartily. "As if four walls have any control over who enters them? Their Lord controls their minds not their buildings." He took my hand in his, holding it gently; nothing like his usual demeanor. In the light of the church, he seemed almost... friendly.

The preacher worked his way over to us, holding his hand out with a welcoming smile. Greeting Zandros warmly, he turned to me. "It's always good to see our youngsters bringing a friend to service. I'm Pastor Dan." He introduced himself.

"I'm an old friend of Carina's." Zandros replied. "You gave a lovely sermon. It's so sad how right you are about people forgetting what's truly important." He spoke clearly, annunciating every syllable.

Pastor Dan nodded enthusiastically. "Well the Lord gave us a promise that day, and it's one that I am grateful for."

Zandros smiled again and wrapped a protective arm around my shoulders. I stiffened in his embrace. "No promise is ever small enough to break. Is it Carina?"

I pressed my lips into a tight line and remained silent.

"I'm sorry, but I never knew Cadi was short for Carina." Dan looked at me quizzically.

"It's not," I muttered.

"We've been friends for a very long time." Zandros reminded the preacher. "Since long before she was Cadi Matthews."

"Well it was very nice to meet you..." Dan let the question dangle in the air.

"Alex. Alexander Zandros." He replied, squeezing my shoulder, digging his fingertips into the flesh.

My heart sank. There was no way he chose the name randomly. After Dan walked away, I braced myself for his outburst. The evil glimmer was in his eye, but his face remained friendly. The only thing that I was truly fearful of was the tight grip he still held on me.

"What are you doing? I still have twenty-four days."

"Ah," he cheered. "You've made a countdown to the day you become a blushing bride."

"Prisoner, bride, whatever," I spat. "You said I had a month, so I'm taking it."

"And I told you that even during that month, you still belong to me. You remember that promise, right?" He pushed my chin up with the crook of his finger, forcing me to make eye contact. "Just remember, the very moment you decide to break your word, I will know. And then no amount of Veduny magic can hide you from me. When the time comes, you will come to me, just like you promised."

I pulled away from him sharply. "Just leave. You don't belong here."

"I belong just as much as you, Carina. Before I forget my manners, please have your friend Alexander relay my best regards to his father."

Without another word, Zandros departed the building, politely greeting people as he passed. I would never understand how he managed to do that without everyone recoiling at the sheer evil of his nature.

My world spun inside of my head.

He knew about Alex.

He knew I was hiding from him.

That meant that our plan wasn't working at all. No matter what we did, I wouldn't be able to get out of this. My heart fell with resignation. The least I could do was warn Alex that Zandros knew about him. I braced my nerves. If my fate was sealed, there was no reason to let Alex get hurt in the meantime.

I quickly joined my parents. "Mom, I'm going to take off, if that's okay?"

She looked confused. "But we all rode together. Where are you going?"

"I just want to go for a walk, maybe hang out with the girls here in town for a while. I'll have someone bring me home."

"What about dinner?" Mom complained.

Dad wrapped his arm around his wife's waist. "She'll be fine. Missing one Sunday dinner won't kill anyone." He smiled warmly at me. "Call me if you need to be picked up."

I nodded before walking out into the bright sunshine. Nervously, I looked around, expecting to see Zandros standing close by, waiting to strike. I felt like taking off, running at full speed. But with the small town we lived in, there was no way I could do that without people noticing. Instead, I started a brisk walk in the direction of the country road that took me home.

There were more people out and about as I passed through the side streets. For the first time I paid attention to the little town around me. Parents and children meandered to and from their cars and houses as if all was right in the world.

How could they not know of the dangers that lived among them?

Monsters were everywhere.

Hell, there was a monster living inside of me.

Who was going to save them all?

Passing through the neighborhood, I saw a family playing in their yard. The little girl squealed with glee as her father picked her up and tossed her into the air.

"You caught me daddy!" she exclaimed.

"I'll always catch you baby girl."

My thoughts skimmed over the times I'd horsed around in the yard with my own family over the past few years. Water balloon fights happened every summer, snowball fights in the winter. We would split into teams, usually the twins versus our dad and me. It wasn't fair, really. The twins seemed to have some kind of telepathy and knew when a shot was coming. Dad and I had to develop our own strategy, which always included a code word.

If you hear me say draw, drop to the ground! Don't forget!

I knew every time I heard it that I had to duck. Then Dad would nail whichever sibling was holding me hostage. We would double over in laughter afterward.

Tears of happiness streamed down my cheeks as I neared the outskirts of town. I would miss those days the most.

By the time I reached Alex's driveway, I could feel an oppressive presence in the area. Zandros was here, I was sure of it.

Pushing myself faster, I made it into the living room without looking behind to see if he was following me.

Crevan bolted straight up off the couch as the front door slammed. "What the…"

"Zandros…" I couldn't catch my breath. "He… was… there. He knows…"

After I caught my breath, I took a big drink of the water Crevan had on the coffee table.

"Sure," Crevan said. "Go ahead; I didn't want that anymore anyway."

"Where is Alex?" I put the empty glass down.

Crevan shrugged. "I dunno. He left right after you did. Didn't say where he was going. What's the problem?"

"It's not working." I stood up and paced back and forth through the living room. "Zan… He was at my church. How was he at my church?"

Crevan rolled her eyes. "How were *you* at your church? What's the difference really?"

I shook my head. "You don't understand. He knows about Alex."

"So what?" Crevan got up and went to the kitchen to refill her glass. "Most demons know about us. If they don't, well that just makes our job a little easier."

I couldn't listen to her flippant attitude. This was a big deal and it was infuriating that Crevan wouldn't recognize it for that fact. I was angry. Fire burned in my gut, begging for release.

"He knows about ALEX!" I shouted at the top of my lungs. "He's here! Can't you feel him near?"

Crevan stepped back, a look of surprise spreading over her face. "Well look who isn't a little lamb after all? Why should I think Zandy is any more of a threat than you?"

"What?" I stopped dead in my tracks. "Why would you even say that?"

"Why did my brother look so guilty before he took off? Twenty bucks says he's going to go repent for something." Her tone was calm, but ice cold. "I didn't give you all that personal information last night just so that you could use it and seduce him."

"I DIDN'T SEDUCE HIM!" I felt like throwing up, I was so pissed off. "Don't you even care that Alex is out there, while Zand... while *he* is here watching?"

Crevan plopped down on the couch and kicked her feet up on the table. "Not really," she said casually. "We've had an awful long time to learn how to take care of ourselves. Seems the only thing I can't protect my brother from is standing right here in his house."

Every breath left my body in an instant. It was like being punched in the gut, only worse. I knew Crevan was right. Before the tears could spill again, I ran out of the house.

Ignoring the darkness that surrounded me, I ran toward home. I went straight to the garage where Spencer had his weight set and a heavy bag. Punching with all my might, I wore my body out, pummeling the bag until my knuckles were bloody. Sinking to the floor, I tried desperately to collect my thoughts and emotions.

There had to be a solution.

If Alex wasn't safe, neither was my family. He might be able to defend himself, but could they?

The smells of Sunday dinner wafted through the air. I could hear my dad cooking on the grill just outside of the garage, but no one was any wiser that I was home.

If I ran away, Zandros would follow me. He would leave them alone.

I sat in the garage and waited for what seemed like forever before the sun fell so that I could go inside.

"Cadi?" Mom out called from the living room.

I stopped in the doorway, tucking my blood stained hands behind my back. My entire family sat in there, absently watching television. "I'm going to go upstairs and finish my Biology essay," I said weakly. My voice cracked, hoarse from crying so much.

"You okay?" Dad asked.

I reassured him before heading up the stairs. After washing my hands and splashing water on my face, I felt a little refreshed and a lot more determined. I had a little over three weeks until the deadline came. I would stay until graduation so that my family wouldn't be too disappointed when I left. Then I would make up some grand excuse as to why I was going. I would run as far away as I could and leave everyone I cared about safe from Zandros.

A soft knock on the door brought me out of my reverie. Dad came in slowly, a pensive look on his face. "I know you said you're fine, and I know a dad's not supposed to pry nowadays, but... Did something happen with Alex or with that Nick boy?"

I shook my head.

"Because if one of them hurt you..."

"Dad it's fine," I lied. "They're fine. I'm okay." I attempted to give him a smile, but it probably looked faker than a school picture.

"I guess Biology homework can be upsetting, but I doubt that's all that is going on," he insisted.

"Dad, really..."

"Because you can talk to me, Cadi. About anything. Anytime."

"I know, thanks." I toyed with the pencil I'd picked up.

What could I say?

I've promised my soul to a demon and I've hurt the reputation of an angel?

"Maybe you should call Alex. He's a nice boy. Maybe he could cheer you up?"

I shook my head and looked down, ashamed. "I don't know that I'll be seeing him again." It wasn't a lie. Would I bother to stop and say goodbye to him on my way out of town?

Dad fell even quieter than normal. "That's too bad. I liked him." He fumbled for the door handle. "Well I hope you kids work it out. Whatever it is that needs to be worked out. Just remember I'm here to help if I can."

Maybe my dad could go on a 'Zandros hunt'. He'd killed plenty of deer and turkeys in his life. I sarcastically wondered what time of year demons were in season.

I nodded as he left and pulled the notebook into my lap.

Creation versus Evolution...

I'd intended to write a long tirade stating the legal violation of the assignment. Maybe I should write about Creation. If I was a demon, and angels existed, then maybe the stories of Genesis were true. Maybe an Almighty created our world. For that matter, even if evolution was correct, who cared that humans evolved from monkeys? Somehow, monkeys were created in the first place. That expanding, hot, and dense thing from the Big Bang Theory had to have come from somewhere. Maybe Evolution and Creation existed side by side. Maybe some God created a place that evolved into the world we knew.

Creation was the ultimate winner by the time I finished rambling through five pages. My eyes ached from staring at the computer screen, gathering information and sources; my hand cramped from writing so much. Everyone was quiet downstairs when I looked at the clock. It was nearly midnight.

Sighing, I headed to the bathroom to shower and get ready for bed. Checking the window, I locked it before climbing under the hot steam. Half expecting an interruption, by either Zandros or Crevan, I finished quickly and pulled on my pajamas.

Tucked in bed, I laid there for hours. Unable to sleep and face the dream visit that was sure to come, I began wishing I was at Alex's house.

"Awe," his cruel voice soothed. "Are you afraid of being alone?"

No one was there, but I heard it clearly, as if he'd spoken it to my face.

"I'm always here, Carina."

"Please," I whimpered. I just wanted him to leave me alone. "I'm doing everything you asked me to. Please just leave me alone."

His face appeared, standing over me and looking down with disapproval. "We've been over that before, Carina. I cannot even entertain the idea."

I pulled myself up to a sitting position, gathering the sheets around me. "What's going to happen to me? When you take me?"

Zandros sneered. "Would you like all of the dirty details? Or would you prefer I just show you?" He climbed onto the bed, roughly pushing me back, pinning me underneath of him. "So sweet, so naive," he snarled, running his lips across my chin.

I turned my face away from his. "I just want to know."

"We all want things, don't we?" He laughed before disappearing into the darkness around me.

By the time morning came, I was more tired than when I'd gone to bed. Although I had gotten a few hours of sleep, I woke up several times with bad dreams. Even when Zandros wasn't there, I dreamt he was. Now I had two tormentors to deal with.

A demon and my own subconscious.

After I drudged through all of my morning classes, I was grateful for the break lunch hour would give. Sitting down at a table toward the back by myself, I carefully picked at the food in front of me. I didn't want to gorge myself in public that was for sure. Then again, if I did, I could just run to the bathroom and be yet another teenage tragedy. I could imagine the rumors that would spread. Even though I was leaving soon, I didn't want to leave Sarah and Spencer with that kind of legacy.

"Hey there pretty girl," Nick said, sliding into the empty chair next to me. "You look beat."

131

"I am," I admitted.

He took my hand in his gently, resting on top of the table. His finger traced the leather band on my wrist. "What happened to the diamond?" I could tell his feelings were hurt that it wasn't there.

My mind raced. I'd forgotten to get it back from Crevan the day before. "It's in my jewelry box at home. I didn't want to risk losing it," I lied. "I figured it would be my luck."

Nick nodded. The hurt look went away as quickly as it had come. "I have just the thing to cheer you up." He grinned playfully as several students passed by, commenting on the great party. With great flourish, Nick pulled some stapled papers out of his satchel and handed them to me.

Turning them over, I saw the Biology exam that Crevan had taken in my place. A bright red A+ marked the top. "And..." Nick continued. "Dr. Robinson said I could tell you the big news."

"Tell me what?" I asked nervously, tucking the test into my backpack.

"They want you to make the Graduation Speech." He smiled so big it was impossible not to share his happiness.

"Thank you," I said sincerely, hugging him. "I never would've passed that test without your help. I'm surprised Blackburn turned in my grade already. I just turned the paper in first thing this morning."

Nick shrugged. "He must've been impressed," he commented. "Are you the typical straight A student who writes her speech freshman year?"

A speech...

Blessing everyone's futures...

Great.

"No speech yet, but it won't take me long to write one." I had plenty of confidence that I could whip up a three-minute blurb in a matter of a few hours. "I guess I know what I'm doing tonight!" I laughed.

"Well I'm a little jealous," Nick admitted.

"Dr. Robinson told me your GPA was ridiculous. Did you make valedictorian?"

"No way. I wouldn't do the speech even if I did."

"Why not?"

He winked as he stood up. "I guess I'd rather sit in the audience and watch you. Besides, who moves to a new town two weeks before graduation and gives the big congratulatory speech to a bunch of strangers?" After quickly kissing the top of my head, he sauntered out of the cafeteria.

Watching him leave, a new pang hit my heart. I'd miss him, too. As little as I knew about him, at least I felt there was some kind of connection there. If only I had time to figure it out.

I had so much to do this week. Lists began to form in my mind as I went from class to class the rest of the day. I still hadn't gone shopping for my graduation dress. I needed to figure out what to take and what to leave behind when I left. I needed to figure out how to keep it a secret but still pack it all. In addition to all of that, I had to go get the bracelet charm back from Crevan.

I drove separately from the twins. In a perfect world, I would spend every possible moment with my family before it was all over, but I couldn't risk Zandros coming around when they were there. The wind blew through the open car windows, lightening my mood a bit. The ride through the countryside was peaceful. It almost made me forget about what was out there waiting for me.

Almost.

As I pulled into the driveway at Alex's house, my heart raced. Nervousness waved through my belly at the thought of seeing his face again. It was best for me to stay away, and I would after I got my charm.

Instead of walking right in, I knocked on the door. A minute passed before I tried again. Frustrated, I checked the handle when no one came. It was locked.

Peering through the windows, I saw that no shadows danced in the usual candlelight. It was daytime, so that didn't necessarily mean anything. Walking around toward the back of the house, I hoped he was in the backyard again.

Near the tree line, I found the remnants of the other night's small fire filling a stone circle. Nevertheless, there was no Alex. There wasn't even that peaceful feeling that came over me whenever I was here. Before, I felt safe. Now I felt nothing.

Emptiness.

Did he leave for good? Maybe he just hadn't come back yet. I tried opening the garage door. It groaned in protest, but slid up on its rails. The Rover sat inside, parked and dusty. Wherever he'd gone, he didn't drive.

I tried knocking on the front door one more time before admitting defeat and heading home.

"Tsk, tsk," he said from behind me. Zandros was leaning against my car, arms crossed tightly across his chest. "Seems no one is home," he chided.

I remembered Alex said Zandros couldn't find this place. He had said it was safe. "How did you find me here?" I wondered out loud.

He stroked his chin dramatically. "I do believe you called out to me. And who am I to ignore my sweet Carina?"

"Where is Alex?"

Zandros tossed his head back in laughter. "I suppose that answer is between him and his maker. Such a shame he isn't here. But tell me, is this the reason you came?" He held the delicate charm between his fingertips and let it dangle in the sunlight.

My heart sunk for the umpteenth time that day. If he had the charm, he'd either been inside the house, which Alex said wasn't possible, or he'd gotten it from Crevan.

No matter what the girl thought of me right now, I hated the thought of Zandros getting ahold of her. "Where did you get that?"

"Second room on the right." He grinned, arching his eyebrows impishly. He seemed to enjoy seeing all of the color drain from my face. In the blink of an eye, he was next to me on the porch. "Come, I'll show you."

He grabbed me by the arm and kicked open the door. He knew exactly where he was going, like he'd been inside the house before. Up the stairs and down the hall he pulled me past Alex's room, then past Crevan's. Ending in the room I used, he threw me to the floor.

Released

Grabbing the discarded nightgown that was on the floor from the other night, he threw it in my face. "So this is what you do while you hide from me?"

"I didn't do anything wrong," I protested, cowering from him.

"Oh I know exactly what you have done and what you haven't done."

He was on me in a flash, his hand striking my face before I had time to react. The sting burned all the way into my bones.

"Say it!" he scorned.

"Say what?" I cried. This was the angriest I'd ever seen him. If only Aniketos could come and save me again.

"Tell me…" He pulled me up to my feet using my hair as a handgrip. "Tell me who you belong to."

"You." I whispered.

"That's right. You belong to me. I will eat his soul. Right after I've made you mine."

Loud footsteps running up the stairs caught Zandros' attention and he spun on his heels. I dropped to the floor with a heavy thud. He'd disappeared by the time my head hit the floor.

"Cadi!" Alex's face came into focus when I opened my eyes. "Are you okay?" His fingertips lightly brushed the welts that had formed on my cheekbone.

"He has a thing for pulling out my hair," I tried to joke, sitting up. The room around me began to spin so I started to lie back down.

Alex lifted me like a child and carried me over to the bed. "Just stay still," he said, gently stroking my hair. "I'm sorry I wasn't here."

"You can't protect me, Alex." I forced myself to sit up, fighting away the vertigo. "He was here because of me. I brought him here."

"I don't know how he got through, but I'll find out and fix it. You'll be okay here."

I shook my head, regretting it the minute I moved. "I just came to get my charm. He said I called to him."

Alex stood up and thrust his hands in his pockets. "Did you?" He looked questioning.

"I don't know, maybe. Maybe I said his name yesterday after he came to my church, when I came here." I rubbed the back of my head, willing the pain away.

"You came back yesterday?" A completely new range of emotions played across his face: confusion, anger, denial. "Crevan didn't tell me you were here."

"I'm not surprised," I muttered. "I'll go now. He has what I came for, so there's really no need to stick around." I stood up. "I can't apologize enough for being such a pain, for bringing him here."

Alex looked me in the eye. "This isn't your fault, Cadi. Zandros is someone I should've take care of a long time ago. You should lie down and let that headache go away." He gently brushed the hair from my eyes.

I wanted to stay, but I knew better. The longer I was here the more danger I was bringing to my friends.

"No thanks." I walked toward the door. "I've done enough. Besides, I need to get home and do my homework."

Alex chuckled quietly. "I don't think I've ever met someone who could get attacked by a demon and be worried about homework."

Released

I nodded politely and wordlessly made my way down the stairs. I had never experienced a longer ride home.

8

Tuesday morning came without any dreams. Maybe Zandros wasn't coming at night anymore since he was here in real life now. Maybe he took more delight in terrorizing me in public. I found out I wasn't wrong when I pulled into my parking spot at school and saw him leaning against a utility pole across the street.

He didn't say a word or move toward me. He just stood there, smugly watching me as I walked into the building.

Nick met me at my locker. "Good morning," he smiled. "You look better today."

"Thanks." I sorted through my locker and got my books organized for morning classes.

"Do you want to go out Friday? Maybe catch a movie and dinner?" He looked so hopeful and friendly.

"I'm not really into the dating scene," I said blushing a little bit. The little kisses he'd given me were enough to make me daydream about more, but I couldn't lead him on if I was running away in a few days.

"That's exactly why I didn't ask you to marry me." Nick laughed at his own joke. "There's no reason two people can't hang out just because they're the opposite sex, right?"

My mind shifted to Zandros. If I spent too much time with Nick, would he become another possible target? "I'm actually busy Friday, sorry."

"So long as your mom doesn't make liver and onions, I'll come over for dinner on Thursday then." Nick grinned.

I couldn't help but lighten up a little bit. Even in the midst of everything, Nick Vikenti always seemed to know how to make me smile. "I guess it's a date then."

"No." He corrected me with a tap to the nose. "It's just two friends hanging out. Don't read into things, Miss Matthews. I'm not into the dating scene."

I shook my head, amused, and watched him saunter away. There was something so simple, so comfortable about him. He certainly was beautiful, smart, and polite. The perfect man... if I was looking for that. I wasn't looking for anything but time, and falling for someone was a huge waste of that very resource.

The bell rang, startling me and making me rush to class. By the time I slid into my seat, the tardy bell was already ringing. Mr. Blackburn scowled at me for the briefest of moments. I rolled my eyes and grinned at him, wiggling my fingers playfully in his direction. Instantly, his demeanor changed and his face softened. For the rest of the class, he left me alone, even skipping over my name when he was asking review questions for the final exam.

It was just like the day the police officer pulled me over. With nothing more than a silent wish, the men were doing exactly what I wanted them to. This must be another side effect of being a demon's child. Just the thought made my stomach churn.

I wasn't the only one who'd noticed that Mr. Blackburn was letting me slide. Several of the girls that I considered friends were shooting me some rather nasty looks.

Nice boob job.

I bet she's sleeping with him too.

I bet she'd do her own brother.

God when did she turn into such a bitch?

Stunned and hurt, I quickly stopped listening to their thoughts and tried to focus on the lesson plan.

The rest of the morning went by the same. All of the girls were thinking nasty thoughts, but the boys… Their mental images made me sick. I had to concentrate to hear the female thoughts, but the boys' bombarded my senses without warning. It was all I could do to remain sane.

At lunchtime, I sat alone against the brick wall outside of the school, slowly picking at the sack lunch I'd brought. There was no sign of Zandros anywhere nearby, but I could feel that the electricity in the air was shifted and was positive he wasn't too far away.

"Hey, I was looking for you," Nick said, joining me. "Everything alright?"

I shrugged. "Just wanted some fresh air," I lied with a not-so-convincing smile.

Nick pulled one of his legs up and rested his arm on his knee. "I highly doubt that, but since you seem to want me to think so, I'll let it slide." He nonchalantly lit a cigarette, hiding it next to him between puffs.

I just shrugged again. It would be nice to have someone to confide in, someone who understood that there were changes happening to me that I couldn't control. It wasn't as if I chose this for myself. A week ago, I was just Cadi Matthews, normal girl.

At that moment, I was becoming a monster that I didn't recognize in my own mirror.

A familiar dirty red pickup pulled up in front of us, coming to a loud stop. The muffler belched as my dad turned off the ignition and got out.

"Dad?" I called to him, worried. Why would he be at our school unless something bad had happened? "What's wrong?"

Nick tossed his cigarette into the bushes. We got up and met him halfway to the door. "Spencer is in the dean's office," Dad explained.

I couldn't imagine such a thing. My brother was a star athlete and honor roll student who never got into trouble. If anything, his teachers loved him just as much as the other students did. Spencer Matthews was one of the most popular kids in school. "What'd he do?"

"He got in a fight." Dad replied. He stopped and looked at me, his gaze flashing toward Nick before dismissing him quickly. "You okay? You look like crap."

"I'm fine," I lied again. I watched as he turned back toward the boy standing next to me and held my breath. Nick remained silent.

"Well I'd better get in there." He paused at the doorway without addressing Nick at all. "Any chance Alex is coming back to the house soon?" His tone emphasized Alex's name.

"Uh…" I stammered. Blushing, I shot a look at him that meant he needed to go away. "I don't know, Dad."

Steven pulled the door open. "That's too bad. You two make the perfect couple."

I rolled my eyes after my dad turned his back. Embarrassed, I wished the sidewalk would eat me alive.

Nick just laughed. "I take it your dad sees a different guy in your future?"

"I'm sorry. I don't know where that even came from," I reddened even more.

Nick just smiled. "Don't worry about it. He's just trying to protect his little girl. Maybe it would help if you told him I'm not after your heart?"

"Maybe. I wonder what Spencer was fighting about?" I absently spoke my words, not expecting an answer.

"Rumor mill says there was a big blow-up in the locker room. There's a dozen guys getting suspended for it." Nick informed me. "From what I heard it was one guy against the rest of them." He looked a little impressed.

I wasn't.

It wasn't like my brother to pick on an underdog. It was impossible to believe he was part of a big group beating up one kid, but what could have happened to make everyone else attack Spencer?

Making my way back inside, I tried to catch a glimpse inside the dean's office as I walked by. I couldn't see anything through the closed doors. Settling down in class, I started eavesdropping on conversations around me to see if anyone knew anything about it.

"I couldn't believe it," marveled one of Spencer's teammates. "He just flipped out and started wailing on Andrew."

"What for?" The wide-eyed blonde girl seemed fascinated by the scandal.

"I guess Spence overheard the guys talking about the party Saturday."

"She really did that with the entire basketball team?" The girl's mouth hung open when the boy nodded. "What... a slut."

He glanced back and caught me looking at them. *I'd risk getting my ass beat if I could tap that* his mind sang across the room to me.

I ground my teeth, doing my best not to react. I only had a few more days left of school to get through. If I screwed up now I might not be able to graduate. It was best to keep my head down and try to ignore it.

It was hard not to notice how the entire student population seemed to hate me now. As I walked through the hallways, I held my books tightly in front of myself and stopped attempting to greet anyone. Even my closest friends were ignoring me.

Tramp.

Whore.

Slut.

Bitch.

If there was a foul word in the English language, by the time the day had ended, I had heard them all. It was as if I had become a social zero overnight. I ignored Nick's friendly attempt to lighten my mood each time I saw him in the hallway.

I just wanted to go home.

Slamming the back door behind me, I stomped into the house and found Dad and Spencer in the living room. Their conversation abruptly stopped when I walked in.

Released

"Mind telling me what happened today?" I had a hard time not taking out my anger on them.

Spencer looked up at me through swollen and blackened eyes. His split lip was already scabbed and there was an ice pack wrapped around his hand.

Dad sat back against his chair and casually looked at his son. When Spencer said nothing, he answered for his son. "You brother got upset at some people who were saying some not so nice things about you."

I swallowed my groan. Great, now my family suffering from my mess, and it wasn't even Zandros doing it to them. "I'm sorry," I apologized. "Is there anything I can do?"

"Can you turn ugly overnight?" Spencer joked. His smile was genuine. He didn't seem angry with me in the slightest bit. "Don't worry about it. I might have gotten suspended, but I know a whole lot of guys that learned to keep their mouths shut and their minds out of the gutter."

"I hear you'll be making the big speech next Sunday at graduation." Dad changed the subject.

"Yeah," I nodded, now dreading the thought of standing up there in front of a crowd of people that suddenly hated me. "I better get working on that."

I went to my room and fumed.

So much for living it up before I die...

Now that I had zero friends left, there wasn't a whole lot I could do other than homework. Since it was the last few days of school, assignments were rare.

145

Released

I convinced myself that I needed to rewrite my graduation speech and sprawled out on my bed, letting the hum of the laptop lull me to sleep. I woke up disoriented a short time later and took quick look around to see where I was. When I decided I was still safe in my bedroom, I grabbed the front of my shirt, as if to make sure I was still dressed. A wave of crimson heat washed over me as the intimate images I'd just dreamt about replayed in my mind. Panic replaced the embarrassment almost instantly.

I couldn't remember who I had been dreaming about, but what if I'd gone to him in his dreams, just as Zandros came to me? I'd only scanned Alex's book quickly that one day, but I remembered that the succubus haunted the dreams of men, stealing their souls in the process.

Grabbing my phone, I dialed one of the only two men I thought I might have dreamt about. "Are you okay?" I didn't even bother to wait for Nick to say hello.

"Uh, yeah? Who is this?" Nick didn't sound like he just woke up.

That meant I hadn't hurt him with my stupid demon dream thing.

I hung up without another word. I was relieved, but still panicked.

I grabbed my jacket and headed down the stairs quickly. When a confused Mom called after me, I just yelled back that I'd be home by curfew. All that mattered right now was finding out if I had hurt anyone.

Crevan answered the door when I knocked.

"Is Alex here?" I expected to get the door slammed in my face. Instead, Crevan walked away, pointing toward the stairs.

Taking them two at a time, the dread in my gut grew. If he was in his room, he was probably sleeping. If he was sleeping now, he may have been before. Did I visit his dream and do anything... wrong?

Alex's bedroom door was open just a crack. Peering in, I saw the still form of a statuesque man sitting in the middle of the floor in lotus position. Quietly, I entered the room. I hated to disturb him, but I needed to know.

Coming around in front of him, I could see his relaxed face, lost in quiet contemplation. His eyes were closed; his mouth opened just the slightest bit. His hands rested gently on his knees while he sat with his spine straight and absolutely still.

"Alex?" I whispered. He didn't respond and my heart dropped.

What have I done?

I touched his shoulder and jumped back when he was startled awake.

"Cadi," He quickly realized who was there. "What's wrong?"

His expression crumbled as he stood, looking into my terrified eyes. "I had a dream..." I flushed, too embarrassed to go into the details. "I just needed to make sure you were alright. And when I came in, you were..."

He hushed me, gently placing a fingertip on my lips. Softly smiling, he assured me that he was fine. "I was meditating, that's all."

I threw my arms around him, the tremors in my body dissipating as he held me against his strong form. "I'm sorry," I muttered. "This whole mess is entirely my fault. One minute I think everything is going to be okay, that I'll just run away. Then the next, I can't even stand the thought of leaving."

Alex led me over to the bed and sat down, pulling me down next to him. "How about you take a deep breath and start from the beginning."

I closed my eyes, collecting my jumbled thoughts. "A week ago, I was a totally normal girl. I liked school, I liked boys and I dreamt about college. Now everything has changed. I always thought the dreams I had about him were just dreams, but now that I know it's real I'm scared. Part of me wants to run away to keep him away from my family, but the other part can't stand the thought of leaving them. I want to spend every day possible with them, but then I'm scared that he'll come after them now, too."

"That's completely understandable," Alex soothed me, rubbing small, gentle circles on my lower back as I spoke.

"I don't want to be the person I'm tempted to be."

Alex stiffened. "What temptations are you talking about?"

"Not just what you think. I mean, I wonder what it would be like to break the rules and party and stuff like that. Hell," I groaned. "I don't even know what I mean. Sometimes it feels good to get what you want without asking for it, but everyone acts like they hate me now. I just know I had a dream where I was breaking some big rules and when I woke up, it didn't seem like it was all fun and games. I was afraid I'd hurt someone."

"Well," he relaxed a little bit. "I am perfectly fine. I think the biggest problem we need to address is the hold Zandros has over you."

He took my hand in his and ran his thumb over the leather strap on my wrist. "Did he give this to you?"

I had forgotten all about the mystery behind the gift. "I don't know who it's from. It was in my locker on my birthday."

"Let's assume it is from him. Can you take it off?"

I shook my head. It was too tight to slip off after I'd worn it in the shower and the thought of cutting it had never entered my mind. I watched as Alex got up and went to an antique dresser.

The top drawer squeaked as he opened it and removed a satin pouch. Returning to me, he sat back down and opened it. Withdrawing a small black dagger, he placed the blade near my wrist and hesitated, as if he was waiting for my permission.

When the cold metal touched my skin, it felt like my arm was on fire. I pulled back sharply. "Ouch," I yelped.

"It's a Soul Dagger, expressly blessed to battle demon magic. That's why it burns."

The way he explained it was so sterile, I didn't know how to react. "If this bracelet is a gift from Zandros, no other knife could remove it. And if it isn't from him, the blade wouldn't react that way."

I took a deep breath and braced myself. "Take it off," I commanded, closing my eyes and steadying my nerves.

Alex slid the blade under the leather again and pulled up quickly. The leather shrieked as a thin wisp of blood red smoke came from it. When it hit the ground, it took a life of its own and began to slither across the floor like a snake. Alex expertly threw the dagger, piercing it against the oak floorboards. The once inanimate object let out one final cry before disappearing into thin air.

My heart pounded harder than I'd ever felt before. If I didn't calm down, I would have a heart attack.

Alex looked over at me casually. "Looks like I was right." He took my hand in his again and examined my wrist. The small bracelet left a small pink ring around my arm. There was a blistering burn mark where the tip of the dagger had touched my skin.

Alex wrapped his hands around my wounds and closed his eyes. As a soft chant filled the air, the burns began to cool. He didn't let go until the pain was gone. For the first time since I'd met him, his touch didn't send electricity through my body.

"Well that explains the shock every time I touch you. The Veduny don't react very well to demon magic. Now that that's out of the way, let's see what else I can do. It won't take long before Zandros realizes you've figured that part out."

"What was it?" I knew the answer would be terrifying if I thought about it too hard.

"I'm not sure really. But he had to have given it to you for a reason."

"So he can't find me at school anymore? It was awful today when he was there; like every girl hated me and every boy wanted me."

Alex smiled and shook his head. "You'll have to get used to that. It's not his doing. It is jealousy and desire. In time, I'm sure you'll learn to control the way people see you. You should be able to mask your influences. There will be people you meet in your lifetime that will give you a fair shot, don't worry."

"I doubt I'll be meeting very many new people in the next three weeks." I fell back onto the bed, throwing my hand over my face to cover the threat of tears.

Alex patted my leg lightly. "How about instead of feeling sorry for being beautiful, we figure out a way to make that three weeks last a whole lot longer."

I dared peek out over my arm. "Is it even worth wasting my time hoping?"

"Of course it is," Alex said. "If you don't have hope, what do you have? Do you think it's just an accident that you met someone who has spent most of his life destroying demons?"

The thought made my skin crawl.

He killed demons.

He could kill me.

"You retired, remember?" I shot back at him. A part of me was glad he was there to help, but the other half was terrified. Zandros was powerful. He could kill Alex just as easily.

"Meh," he said playfully. "People come out of retirement all of the time. I'll do one more and then re-retire."

"What do we have to do?"

"*We* have nothing to do. *I* however, have a lot to do." He patted my leg again, this time to get my attention. "I'll be right back."

He disappeared for a few minutes. By the time he'd returned, he had an armload of books and spread them out on the floor. Flipping open his notebook, he began scribbling notes. "I need to know everything Zandros has said to you."

I groaned, joining him on the floor. "Everything?" There was no way I was going to tell him everything. Some of it was too embarrassing to think about, let alone say aloud.

Alex looked at me, apparently stunned that I would even question it. "Of course, everything. I have to figure out what he wants, what deal he made, what his weaknesses are, and his strengths. You're the only connection I have to him, so you have to fill in the blanks."

"Fine," I conceded. "What do you want to know?"

"When was the first time you remember seeing him?"

Images flashed through my mind. I was in the back seat of my mother's Mercedes. Buckled tight, I couldn't reach the brand new iPod that had fallen to the floor and was begging my mother to get it for me. When Melantha had grown tired of my incessant whining, she started yelling at me. I dissolved into silent tears, trying to tune out the hateful words of the woman in front of me. Pouting into the window, I drifted off into a daydream where Zandros appeared to me for the first time.

"That isn't very nice of her, is it?" he asked, handing me the iPod. I just pouted and shook my head. For a ten year old, I acted as if I were no older than three. "I would never treat you like that. I think someone should stop her from being so mean, don't you?"

I nodded, but said nothing. My mother always taught me to be wary of strangers. He brushed the tearstains from my face.

"If she was gone, she'd never be able to be mean to you again."

My young mind raced with the possibilities. I was so mad at my mother, it sounded like a good idea; good enough to listen to a stranger. Even as young as I was, I knew it was just a dream, so I wasn't really breaking the stranger-danger rule. "I hate her," I complained.

Released

"Then I'll get rid of her. But you'll have to do her job when you grow up."

The man with the blue eyes and big scar on his face smiled kindly. I reached up and traced the length of the red gash with my fingertip. "What happened to you?" I asked.

"A very bad man tried to kill me," Zandros replied, taking my petite hand in his. "But he found out that no one can hurt me. So what do you say? No more yelling and you'll get everything you ever want. How does that sound?"

"It sounds good," I said with a smile.

I woke up to the sounds of my mother screaming. The brick crashed through the windshield with an explosion of glass. I put my hands over my face to shield myself from the onslaught. The headphones of the iPod were nestled on my ears, soft music playing.

Alex interrupted my reverie after a moment of silence. "He never told you what you had to do in return?"

To this very day, I still didn't know what his exact intentions were. "The first day, he just said I'd have to do her job, but he never said what that meant. In the past few years, he's been using words like betrothed and wife."

Alex pulled open a book. It looked like a handwritten journal. He flipped through a few pages before stopping. "Here's an old story that tells about a demon's search for a child. He's looking for the right man and woman to become one. He thinks that their offspring can overrule the Dark One and control the Earth."

I shuddered at the thought.

Alex sat back on his haunches and closed the book. "Hang on." He grabbed another book and quickly scanned the pages. Thrusting it toward me, he grinned. "What if your mother isn't really dead?" he said. "If she isn't, you can't be forced to take her place."

"I can't read this," I sighed, frustrated. "Tell me in plain English."

"Zandros never said he would kill her, just that he would get rid of her. The only way a soul binding can be transferred is through death. If she were dead, her name would be in the Book of Lost Souls. And it's not." He seemed excited at the prospect.

I wasn't sure what to say. "I watched them bury her," I said quietly.

Alex shook his head vehemently. "You don't bury a demon. You burn them and send them back to the hell fires where they belong."

The hairs on the back of my neck stood on end. "That sounds awful."

"It should," Alex replied coldly.

Apparently, he'd forgotten that I was one of the people he was so casually talking about burning to death. "Do you actually enjoy doing that to them?"

Alex looked stunned. "When it comes to ridding the world of evil, I don't think enjoy is the correct word. It's a privilege and an honor."

I stood up and went over to the bed where I took a tentative seat. "What if you're wrong about them? What if DNA isn't what makes them evil? Do you consider their actions first, or is their family name just an automatic ticket to Hell?"

Alex was silent. I could see in his eyes that his mind was racing, but I didn't dare look into his thoughts. I was too terrified to see what was there. It was bad enough knowing what his past was like, but to see it would be completely horrible.

"Even if I do survive whatever... he has in store for me, what's to keep the rest of the Veduny from coming after me someday?"

"I promised you." He came over and sat next to me, taking my hand in his.

"You promised, yes, but are you the only one who hunts people like me?" I could tell by Alex's expression that I was right. "Even if I do everything in my power to live a good life, I'll still be a target just because of my DNA."

Alex shook his head. "Let's worry about Zandros for now. Everything else will work out in time. Right now, we need to focus."

Crevan's voice shouted from downstairs, startling both of us. "I found it!"

Bewildered, I followed as Alex hurried downstairs. Crevan was lying on the living room couch. She had her feet kicked over the back while her head dangled off the front of it. Popping her bubble gum, she grinned at us when we walked in.

Alex was the first to approach her. I held back, not sure what was behind Crevan's coldness toward me in the past few days.

"Melantha was Vadim," she grinned.

Alex sat next to her, slapping her legs off the couch and forcing her to sit up right. He took the journal from her hands and began scanning the pages. After flipping through a few, he looked up at me. "That explains a lot."

"Mind filling me in?" I asked from the doorway. "What's a Vadim?"

Crevan looked delighted in her discovery and seemed more than happy to elaborate as her brother continued reading. "Our folklore says that Vadim are traitors, members of our family that have turned against our ways. In a really strange twist, they even refer to demons who refuse to do the Dark Lord's bidding as Vadim. It's pretty much our worst cuss word and I'm positive that your mother was Vadim."

"So you mean she was... Good?" I sat in the chair across from them.

"Not necessarily," Crevan said. "Maybe she was in the process of finding a happy medium?"

"It says here that Micah was Vadim." Alex muttered. "Now I know why no one ever speaks of him."

"Even if Aniketos had a brother, no one would ever recognize him," Crevan added. "Not once he turned to the dark side." She rolled her eyes, speaking dramatically.

"English?" I begged.

"There's a couple different ways for Veduny to be outcast as Vadim. If you fraternize with someone who isn't one of us, or if you refuse your duties, stuff like that."

"Wait," I interjected. "So you're telling me that if you're given an assignment to kill someone and you know it's wrong and refuse, they kick you out?"

Crevan's eyes sparkled. "Oh no, it's soooo much more than that. Not only are you kicked out, but you are forever considered more evil than the Dark One himself and then all of the Veduny hunt you down! Our people take their shit pretty seriously," she laughed.

"Crevan!" Alex scolded.

"Well my mother wasn't Veduny, but she could still be this Vadim thing?"

"Psh," Crevan sniffled. "We practically think anyone who isn't one of us is Vadim." She popped her gum. "We're a pretty stuck up kind of people."

I digested everything I'd learned in the past hour.

My mother might still be alive and she may not have been completely evil.

Somehow, this Micah guy mattered.

Was he my father?

Was I only half-bad?

Would Alex be ordered to kill me and then became hunted himself if he refused?

My mind spun right along with the world around me. It was all too much.

"Is this Micah guy my father?" I asked.

Alex shook his head. "I would have sensed it if you had Veduny blood in you."

"Tough luck for you big brother." Crevan smacked her gum. "You might've been able to bend some rules if she was a half-breed at least."

She dissolved into a fit of giggles while Alex remained silent. He was scanning pages so quickly it was amazing that he even could read the words on them. "Where do you get all of these books and journals?" I asked.

"I've collected them over time," Alex replied, trying to ignore his sister's antics. "Can you be serious for more than five minutes, please?" He finally snapped at her.

Crevan sat upright, a look of fear frozen on her face. "Elric is coming," she warned.

It was Alex's turn to look frightened. "Are you sure?"

Crevan nodded and jumped up from the couch. Grabbing every candle she could find, she began lighting them all. "Get her out of here!" she commanded

"What..."

I didn't have time to finish the question before Alex was pulling me to my feet and leading me to the front door. "You can't be here right now. Can you make it home by yourself alright?"

I was confused. "Why?"

"I'll explain as soon as I can, maybe not until tomorrow. I promise as soon as I can come to you, I will." There was a sense of panic in his voice. "Go home now. I'll come for you soon."

9

I saw that Alex waited until I pulled out of the driveway before he ran back into the house. I couldn't help but wonder what was happening, but I had to trust him. I knew that worrying and wondering wouldn't bring answers any quicker.

Mom was just finishing the dinner dishes when I walked in. "There's leftover meatloaf in the fridge for you if you're hungry."

"Thanks," I gave her a brief hug. "Tomorrow is senior ditch day. Would it be okay if I didn't go to school?"

Mom smiled at me. "Well maybe there's a little bit of a rebel in you yet," she laughed. "Is there anything going on at school that you'll miss?"

I shook my head. "Graduation practice is on Friday, and my speech is done, so I don't really have anything to do."

"Are you planning to do something with that Alex boy?"

"No." It wasn't a lie. I didn't know that anyone would be accompanying me tomorrow. "After what happened at school today, I'd just rather not be there if I don't have to."

The look on Mom's face was priceless. The entire side of her face twitched at the mere thought of her baby boy being involved in any sort of unrest, especially the permanent record kind. "I'm fine with it as long as you stay out of trouble. And don't let those kids at school bother you. They're just jealous that you're so much prettier than they are."

"Moms have to say that," I countered before going up to my bedroom. I'd just fired up the laptop when my brother knocked on my door.

"I hear we have plans tomorrow?" Spencer said from the doorway.

"Do we?" I smiled. I couldn't help but feel a little bit guilty looking at the bruises on his normally pretty face.

"Mom said you're ditching tomorrow and decided you get to make sure I don't wind up in prison." His grin broadened. "So what are we going to do?"

I shrugged. It depended on whether or not I could find what I was looking for. "They really did a number on your face."

"Pshaw," Spencer waved it off. "Anything for my sister."

I threw a pillow at him. "Don't go getting yourself killed over stupid idiots and rumors."

Spencer straightened up, getting a little more serious. "Defending my family is something I don't take lightly. Let me know if you come up with something cool to do tomorrow."

I nodded, speechless, as he closed the door behind him. I turned my attention back to the laptop and found the internet to be a valuable resource when it came to storing old newspaper articles. It was almost midnight by the time I'd sorted through enough of them to find the information I wanted.

I woke with the dawn after a quiet, uneventful night. I was grateful that Zandros hadn't made an appearance, but it bothered me that Alex hadn't either. I couldn't help but wonder what was going on.

Released

After pulling on my tennis shoes, I took off down the lane for a quiet run. Thoughts of how I planned to spend my day swirled in my mind. My heart raced faster in nervous anticipation every time I thought about it. By the time I made it back home, both of my parents had already left for work, Sarah not far behind them.

Spencer was still asleep. I kept quiet so that I wouldn't wake him up. Grabbing my cell phone, I dialed a number quickly.

"Yeah?" said the gravelly voice on the other end after a few rings.

"It's senior ditch day," I said nervously. "Got any plans?"

I could practically hear the smile spread across Nick's face as he replied. "I was thinking about hanging out with this one chick, but she waited until the last minute to call me, so I'm not sure what we have planned yet."

"How do you feel about road trips?" I paced the floor, refusing to let my nerves get the best of me. I needed to do this, and there was no way I could involve my family.

"I love them, but not in your piece of crap car. I'll pick you up."

I hung up and grabbed my purse before heading to the kitchen to grab a quick breakfast. My stomach growled loudly, making me wonder when the last time I ate was. Grabbing an apple, I pulled the gallon of milk out of the fridge and drank almost all of it.

By the time Nick pulled up in his white Jeep Wrangler, I was pacing outside. I jumped in before he had a chance to turn off the engine and smiled sheepishly at him. "I have gas money."

"No need. Where are we headed?" Nick's face gleamed with curiosity and excitement.

"Springfield." The word was heavy as it left my lips. The last time I was there was eight years ago.

Even when my class took a field trip there, I'd skip school to avoid going. The town held many memories for me, and none of them were good. Now that I'd said it aloud, I was more tense and nervous than ever.

"What's in Springfield?" Nick asked as he put the Jeep in gear and started driving.

"Can you keep a secret?" I peered over at him, judging his reaction.

"I don't know. How good is it?" His eyes lit up like stars, excited at the prospect of scandal.

"I want to go to my birth mother's grave today. I just don't want Mom and Dad to know. I don't want to hurt their feelings."

Nick smiled warmly. "Finally ready to say goodbye?" he asked.

I didn't answer. I couldn't lie about it, but I couldn't admit that I really just wanted to see if she was even there after Alex had said demons had to be burnt not just buried.

"We'll see," I muttered, absently watching as the scenery passed by.

Nick gently placed his hand on mine; silently letting me know that he wasn't going to question my motives. "So you remember where this place is after all these years?"

"No, I had to Google it," I replied. "You sure you're okay with going with me?" They weren't too far away from home yet. There was still time to change his mind.

"I'm cool," he replied casually.

Released

We were just passing Alex and Crevan's house. There was a dead calm in the air, like a heavy, oppressive weight in the atmosphere. It was the exact opposite of the electrical charge that I was so used to feeling. Whatever was going on inside that house was bad. At least, it felt that way. I turned up the music as we headed for the interstate.

"You look like you're gonna explode," Nick observed. "We could just hit the mall or go back home if you want. Nobody will ever be the wiser."

I punched an address into the GPS. "I will know."

"Well I'm at your disposal, just let me know what you need me to do." He followed the directions on the screen in front of him during the awkwardly silent drive. He finally slowed down when the large wrought iron gates came into view.

The cemetery entrance loomed ahead of us. I had no idea where in this vast place my mother's grave was. I only found the name of the cemetery. After pulling into the parking lot, Nick suggested we go into the sexton's office and inquire. Nervously, I grabbed his hand when we entered the aged stone building.

The marble floors echoed under our footsteps as we walked with a determined pace through the mausoleum toward the office in the back. I wasn't fond of the idea of two-story walls of dead people surrounding me on both sides. The large oaken door was ajar at the end of the hallway.

We entered quietly and found a very old, funny looking man. He had a pointed nose, long fingers and was tall and extremely skinny.

He was balding with about five hairs combed over a shiny patch of skin, like Riff Raff from The Rocky Horror Picture Show.

"Welcome, children." He said with a grin, revealing yellow, crooked teeth.

I didn't want to get close enough to find out what kind of breath a mouth like that made. "I need to find a grave here, but I'm not sure where it is. Can you help me?"

He scurried over to a large shelf filled with enormous leather bound books. A sense of purpose filled his movements, as if he'd been waiting for years to be helpful to someone.

"Of course, of course," he said. His hands hovered in front of the bound records. "Tell me, child. In what year did your beloved part?"

"Eight years ago," I scanned the room nervously. The cobwebs that lined the ceiling were god awful, increasing the creepy level to a completely new height.

He pulled down a book and laid it on the table in front of him. Based on the thud it made, it had to have weighed more than he did. Dust danced in the light as he opened the tome. "And the name?"

"Copeland." I steeled my shoulders, faking assertiveness. Nick stood behind me and gently squeezed my shoulders, loaning me some extra confidence. "Melantha Copeland."

The sexton looked up sharply for just a second, cleared his throat, and turned his attention back to the book. I couldn't help but shiver when he turned to the exact page. "Shall I take you?" he offered.

I shook my head. "No thanks. If you can just show me on a map or something, I should be able to find it just fine."

"Very well," he croaked out. He pointed over to the wall where a huge parchment map hung. There were thick black lines marking areas with numbers. "You shall find what you seek in section seventeen. It's hard to miss."

I scanned the map, noting the different numbers. Seventeen was toward the back, along the property edges. There was nothing but mausoleums marked in that area. "I'm sorry, that can't be right," I said. "I was at her funeral. She had a normal grave, not a mausoleum."

The man snickered. "She was moved not long after her interment. What a pain that always is. Put them in the ground; take them out of the ground..." He began muttering under his breath but I didn't stick around to listen.

Nick pulled me out of the room and back to the Jeep, driving toward the back of the cemetery.

"Wow." He marveled at the stonework at each gravesite as we passed. The farther in we drove, the more shaded and ancient it got. It was unnerving, but strangely peaceful at the same time. "These are getting older the farther you go Cad. Are you sure about this?"

"Just follow his directions," I snapped, taking out my nerves on Nick.

He responded with silent, raised eyebrows and a smirk.

Finally, we reached our destination, but I hesitated to get out of the Jeep. There was one long row of stone houses, looking forgotten and ancient. Several of them were crumbled messes. All looked as though they were built to keep the dead inside.

Or the living out.

Carved in the marble above the doorway was a single word.

Melantha.

I took a deep breath and got out. Baby's breath and bellflowers carpeted the ground all around the intact mausoleum, giving it an inviting look. Right next door, another building stood with its door crumbled.

"You'd think vandals would at least respect the dead," Nick offhandedly remarked, joining me in front of Melantha's tomb.

A white cat jumped out of the trees, hissing at us. I jumped back, but Nick laughed.

"Guarding the dead, are you?" He bent down and coaxed the animal toward him. The cat came over, still hissing, but calmed with each step it took. "Aren't you pretty?" He scooped it up in his arms and began petting it.

I looked at its eyes. There was nothing friendly or pretty about the creature. It hissed at me again before rubbing its face against Nick's hand with a loud purr.

I left him to his new friend and began walking toward the mausoleum. There was a wrought iron rail firmly bolted to one side of the door. I grabbed it and pulled. Surprised that it opened with a groan, I peered into the blackness and saw nothing but dust flying in the sunbeam that I had just let in.

When I stepped inside, the door slammed behind me. Trapped in total darkness, I pushed on the door, but it wouldn't budge. It only took a few moments before I heard Nick yelling to me from the outside. I could hear him struggle against the door. Even though I joined his attempts to open it, the door remained sealed. Panicked, I tried to calm myself. Alex had said we could see in the dark, so I tried to focus. Soon, the form in front of me began to take shape and I forgot all about Nick.

The woman lay on a marble table, her hands crossed neatly on her chest. Her auburn hair draped down the sides of her beautiful face. No amount of decay had taken over the body in the years she had been dead. Instead, she simply looked asleep. It was the most peaceful I could ever remember my mother being and I couldn't resist the temptation to reach out and touch her.

The same shock I'd gotten used to coming from Alex travelled up my arm. I could have sworn I saw Melantha's chest rise, a deep breath filling her body.

"Mother?" I whispered. A big part of me prayed that I'd get no response.

Melantha's eyes blinked slowly. She turned her head to look at me standing near her. A flicker of recognition gleamed in her eyes. "Carina," her hoarse voice coughed.

Tears streamed down my face, tears of disbelief, anger, and relief. "How can you be alive?"

Melantha stayed in her frozen position, watching my every move. "He promised that I'd see you again one day."

"Who?" I demanded.

Melantha shook her head slightly, refusing to say the name aloud.

"Are you trapped here?"

"I never thought of it as trapped," Melantha hoarsely replied. "More like resting."

"Why are you here? Is Zand..." I stopped just short of saying his name. The terror that flashed across Melantha's features said enough. This was my fault. I was the one who wished my own mother away for what, the latest electronic toy?

Melantha's face fell motionless again. "Actually, I am here because of you, if memory serves me correctly."

My mind raced back to the day of the accident. Guilt was a hungry enemy, I thought, as it gnawed at my insides.

"I'm sorry," I cried. "I didn't know. I was just a little kid."

"And here you are now, all grown up. Tell me Carina, what is it that you want?" I never saw her move, but the woman was up and standing in front of me in the blink of an eye, all signs of weakness and sadness gone in that instant.

"I... I..." I couldn't answer.

The woman circled, inspecting me from head to toe. "Do you stutter often when you're afraid?"

"I'm not afraid," I tried to sound strong. "I wanted to know if you were dead, that's all."

"That's not all," Melantha taunted. "You want to know what you are, what you will become."

I waited, a sick feeling forming in my stomach. When Melantha was on the table, I felt bad for her, but now I couldn't sense one ounce of goodness coming from the monster in front of me.

"You are my child, and my attempted replacement. You are demon spawn and nothing can ever change that," she spat.

"But you changed." I hoped aloud that Alex and Crevan had been right. "You were with Micah, you changed."

Melantha laughed the evilest sound I had ever heard. "Ah, Micah... He was such a weak man. Not even his own kind wanted anything to do with him."

"Was he my father?"

She clicked her tongue, tracing her fingers across my shoulder blades as she walked the circle around me again. "Your *father* has nothing to do with us." Hatred dripped from her words.

"Why are you trapped here?" I demanded as I stared into the eyes of the witch.

"I'm only here until the Master calls to me again. And then, we shall prevail."

Anger boiled in my gut. This woman was evil incarnate, not the repentant, changed woman I had hoped to find. "*We* who?" I asked through gritted teeth.

"You, Zandros, and..." she paused and kissed my cheek softly. "Me. The perfect trinity."

I shook my head defiantly. "I won't do anything with you, or with him."

"But you agreed," the woman taunted. "You can't break a soul promise, no matter how much you regret it. I gave up eight years of my life for you. Besides, soon enough you'll find that you enjoy your life. Getting everything you want, disposing of everyone once they've fulfilled your needs, taking what is yours to take, answering to no one."

I took a deep breath, trying to control the fury that had built inside of me. I was getting hot, literally and it felt like flames were about to burst from my body. "Who was my father?" I repeated carefully.

"The Dark Lord is the father of us all," Melantha laughed. "At least, he's the Lord for now. That shall change in a short matter of months I imagine." She reached forward and poked a long fingernail into my belly, a wicked smiled cracking across her awful face.

I grabbed the woman's arms and fought the urge to rip them off her body. "Tell me that Micah made you see the good in life."

Evil washed over the woman's face as she smiled. "Micah is nothing; no more useful than the Veduny filth you spend time with. The day will come when you destroy Alexander's soul, just as Micah lost his." Her laughter echoed off the walls.

I let go of her and backed away into the corner. All of my focus was on the demon in front of me. "I will never hurt him." I tried to regain my composure.

"Awe, such sweet love," Melantha cheered. "It is such a pity to waste it on the unworthy."

"What do you know about love?" I countered.

"I know it's a very, very useful resource. Once you make them fall in love with you, they are mere puppets. I can see in your heart that you've already mastered the unconquerable, finding a bond with a Veduny. I can smell him on you. Poor soul, he never stood a chance against my little girl." She clapped her hands with delight.

"You know nothing. You deserve to rot in here forever." I turned and grabbed the handle of the door. Even though I pushed with all of my strength, I couldn't get it to budge.

Nick still banged against the door and called out. I yelled back and pushed again.

This time, fresh air streamed in as the door flew open. Nick stepped inside and immediately pulled me toward him. He didn't take his eyes off the woman that stood in front of us.

"You okay Cadi?" His voice was steady. Not a bit of fear showed on his face in spite of the fact that he was standing face to face with a dead woman that looked just like an older version of me.

I didn't have the opportunity to answer before Melantha continued her game.

"Maybe, just maybe, you are wrong about me, sweet Carina." Melantha tried to move behind us, but Nick turned to face her, keeping me tucked protectively behind his body. "Why not stay and talk for a while? You should introduce me to your little friend. I'll tell you everything you will ever need to know."

"I wish you'd just died," I seethed. An hour ago, I felt sorry for wishing death upon this woman, but now I felt nothing but hatred.

"That's my girl," Melantha cooed. "Embrace your rage. It will make you become the greatest succubus in the history of the world. Imagine all the souls you will get! You won't even be able to help yourself; it is pure survival instinct for you."

"I would rather die!" I screamed.

Melantha hissed, charging at me like a feral animal. Nick pulled me to the side quickly, avoiding the brunt of her attack, spinning and kicking her from behind, all the while remaining in between the two of us. Melantha kept charging, refusing to back down.

Released

"Run!" he shouted to me, pushing me toward the door while moving forward to engage Melantha. The woman shrieked again, trying to get to me before I made it through the door. Nick stopped her just in time, throwing her body against the back wall before escaping himself.

Outside, he pulled the door closed behind him. We both took a minute to catch our breath and listened to Melantha's repeated screams of agony and anger.

The sexton was standing near the mausoleum, half hidden in the shadows. "What the..." he gasped.

"What the Hell indeed," I replied coldly as I walked toward the Jeep. My gaze wandered to the vault with the broken door where I could read the name etched in marble.

Micah

Nick jumped into the driver's side and turned on the ignition. With white knuckles, he grabbed the steering wheel and spun the tires to get out of there as quickly as possible.

I cursed myself for bothering to go in the first place. At least now, I had the answer to the biggest question I'd ever had.

No longer did I feel guilty. That woman deserved to die. It would be a blessing upon the whole world to be free of a soul like Melantha.

I didn't pay attention to where we were going until Nick pulled the Jeep to a stop at a rest area along the interstate.

His face was pale, sweat beads formed on his forehead. His chest heaved as if he was struggling to get his breath. "I don't think I can drive anymore," he said cautiously.

"I can drive us the rest of the way." I looked around and hoped to find something familiar enough to tell me how far away from home we were.

"No," Nick replied firmly. "I think I earned an explanation back there."

I sighed heavily. How could I tell him everything without scaring the hell out of him? "Nick..." The words wouldn't come.

He turned in his seat to face me. "How about I start? It could go something like this: Gee Nick, I'm sorry you had to meet my dead mother today while she tried to kill me, but hey, wasn't this a fun road trip?"

I cringed at the angry tone in his voice and became instantly defensive. "Like I expected to find that *thing* in there?"

"Well you had to have some kind of clue. Who the hell walks into an old crypt like that anyway?" He reached into his jacket pocket and withdrew a pack of cigarettes. Lighting one, he took a deep drag while waiting for me to answer him.

"Please, Nick. I swear I had no idea."

"Bullshit." He wasn't amused and there didn't seem to be any patience left in him. "I'm supposed to be your friend. You could at least give me an honest answer."

I couldn't stop the tear from falling down my cheek. "What do you want me to say Nick? I'm sorry that my mother is a demon and isn't dead?"

"She said you were a succubus. Is that true?" He didn't take his eyes off of me for a second.

"What do you think?" Maybe I would be better off if he answered his own questions.

"I think..." He exhaled and watched the smoke curl out of the open window. "I think that if you are, I'm seriously offended that you've never hit on me."

"You really think this is a good time for joking?" The color came back to his face as he calmed down.

Nick shrugged his shoulders. "Every myth has some kind of basis in reality. Maybe vampires and werewolves exist too."

I shook my head in disbelief. "So you're okay with the fact that you might be sitting in a car with a demon?"

"I dunno," he replied thoughtfully. "I guess that depends on whether or not you're gonna try to kill me. Are you?"

"Not that I know of." I let a small smile escape. Maybe Nick could help me get some answers too. It might be nice to have more people know my secret other than just Alex and Crevan. "I honestly don't really know what is going on. This is all kind of new to me."

"Well then, let's go somewhere and figure some stuff out, shall we?" He tossed the cigarette out the window and drove the Jeep back out onto the highway. "When do you have to be home?"

"Whenever I get there I suppose. Where are we going?"

"My place. I have lots of privacy. We'll get to the bottom of this, don't worry."

I couldn't help but wonder how many times I'd have to hear that promise before it came true.

10

Nick cranked the music up loud and sped home, not slowing down until he pulled the Jeep into a winding driveway that led to a very large estate. I had passed by the old gates many times and had always assumed the property was abandoned.

A ten-foot tall wall of stone that was partially covered with creeping vines enclosed several acres and a two-story Victorian house rested in the middle of it. A veranda porch wrapped around to the back and I could see that some of the balcony railings were broken. The yard was overgrown and weeds filled the landscaping and once decorated flowerbeds. Even though it was a run-down and neglected structure, it wasn't hard to imagine the home in its glory.

"Is this your parents' place?" My voice spoke in a hushed tone.

"It was my grandmother's. Now it's mine I guess." He got out of the Jeep and led me to the front door.

My footsteps creaked against the old wooden porch that was in need of repair. I followed him into the dim entrance hall. Dust covered the elegantly decorated surfaces. A huge gilded mirror hung on the wall next to the door; a spiraling staircase led up the stairs in the front turret. The foyer was grand with vaulted ceilings and a lavish crystal chandelier.

"Tacky, I know," he excused, grabbing my hand and leading me to the staircase. As we passed the sitting room entrance, I noticed someone lying on the sofa. I could hear the loud snores but didn't bother to ask. The empty booze bottles that littered the floor around the man spoke volumes.

Once upstairs, he led the way into a large room that looked like it was once used as a library. My first thought was how much Alex would love to have the shelf space that was in here, over twice the area he had in his living room. Very few books remained, and the ones that did looked like they were in horrible shape. At one end of the room was a fireplace and sofa. French doors that led out to a balcony dominated the wall on the other side of the room.

I walked to the doors and peered out. From here, I could see the wall that surrounded the property. It disappeared into a thick grove of apple trees.

"I bet this place was incredible once." I looked out at the sprawling lawns and enormous in ground pool that was empty except for a small amount of dirty water and debris.

"Maybe," Nick shrugged. "I wouldn't know. I wasn't here then." He smiled and sat down on the sofa near the fireplace. Grabbing a MacBook from the table next to him, he powered it up and patted the leather cushion next to him. "Grab me another pack of cigarettes out of my bag."

I picked up his bag as I walked over and sat next to him. "What are we looking up?"

I looked over at the computer screen. He'd gotten online already and had typed in the address into a search engine. Cringing, I held my breath while he typed in the word succubus.

The first thing that popped up was a definition. Nick read it aloud.

Released

"A succubus is a lady temptress and the female counterpart to an incubus. She seeks sleeping men, stealing their souls through the act of intimacy. The succubus was once thought to be a fallen angel, looking for revenge against God. Demons, witches and deformed children are the supposed result of such couplings."

He wiggled his eyebrows at me playfully and lit a cigarette. "Well that sounds scary, yet strangely enticing."

I smacked him on the arm. "That's not me at all, thank you very much."

He clicked on the next link and scanned the words. I tried to keep up with him, but it was too hard when he kept clicking on new links, speed-reading the pages as he went. Finally, he stopped on one.

"Cambion?" I had never heard the word before.

"Why not?" Nick shrugged. "Look, it says here that Cambion can be human children that are more susceptible to supernatural influences. How do you know what you are unless you look at all the possibilities?"

I warmed to the idea, but I knew he was wrong. Alex would've known if there was no reason for me to worry, and he seemed very concerned. "Look up the word Veduny."

He typed it in slowly and the screen filled with such a random mix of websites it was hard to navigate through them all. Mostly, it was listings of people with the word as a last name or characters in online fantasy games. My heart skipped a beat when I saw one page, toward the bottom of the screen.

"Click on that one." I pointed to the link and Nick poised the mouse over it.

"...The Veduny are a hidden sect of angelic warriors who hunt the souls of Satan's spawn. Known to be duty and honor bound, these people keep their traditions more closely guarded than the highest order of the Masonic temple.

From the few tales about the Veduny, it is known that any living being is a potential target. They act as judge, jury, and executioner in a very quickly conducted trial. It is rumored that a trio of leaders have the ultimate say over the fates of all who come across them. A common tactic they employ is to assume any soul not of their bloodline is demonic.

The Veduny have no ability to feel emotion, and cannot be swayed from their mission. They know nothing of fear or friendship, only loyalty to their own and slaughter..."

The article continued to talk about the supposed history of a people that dated back to the beginning of humanity. I tried to wrap my mind around the information. Alex was nothing like the cold monster that the author described. It wasn't until the end of the page that it discussed their supernatural abilities such a shape shifting and mind reading. That was the only thing that seemed familiar to me.

"They can put anything on the internet." Nick appeared amused by the mythical tale we'd just read. "Where did you hear about them?"

I didn't want to answer him. Deciding to test his willingness to accept me, I challenged him.

"Don't say it out loud, but think about your favorite childhood memory."

Released

Nick leaned back into the couch, a dreamy smile spreading across his face.

I concentrated. It was a little harder than the kids at school, but the image played clearly in his mind and I couldn't help but grin. "You named your cat Dog?"

Nick laughed. "Hey, I spelled it d a w g, so it was cool. He was awesome."

I watched his mind replay the day he'd found him. The cat was skinny, abandoned and lonely. With gray fur matted to his body, when Nick petted him, the young boy could feel every bone in the cat's body.

"It doesn't bother you that I know that without you telling me?" I watched him carefully as I left his mind.

Nick put the computer back on the table and grabbed my hands in his. "I'm not going to lie to you, Cadi. Is it weird? Of course it is. Am I going to go running out of the room to find a crucifix and a priest? No way. Like I said before, I'm your friend and I'm here to help. Anytime you need it."

I smiled, gently squeezing his hands. Leaning forward, I gave him a quick kiss on the cheek. "Thanks. That means a lot."

He flashed another prize-winning grin at me and pulled his hands away playfully. "I said we're friends, not that I wanna make out with you. I don't need you sucking out my soul or something."

"Very funny," I chided. "So how do we find out what I really am?"

"Well, are you sure that was your mother back there?" Nick got serious. "What all did she tell you before I came in?"

"She said I was her replacement, I was demon spawn, that my father was the dark lord, and that I was supposed to be a part of some unholy trinity."

"Well that's a light conversation if I've ever heard of one." He absently replied. "What trinity? Who are the other two? Did she say?"

"Me, her and... a demon I know of. But I can't say his name or he can come here."

Nick laughed. "If a demon wanted to come into my house, I'm sure he would without an invitation. I don't exactly have garlic and holy water covering all of the exits." He picked up the computer again and began clicking on different websites. "Tell me the story from the beginning."

"I didn't know anything was different, until last week when I got so sick. That's when things started to change."

"Nothing weird has ever happened to you before that?"

I sat back and looked at him closely. He was so good looking, with perfect bone structure and hair that made you want to run your fingers through it. He oozed sex appeal, but didn't act as if he knew it. His personality was so engaging it was hard not to confide in him. "What about you? I don't really know anything about you. Has anything weird ever happened to you?"

Nick looked up, surprised at my question. "What do you want to know? I'm an only child. My mother died when I was a kid and my father drank his way into oblivion. I live off a trust fund my grandmother set up for me. I hate dogs but can't resist a cat. I can't cook but can order a pizza in four different languages. I play the guitar well but sing badly, and I have a lot of unhealthy habits."

"Like what?" I pressed when he stopped talking. I could see him becoming defensive.

"I drink occasionally and smoke cigarettes." He stared directly into my eyes, refusing to back down from the confrontation. "I get high about twice a year and lost my virginity when I was fourteen. I think curfews are a joke. I got caught shoplifting when I was twelve. How about you?"

It was my turn to go on the defensive. "I haven't done any of that," I admitted with a blush.

"Liar," Nick countered. "You got drunk last weekend. I'd have to say that meeting a dead woman ranks higher than anything on my list of weird experiences."

I took a deep breath. "I'm sorry. I didn't mean to…"

Nick cut me off. "Don't sweat it. Let's get back to this. There are tons of stories about people making a deal with the devil and that's how they become demons. Like, when they die, their soul belongs to Satan. Maybe your mother wasn't born that way. If she just made a deal, I don't see that you have anything to worry about because she was completely human."

"But what if I made the deal? What does that mean?"

He cringed. "I guess you'll find out when you die. If you go to Heaven, it means nothing. If not, well… What was the deal?"

I looked confused.

"What were the terms? No deal is made without terms." He seemed frustrated when I still didn't know how to answer his question. "Okay, you agreed to give this demon your soul in return for what?"

"I wanted her to stop yelling at me." I spoke in a whisper.

Nick just looked at me, a stunned expression filling his face. "You bartered your soul over parental discipline?"

My entire body shook. "You don't understand. She was horrible. I didn't want her dead. I just wanted her to stop screaming. I was too young to know any better."

My words seemed to spark an idea and he turned back to the computer. Nick typed in random words on a mission that I couldn't follow. "I wonder if the Supreme Court holds any power over the devil. If so, it's not legal to enter into a binding contract as a minor."

I smiled weakly, knowing he was just trying to lighten the mood a little bit. I remembered Aniketos saying something similar in a dream. "There are laws," I said excitedly. "He said it was against their laws for him to be betrothed to a child."

"Whoa, wait up. Betrothed? As in married?"

I nodded slowly. "I think so. He said Aiyana would remind him of the laws."

"Who said? I'm so confused."

"Zandy," I said, referring to him the way Crevan had. "He said we were betrothed. But then Aniketos told him Aiyana could remind him of their laws."

"Zandy? Your devil's name is Zandy?" He struggled to bite back a chuckle.

"No, that's just what Crevan calls him." I laughed at the silliness of the name.

"Who's Crevan? Should I be taking notes?"

How could I explain this part without betraying the Maxwells' secrets? "She's just a friend who knows what is going on. They are trying to help me figure out what to do, too."

"Okay, so this Zandy guy says you have to marry him? When?"

Disgust filled my body. "I have twenty three days left. And then I'm his."

Nick grinned. "So we have three weeks to figure out how to stop a demon. How hard can that be?"

I wondered if it would be easier if Nick met Alex and Crevan. Then again, knowing how threatened Alex was about the mere idea of Nick, maybe that wasn't the best idea. Selfishly, I couldn't help but want them to work together anyway. Nick was my friend. Alex was my friend too, wasn't he? If only he'd call and explain why I had to stay away, we could figure this out quicker.

"So that's your plan? You just want to stop the demon. What about what's happening to me? How can I stop it?"

"Why would you want to stop it?" He practically glared at me. "You have a gift. It's up to you how you use it. From what I can tell, you're a pretty good person. Who says that has to change?"

"What about when I become glutinous with everything like the books say I will?"

"Then I suggest you surround yourself with people who can handle you. All you have to do is believe in yourself, Cadi. Don't you know that? Mind over matter is a good way to live. People can cure themselves of cancer with the right mindset. You can control this, I know it."

I smiled warmly. "You've known me for less than two weeks. How can you have so much faith in me?"

"Maybe I'm just that damn intuitive. Speaking of which, I bet your parents have rules about how late their beautiful young daughter comes home at night. So unless you're ready to start breaking rules, I'd say it's time to get you home."

I looked toward the French doors and noticed the sun had already set. Time passing was something that seemed to escape my notice lately. Checking my phone, I saw that it was nearly ten and I'd missed several phone calls. Three texts were waiting for me to read.

8:32 Alex wants to see to you. We can do the switch. Let me know when to come.

8:46 Ignoring my calls is making him grouchy. Don't leave me here to deal with him!

9:12 If you're ignoring me while I endure this wrath, Zandy will be the least of your worries!

"I have to go," I said as I quickly headed for the door without thinking.

Nick grabbed my arm and pulled me back into the room. "Wait a minute. What's wrong?"

My finger was on the phone ready to dial Crevan's number. "My friend... I forgot she was coming over tonight," I lied. "I've missed her calls for the past three hours."

Nick's face softened, the worry lines smoothing out of his forehead. "Let me drive you home at least, okay?"

Of course, he'd want to drive me home. He didn't know how fast I could run. Instead of explaining, I waited for him to grab his leather coat off the floor next to the sofa before walking out with him.

"Nikita!" A slurred voice bellowed as we reached the front door. "Where the hell is my…"

Nick cut him off and rolled his eyes. "There's a new bottle right next to your head," he yelled back before closing the door behind us.

"Nikita, huh?" I smiled when he climbed behind the wheel of the Jeep. "I'm not the only one with secrets."

"You're right. I'm a Russian spy. My whole family has been part of a sleeper cell for ages."

We both laughed as he made his way back to my house. I'd never realized how close Nick's house was to mine. If I had my direction sense right, he was less than a mile away if you were a bird flying through the woods. That made him my closest neighbor. When we reached the back of my house, he put the car into park.

"Everything's going to be fine," Nick assured me. "I'll keep looking and let you know what I find tomorrow at school."

I hugged him tightly. "Thank you. I know I don't have to ask, but you won't tell anyone about this, will you?"

"I solemnly swear that you can suck out my soul if I should ever make a peep." He held his hand up as if he was taking an oath.

"Something tells me you'd like that too much," I laughed.

His face shifted. I couldn't tell what he was thinking. "Good night Cadi. I'll see you tomorrow."

Nick kissed me tenderly on the cheek.

Released

After an awkward moment of hesitation, I climbed out and waited for him to pull away before dialing Crevan's number.

"No need," the girl's voice called out from behind me. "I've been waiting here in the weeds for the past hour. And to think you haven't just been ignoring me, you've been with my Bio-Boy!" Crevan looked offended.

"Don't read too much into it. We're just friends. Would you do me a favor though?" I prayed Crevan would agree to my next request. "Could you please not fawn all over him while you're pretending to be me? I really don't want to ruin a good friendship."

"Psh," Crevan was indignant. "He's only interested in you. I have no chance if I don't look like you."

"Please?" I repeated, ignoring her complaint.

"Fine," Crevan agreed reluctantly. "Now you do me a favor and go settle my brother down. He's waiting at the house for you. Our father's been breathing fire down our throats all day and finally left a bit ago."

I nodded in agreement and headed down the road. Instead of running, I walked and dialed Nick's number. I knew he wouldn't be home yet, but planned to leave him a voice mail. When he answered, I laughed.

"You know it's against the law to talk on your cell phone while you drive, right?"

"What can I say," Nick joked. "I'm a deviant. Miss me already?"

I grinned at no one. "Duh. Listen, we need a code word so you know it's really me when we talk."

"Uh... Okay. Why?"

"Well, demons can change shape, right? I just want to make sure no one messes with you and you think it's me, that's all."

Nick chuckled into the phone. "Your fiancé isn't going to try to seduce me, is he? I'd hate to be Zandy's new toy."

"Not funny Nick. I'm serious."

"Well if we say a word on the phone, he could overhear. How safe is that?"

He had a point. "Think of something. I'll try to hear you." I stopped walking and concentrated. It took effort to sort out the massive energies of all of the people tucked in their houses but I finally found his mind.

Purple dinosaurs. Purple dinosaurs. Purple dinosaurs.

I burst out laughing. "Really? That's the best you could come up with?"

"Hey, I liked that guy when I was little Nikita. You know, 'we're a happy family'..." Nick sang into the phone. "Good night."

I hung up and quickened my pace, anxious to see Alex and find out what had happened with his father.

I was halfway there when I felt Alex's thoughts calling out to me.

Don't come. Don't come.

Repeatedly, his mind chanted the mantra. Panic framed his words. Something terrible must be happening. I quickened my pace and ran as fast as I could to his house, ignoring his pleas.

I threw the front door open without knocking and paid no mind to the older man that stood in the living room. Alex jumped up from his submissive position on the couch and ran over to me.

The older man glared at me, but after a decade of Zandros, not to mention what had happened today with my mother, I couldn't care less. Whatever threat this man posed couldn't be much worse.

"I tried to tell you not to come." He grabbed hold of my waist and steered me back toward the door. He pressed something cold and metallic into my hand. "Don't let go of this," he whispered into my ear.

The man approached us. Alex stayed by my side, keeping a protective distance from the man with the terrifying, cold blue eyes. Every frightening thing that website said about the Veduny was standing in front of me.

"Ah, tell me this is the girl in question?" The glare was still on his face, which was an older and much icier version of Alex.

"She'll go." Alex didn't directly address the man's question.

"Oh no," the man interrupted. "I think I deserve an introduction in the least. Don't you agree Alexander?"

Alex slowly looked up at the man. "Cadi Matthews, this is my father, Elric." His hand found mine behind his back and he squeezed it lightly. When I didn't respond immediately, he did it again.

I looked from father to son, trying to assess the situation but failed miserably.

Be polite. Be brief. Don't touch him or accept his touch. Alex's thoughts cried out to me.

"It's nice to meet you." My voice shook. Every ounce of bravado I'd walked in with was now completely gone.

"I wish I could say the same." His tone dripped with disgust. "Tell me Cadi Matthews. Exactly what is your intention with my children?" His silent judgment never took a break.

Tell him you want to help me trap the demon.

"I can help Alex get Zandros." I cringed, knowing that I had just called out to the demon again.

Elric scoffed. "And you think you can help him how?"

Alex squeezed my hand again. *Don't engage him anymore. Stay silent.*

I ignored his instruction. "I have what Zandros wants. I can lure him into the open; trick him and give Alex the chance to kill him."

Alex groaned.

"Filthy Vadim!" Elric screamed. "My son needs no help from your kind!"

"She's right," Alex stated calmly. "Zandros has been in hiding far too long. If she can help end his reign, I say we let her."

Elric shook his head while his face reddened. "We do not take assistance from evil."

I pulled my hand away from Alex. The same fury I'd felt with my mother threatened to resurface. "I am not evil! I've never done anything even remotely evil, or wicked, or... You can't blame me for the actions of my mother!"

Elric seethed. "You are the devil's spawn, nothing more."

I steeled my nerves, wishing I could smack that smug look right off his face. "What God do you serve? The Bible clearly states that the soul who sins is the one that shall die. Don't you know your own teachings?"

"*You* dare quote scripture to *me*?" He seethed with anger.

Please stop this madness. It won't do any good.

"My father taught me well. In the Book of Ezekiel, it says that 'the son who has done what is just and right shall surely live. The son shall not suffer the iniquity of the father, nor the father suffer for the iniquity of the son. The righteousness of the righteous shall be upon himself, the wickedness of the wicked shall be upon himself'." I stared him down. "I have not sinned, so I will not be judged for the sins of my mother by you or your God."

Elric paused in contemplation. He shook his head slowly and spoke softly. "You quote the prophet well, but you do not speak the words of the Creator. *His* law clearly states that He shall punish the children for the sins of the fathers to the third and fourth generation. Your time shall come." He turned away but paused just short of walking out of the room. "We have an agreement Alexander. Do not forget the terms."

The house was eerie silent. The heaviness in the air lightened after the man left and Alex took a visible deep breath.

"You shouldn't have baited him like that." Alex quietly scolded. "I'm sorry you had to meet him."

"What arrangement was he talking about?" My mind raced back to my earlier conversation with Nick about deals and terms.

Alex sighed heavily and went to sit on the couch. "I've agreed to go back into service for the Veduny."

"In return for what?" My heart melted. If he was going back to hunting like he used to, that meant he was leaving.

"In return for your safety. No Veduny will ever hunt you so long as I remain true to my word. And my father has agreed to allow Zandros to be my first priority."

I sat down next to him and opened my hand. My fingers wrapped around an ornate black iron ring with a delicate red and black opal nested inside the setting.

Alex took it from me and slid it onto my middle finger. "This is the other part of the deal. He gave my mother's stone to me so that I could make this. Never take it off. So long as you wear it, no demon or hunter can sense your soul."

I held my hand up to gaze at the swirling stone. The colors wrapped around each other as if they were swimming. "Does this mean you can't find me either?"

Alex shook his head. "As the maker of the ring, I will always know if you are safe or in danger, even if I am nowhere near you."

I sighed. Nowhere near meant he planned to be far away. "So where does that leave us?"

Alex smiled and gently traced his fingertip over the back of my hand. "That leaves us in the exact same place as always. I will rid you of Zandros' threat and you will live a very long and very happy life. Nothing would make me happier."

"Nothing?" I didn't want to believe him. In the few short days since we met, I'd come to think of him as a true friend, a best friend, maybe something more someday. I thought he felt the same way. Now he was acting as if it was no big deal that he was going away.

"Cadi," Alex breathed heavily. "I've always been honest with you. I can't be who you would need me to be, and I'm truly sorry for that."

I didn't know how I was supposed to react. This wasn't fair. "This isn't your idea! This is your father's, isn't it?"

Released

Alex was tired. I could see the resignation in his eyes and didn't want to fight with him, but I didn't want him give up either.

"No," he stated calmly. "It was my offering, although I knew he would agree in order to protect our family's reputation."

I was angry. My only real friend was saying goodbye, and all because I was damaging his reputation. Tears streamed down my face as I stood up and ran out the front door. I didn't bother looking back to see if he was following me. I knew he wasn't. With nowhere else to go, I hit the tree line and ran straight past my own property, into the night.

11

Once I reached the stone walls, I stopped. My breath came in sharp, jagged rasps that made me dizzy. I climbed up over the wall and headed toward the back of the house. I had nearly reached the empty pool before finally falling to the ground, exhausted and out of breath. Curling into a ball, I allowed myself to sob under the clear night sky.

After my self-pity began to ease, I sat up, watching the stars overhead as they twinkled. How could a loving God be so unfair? Then again, I'd actually only known Alex for less than two weeks. I had no claim, no real reason to think we had some life-long relationship forming, but there was a bond there and the thought of it being over already ripped at my heart.

"Cadi?" Nick's footsteps quickened as he approached me. "Cadi! What happened?" He bent down and scooped me up like a child in his strong arms.

The harder I tried to stop crying the more tears fell.

Nick carried me into the house, up the stairs and back into the library. He deposited me gently on the sofa and sat on the floor next to me, silently waiting for me to start talking

It was well past midnight and he looked tired. Why wouldn't he? I'd woken him early and he had quite an eventful day. Now, I was invading his life again. My voice cracked when I spoke. "I'm sorry to keep dragging you into this. I just couldn't go home and I didn't know where else to go."

Nick looked up at me and pushed a stray strand of hair out of my face. "Never say you're sorry, that's lesson number one. Everything happens for a reason, and if you go regretting things all the time, you never really learn anything. But now that you're a little less hysterical, you have to tell me the secret word."

"What?" I watched the crooked smile spread across his face like a child.

"Hey, I'm just playing your game by your rules in your world. What's the secret password?"

My tears stopped flowing as I realized what he was saying. "Purple dinosaurs."

"Good," he said, leaning back against the edge of the sofa. "Now tell me who I get to beat up for making you cry?"

"No one, it's my fault really."

"Lover-boy in the Range Rover?"

I nodded. "Not an appropriate title though."

His brow creased and I could tell he felt sorry for me. "How long were you two going out?"

I gave him my own version of his crooked smile. "We aren't. We're just good friends." It sounded absurd the moment it left my lips.

"Well that's your problem then. Most guys don't fall in love as quickly as girls do."

He was so matter of fact about it, it made me stop brooding and actually think. "That's not what I mean. I mean... I don't know what I mean. I'm so stupid." I threw my arm up over my forehead and slumped back into the cushions.

"No, but you are filthy. And you're getting my bed all gross, so how about you go clean up that pretty little face of yours and you can crash here tonight." He pointed toward the door. "Straight down at the end of the hall," he instructed.

I got up guiltily looking at the dirt stains and rips on my yoga pants that came from running through the woods. "I don't have anything to change into," I stammered, embarrassed.

He stood up and pulled off his t-shirt. "Instant pajamas," he smiled warmly.

I took the garment from him and made my way down the hall to the bathroom. Turning on the showerhead, I stepped out of my ruined clothes and stood under the hot water. I scrubbed myself quickly, not taking time to soak like usual. The last thing I wanted to do right now was let my mind wander. Besides, I didn't want to risk his father coming in.

After pulling on the soft cotton shirt and making sure it was long enough to cover my butt, I went back to the library. Nick was sitting on the couch, still shirtless, scouring the Internet.

"Still looking for demon stuff?" I sat down next to him and curled my bare legs underneath of myself, making my body as small as possible.

"Worse. Facebook."

I looked over at the screen and saw that he was indeed on the social networking site. His newly updated status read 'Hot babe in my shower. No sleep for me tonight!'

He winked at me when I blushed. "I don't know why people do that stuff." I pouted.

"It's a fun way to creep into other people's lives. You'd be surprised at the things people post on here."

"No I wouldn't. My sister has one. It gets pretty ridiculous if you ask me."

His smile turned mischievous. He grabbed his iPhone and pointed it at me. I could hear the click of the camera before I had time to react. Triumphantly, he hit the send button and a moment later, my picture popped up on his profile page.

'Girl of my dreams.' He captioned it.

I was horrified. "How many people from school will see that?" I was just sitting there, my butt practically hanging out, with dripping wet hair wearing nothing but his t-shirt. He'd managed to capture the personal moment and share it with the entire world.

Nick shrugged. "I'm not friends with anyone there. You're pretty much it. And I'm positive your boyfriend won't see it."

"I don't have a boyfriend." A tear escaped me again. I tried not to feel alone in the world, but it was too hard. Alex and Crevan were the only people in my life who knew everything. I just didn't know how I was going to be able to say goodbye to them.

"Well that's his stupid loss." Nick spoke softly, gently wiping the tear away. He leaned back into the cushions and pulled me into him, wrapping his arms around me. Planting light kisses on the top of my head, he rubbed my back gently, soothing my troubles and blurring my sadness.

I rested my head against his bare chest, listening to his strong heartbeat. It was fast, but not as fast as mine was. A deep growl in the pit of my stomach began to grow like a fire engulfing my belly. I pressed my lips against his skin and pushed my body into his, moving my face a fraction of an inch at a time, kissing my way to his neck. I relished the taste of salt, the sweetness of his essence, the desire in his breath as he gripped me tightly around the waist, pulling me into him even tighter.

A low moan escaped Nick's lips when I pulled away just enough to look in his eyes. His need for me clouded his face. He leaned into me, biting my lower lip and raking his tongue across it seductively. I may have started this in an attempt to forget all of my troubles, but I was putty in his hands at that point.

Responding passionately, I opened my mouth enough to let his tongue dart in, dancing around my own. He tasted so sweet I didn't want him to stop. Ever. Melting into him, I let the embrace linger, pulling away slowly.

Again looking him in the eye, I whispered. "I have a confession to make." He raised an eyebrow. "It wasn't always me. I mean, sometimes my friend took my place pretending to be me, and she said she'd spent time with you."

Nick smiled. "I know."

I sat straight up, straddling his lap. "You did?"

"Mhm." He wrapped his fingers in my hair. "You don't pop bubblegum like a thirteen year old." It was his turn to whisper as he nibbled on my collarbone. "I have a confession for you, too."

I moaned. I didn't care what he said, so long as he didn't stop kissing me.

"I plan on taking advantage of your vulnerability issues right now." He said each word between light kisses. "And I don't feel guilty about it at all."

My mind swam. I couldn't even think straight right now. All I wanted was Nick to stop talking and keep kissing. I replied without words.

He grabbed my hips and quickly flipped me onto my back. Hovering over me, Nick began devouring my neck hungrily.

Through drunken eyes, I noticed a strange looking book sitting on the table next to his laptop.

The cracked leather binding looked so familiar, but I couldn't place it. It came to me as Nick's hands began to wander, pushing the t-shirt up on my torso.

"Wait!" I grabbed his hands, stopping him suddenly.

Nick groaned, sitting up a bit. "What?"

I pushed him off me and scrambled to get out from underneath of him. Nick sat back and rolled his eyes. He ran his hands through his hair in frustration.

"What is this?" I grabbed the book.

Nick's eyes narrowed, a strange expression crossing his face. He looked like he was about to become very angry. "Just some book I found on the shelf. Why?"

I picked it up and opened it carefully. The parchment pages looked like they could disintegrate with the lightest touch. Holding my breath, I wasn't sure what to think when I saw the strange writing inside. There was no mistake about it. "This is Glagolitic. Is this yours?"

Released

My mind was swimming again, only this time there was no lust involved. My heart raced, looking into his deep brown eyes. There had to be a clue somewhere, if only I could see it.

He shook his head and shrugged. "It's just an old book, Cadi; nothing more." He reached out and grabbed my waist again. "Now where were we?"

I pushed his hand away. "Just stop for a minute! Why do you have this?"

Nick rolled his eyes again. "I don't know, ask my grandmother. She left it here."

His tone was evasive. Warning bells went off in my head. Footsteps coming down the hallway tore my attention toward the door. I knew those steps. On the table next to the door, I saw a small diamond pendant. My heart sank with fear when I realized it was the same one Nick had given me. The last time I saw it was when…

"Sweet Carina." He stood in the doorway, tall and impressive. The wicked grin that spread across his face made my stomach turn.

Nick looked back and forth between the two of us. "You know her?" he asked Zandros innocently.

Zandros didn't take his eyes off of my terrified face. "Tell him, Carina. Tell my nephew how well you know me."

I shook. "Your nephew?" Hurt, I glared at Nick. "You said you didn't know anything about me, about what was happening."

Nick just stared at Zandros, not bothering to move a muscle.

Zandros just laughed. "Very good my boy," he applauded. "You see Carina, I told you no amount of Veduny magic could keep you away from me. Not even their silly little trinkets."

"Do you mind? We were a little busy here," Nick said with a tilt of his head toward me.

I wanted to cry, but I refused. Standing up, I stalked toward my tormentor. "You gave me your word. I have twenty three days left and I demand you leave me until then."

Zandros laughed while Nick looked impressed. He joined me in front of his uncle. "She's right. If you told her she had more time, you have no choice but abide by your word."

Zandros conceded. "If you ruin her before my plans can take form, you will wish you were in Hell," he said to Nick. With a flourish of movement, Zandros turned and left as suddenly as he'd appeared.

I spun on my heels and slapped Nick across the face.

Nick held his face, rubbing the sting away. "Well that was the reaction I was expecting. I guess I was just hoping it would be different." He went over to the table and started shoving his computer and the book into his satchel.

I stood frozen in anger. "You lied to me."

Nick shrugged. "It's what we do," he said casually. He turned to face me again. "I suggest you learn to do the same if you want to make it out of this alive."

I was stunned silent. How could I be so stupid?

Nick walked over to a chest of drawers and pulled out a pair of basketball shorts. He tossed them to me. "Put those on, I can't have you wandering around half naked."

"Wandering where?"

Playful, sexy Nick was gone. He was angry. "Put them on!" he ordered.

"Not until you tell me where you think I'm going with you."

He raised an eyebrow. "We're going to have a little chat with your boyfriend. If you'd rather walk into his house half naked..." He walked to the door and grabbed me around the wrist, pulling me along behind him. "I honestly have no problem with that."

My heart beat out of my chest. The smell of my own fear washed into my nostrils. I had to stumble and hurry to keep up with his pace as he pulled me down the stairs and out the front door. Nick opened the driver's door of the Jeep and pushed me in, climbing into the seat after I'd moved far enough out of the way.

I sat terrified of what was going to happen to me. "Please, don't do this," I begged.

"There's not much choice Cadi." His face softened, a pang of regret filling his eyes as he drove toward Alex's house. Cranking up the music loudly, he sped away into the night.

I wished I'd brought my cell phone. There was no way to warn Alex or Crevan. I'd made such a mess. I could hear Alex's thoughts; maybe if I tried hard enough I could send a silent message to him.

Alex!

"Stop that," Nick said sharply. "He won't be able to help you if you try to warn him before we get there. He isn't the only one who can hear you."

My big eyes faced him in the dark. "You can hear...?"

"We all have secrets, Cadi Matthews." He slowed the Jeep at the beginning of Alex's driveway. "Put the shorts on. He knows we're here."

His voice was softer so I complied. I had to shift in my seat to pull them all of the way up. "What are you going to do?"

Nick almost laughed. "I have no idea. That's why we're here."

Alex was at the foot of the porch stairs when we pulled up to a stop. Nick got out first and walked around to the passenger side. He pulled me out of the car and I stumbled a few steps before I found my footing. I knew what this must look like. I was wet and barely dressed in Nick's clothing and he was wearing only jeans. We definitely looked like we had been messing around. The worst part of it all was the fact that we were.

"Nikita Vikenti," Alex said slowly as we approached the house.

"Son of Elric, we request asylum." Nick spoke clearly, confidently.

He stood like a statue guarding the gates, considering Nick's request. Alex stepped aside to let us in the house.

"What are you doing?" I hissed.

"He's a Veduny Warrior. They can't refuse a request for asylum unless it comes from a targeted enemy." His hand moved off my arm once we'd entered the house.

Alex slowly followed behind us. Not once did he take his eyes off Nick, refusing to look at me. "From whom do you seek asylum?" he asked.

"Zandros, of the Thann tribe." Nick's speech was so formal.

Alex crossed his arms over his chest. "I have already granted the girl protection. Why would I bless you with the same?"

Nick laughed. "Please, I don't need your blessings. I just need your damn house." He looked around at all of the books on the walls.

"No TV, no lights, no nothing? Jesus, do you not realize what century you're in?"

"I have no need. What protection do you need from one of your own elders?"

I couldn't help but notice Alex still refused to look at me. It was heartbreaking.

"You're too naked," Nick swallowed a laugh. "He doesn't like the thoughts that go through his mind when he looks at you completely covered up, let alone half naked. Isn't that right, Alexander, Son of Elric?"

Alex stood firm and refused to take Nick's bait. "I assure you I have no such problem."

Nick casually sat on the couch and kicked his feet up on the table. "Well I'll give you two a minute. Don't mind me," he said cockily.

I went over to Alex. "I didn't know he was…"

Alex shushed me. "It's okay. I was unaware of who he was until my father informed me this morning. You ran away before I could warn you. I should've made my inquiries better and kept him away from you but I've dealt with worse. Go upstairs and get dressed." He attempted a small smile. "And no, I don't have a problem with your manner of dress I'd just rather not see you wearing his clothes."

"I can explain," I attempted.

"No need." His face softened as he lightly touched my shoulder. "Just go get dressed while I talk to him."

I nodded and headed up the stairs to my room. Once inside, I took no time finding a pair of jeans and a blouse to put on. I wondered what they were talking about and dreaded leaving them alone for too long. Grabbing the discarded shirt and shorts, I hurried back down the stairs.

Alex leaned against the doorframe while Nick still lounged on the couch. I tossed the clothes back to Nick and sat on the chair across from him. He pulled the shirt back on.

"So what exactly are we doing here?" I finally asked, breaking the awkward silence.

"We need your little angel friend to find a Soul Seeker." Nick replied. I was confused, but Alex looked shocked. "And I know you have access to that kind of magic or she would still be wearing Zandros' filthy bracelet."

"You knew about the bracelet?" I asked tentatively.

He gave me an incredulous look. "Why else would I give you a four carat diamond? The power of the pure gem would've blocked his spell if you'd actually worn it instead of giving it away."

"What spell?" Alex asked.

"It was a weakening spell. So long as she kept it on, she would eventually succumb to his wishes, no matter what her heart really wanted."

"And you wish to protect her?" It was obvious that Alex didn't believe him. "Or did you just want her for yourself?"

"You want me to lie?" That cocky look came back. Nick sat straight up and got serious. "Look, you can be mad at me later. The only thing important right now is Zandros. He needs to be stopped."

"And what exactly do you get out of this?" Alex asked.

I looked back and forth between the two men. I wasn't sure what to think. All I knew was that I was terrified.

"There are only two members of our tribe still alive. If Zandros is gone, I would be the only Thann left. I would think your people would like the sound of that enough."

I cringed at Alex's reaction. For a minute it seemed like he'd love to kill Nick himself.

"What about your father?" Alex asked. "Our records show that Zandros' brother Karan still lives."

"He may as well be dead." Nick grumbled.

I had to agree. The man I'd seen passed out with a bottle of liquor didn't really seem like much of a threat. I almost pitied the look of despair that flashed across Nick's face when he heard his father's name.

Alex shook his head. "I guess my only question is what your intentions are."

"I know my uncle better than you or any of your little books could ever know him. I know his strengths, and his weaknesses. I know what it will take to kill him, and it's nothing short of a Soul Seeker."

"You still haven't said what you want in return for your help." Alex still stood over us, his authority hanging heavily in the air.

Nick cast a quick glance in my direction. "I want nothing. It will be enough to know he is gone."

Alex finally looked at me. "Read his mind. See if he is lying."

Nick rolled his eyes and laughed at my hesitation. "Go right ahead. I have nothing left to hide."

The room fell silent as I concentrated. Images swirled from Nick's mind into mine, easier this time than the first time I looked for his memories. I could see the young boy, happily dancing in a garden with a breathtaking brunette woman. She was the most incredible looking woman I'd ever seen.

Everything you do in life is your own choice Nikita. Don't ever let anyone make you think differently.

The image shifted to one of Zandros breaking down a door. A very young Nick cowered in the corner, hiding behind a small bed and covering his ears so that he couldn't hear the man shout at his parents. Fire flew from the demon's fingertips, engulfing his mother instantly. She screamed in agony as the skin on her perfect face bubbled. Nick's father grabbed a blanket, trying to smother the flames while Zandros stood back triumphantly. The fabric caught fire, burning his father as well. Her screams stopped when her body fell to the floor. A sickening gray smoke filled the room. Nick sobbed.

I fought my way through a menagerie of memories, finding one from when Nick was about thirteen. Zandros was at his house, standing in the library. The full shelves made Alex's book collection look like nothing. One by one, he took the books and burned them. Nick leaned against the doorway, disgusted by his uncle's actions. *No one needs this garbage. My mother's diaries might as well be fairy tales.* Nick hoped differently. His mother had read some of them to him. Those stories were the only thing that gave him hope. Now he had nothing.

Another memory not too long after that had Nick sitting across from Zandros. The man was teaching him how to make fire come from his hands. Nick hated every bit of the magic and refused to do it. Zandros backhanded him, screaming that he would never be worthy of the Thann name if he didn't learn. It made him sick to his stomach to think of wielding the same weapon that killed his mother.

A recent image danced to the front of Nick's mind. Again, Zandros was there and Nick's hatred raged. *Soon you will be my son, and I shall bestow a great gift upon you. We will be the perfect trinity, powerful enough to take down the Dark Lord himself.* Zandros looked drunk with greed as he told Nick all about the half-demon girl that was about to become an adult. It was then that Nick decided to inject himself in my life. He would find out if I was deserving of Zandros' evil or if I was good, like his grandmother's stories told. If I was the latter, he would do everything he could to protect me from his uncle's madness.

By the time I pulled myself out of Nick's mind, I knew his biggest desire was to get revenge against Zandros. I nodded at Alex after giving Nick a look of pity.

"Fine," Alex said, pushing himself off the doorway to take a seat in the other chair. "What can you tell me?"

"Zandros doesn't take residence here. He prefers the ether realms. The only reason he comes to the earthly plane is to take pleasure in human delights."

I gulped.

"He has no human form?"

Nick shrugged. "Not that I have ever seen outside of my house anyway."

"I've seen him," I interrupted. "He was in the field that one day. He was at my church. He even shook hands with the preacher and was here in your house, too."

Nick seemed surprised. "Well he must've had a pretty big point to make then."

"He wanted to make sure you knew you weren't safe anywhere," Alex added.

"Why did you act so surprised when you saw my mother today?" I suddenly asked. If he already knew about my world, he was a good actor.

Alex shot me a stunned look.

Nick shrugged. "I was honestly shocked that she was alive. It's not often that you find a demon trapped like that."

"Your mother is alive?" Alex asked me.

I nodded, fearing the memory of the woman in the crypt. "She's in a mausoleum in Springfield."

"Whose binding keeps her here?" Alex turned his attention back to Nick.

"I assume my uncle's."

I nodded in agreement. "She said she was just waiting until he came for her again; that the three of us would be some kind of unholy trinity that would take over the Dark Lord, whatever that means." My mind shifted to Nick's memories. The trinity Zandros spoke of in Nick's memory didn't involve Melantha.

"Look, I love all of this reminiscing, but can you get the sword or not?" Nick was impatient. "The sooner we get him, the sooner this will all be nothing more than a bad memory."

Alex nodded. "I have one, but you know as well as I do that it will do nothing against a demon in the ether realms. He will have to take an earthly form."

Nick sat back, frustration filling his face. "There has to be a way to force him into doing that."

"There is," I suggested cautiously. Four eyes trained on me. "What if he knows I've decided to stop fighting him off?"

"No way!" Alex and Nick both objected at the same time.

"Don't start something you aren't willing to finish," Nick warned. "If we can't stop him for some reason, you'll wish you were dead."

Alex agreed. "We will find another way."

Nick gave Alex a very determined look. Leaning forward with his elbows on his knees, he twisted his fingers together, lost in thought. "What if he were to fight a true Veduny Warrior? He can't do that in the ether realms. He'd have to take an earthly form to engage in battle here."

Alex nodded. "True, but we've been trying for centuries to get to Zandros."

"You never had the right bait before." Nick's solemn eyes turned to me. "Nothing tempts a demon more than the virgin sacrifice."

"We already agreed that she cannot offer herself to him."

"But," I knew exactly where Nick was going with this. "He won't hesitate to intervene if he thinks I'm offering myself to someone else."

Nick's bright grin lit up the whole room. "Well aren't you just a little vixen after all?"

I blushed but Alex seethed at the thought. "So you want to make your dear uncle think you have been with her?"

Nick shook his head and stared Alex down for a minute. "A Veduny Warrior taking a Thann bride would make his blood boil. He would come, I guarantee that."

Alex shook his head. "I will not..."

I knew all of the reasons Alex would refuse. "You don't have to actually do anything. We just have to make him think we are." The blush that crept over my face warmed my whole body.

"If you think you can stop yourself in time to focus. It's not easy, she's pretty hot."

Alex rolled his neck, obviously uncomfortable at the thought. "I have no problem with my self-control." His words dripped disgust toward Nick.

"Good, because I do," Nick admitted without issue. "Now here's the real problem. Cadi has to be the one to take his soul."

"What?" I exclaimed.

"No!" Alex argued. "She has demon blood. Just touching the sword would cause her too much harm."

"She's promised herself to him. If she isn't the one to kill him, the promise transfers to another of Zandros' choice."

"You?" I asked, fearing his answer.

"I haven't read his will," Nick replied sarcastically. "It doesn't matter who it would be transferred to. The point is your soul still wouldn't belong to you and that's wrong. You're going to have to do it."

I nodded, looking for some sort of inner strength. "I'll do it."

"Cadi," Alex reached over and grabbed my hand. "It could kill you."

Released

"I'm dead either way. At least this way I have a chance."

"I can fix her when it's over," Nick said quietly.

"How?" Alex asked, exasperated.

"I just know a way to do it. No problem."

Something about the way he said it told me that it would be much more than no problem. It would be a big problem.

"You can take her wounds? And you're willing to?" Alex asked.

Nick nodded slowly, looking down at his hands. "Zandros has to be stopped. This is the only way. You two have to make him think he has something to interrupt. Then we attack him. Once he's down, Cadi needs to take his soul. After that, we can all live happily ever after."

"The Veduny will know about you. They will hunt you as Vadim." Alex warned.

Nick shrugged. "It's just a name. I've been called plenty of things in my life. What's another title?" He stood up and wandered over to the books. Scanning the titles, he brought a large tome down and carefully opened it. "I bet you can find a lot of titles for us in these books, can't you?"

He turned and looked at Alex who sat there in stunned silence. I wondered if Nick even realized what it meant to be a traitor of his own kind.

"Alex, can I talk to Nick? Alone?" I asked quietly.

Alex nodded. He got up and walked up the stairs.

I waited until I heard his bedroom door close before going over to Nick. He absently flipped through pages but stopped on one when he found the word he was looking for. I read over his shoulder but didn't understand the language. He took a deep breath as his finger traced over the word Aiyana.

"Who is that?" I recognized the name from Aniketos' threat.

"My grandmother," Nick smiled. "It's the Book of Lost Souls." He closed it gently and placed it back on the shelf. When he turned to face me, the sadness in his eyes was impossible to ignore. "I'm sorry I lied to you. I thought you would run away from me if you knew the truth."

"I probably would have." My eyes filled with tears. "You aren't like him, you know. Your mother was right. It's all up to you and the choices you make."

Nick nodded, taking my face in his hands. He wiped the tears away with his thumbs. "Never cry for me, Cadi. I'm not good like you."

My heart dropped as I pressed my face into his warm hands. "I want to help you avenge your mother."

"I don't think you have a wicked bone in your body." He smiled warmly, placing a soft kiss on my cheek.

"Neither do you," I whispered. "Alex has secured my safety already, but the Veduny will hunt you for doing this."

He pulled me into his chest, wrapping his arms around me tightly. "Tell me you forgive me for deceiving you and it will all be worth it."

I hugged him back. "I forgive you, but you don't have to do this. You can leave now and never think about it again."

"Not a chance," he laughed, pulling away from me. "No way am I going to let your little boyfriend take all the credit."

I shook my head, laughing softly. What is it with boys and their competitive nature? Jealousy and pride were obviously not just a human trait.

Alex came back down the stairs and held out a ring toward Nick. It was iron, with the same stone as the ring he'd given to me. "Zandros will assume you are shielded from him due to your close proximity to Cadi. If you wear this, he won't be able to read your thoughts and know that you are planning to betray him."

Nick took the ring and slid it onto his index finger. "What about you?" he asked Alex.

"He cannot read the mind of the Veduny. So long as I never speak of it aloud outside of this house, he won't be the wiser."

Nick nodded and sat down at the dining room table, pushing Alex's books out of the way. "So tell me, what's to say my name won't be the first on your list once Zandros is gone? Your people love to exterminate entire families."

Alex sat across from him and pulled his notebook in front of him. "No promises," he muttered as he opened the book and took out an ink pen. "So how do we convince Zandros to come?"

"Lots of nudity would do the trick." Nick joked but laughed even harder when he saw Alex blush so deeply. "Set it up to look like some romantic interlude and he'll be there, I guarantee it. Just don't screw it up."

Alex stared him down. "There's an open field at the south end of the park. He found her there once, but something scared him off and he ran away."

"How big is the clearing?"

"Two hundred yards. Tree cover surrounds it completely so there would be no random human passing through."

"Good, let's go look at it then so we can get a feel for it." He stood up, pulling his car keys from his pocket.

Alex shook his head. "No driving. It's completely cut off so we'll have to walk." He stopped me when he noticed I was walking toward the door with them. "You should stay here."

"As if," I objected. "This is all because of me. No way are you cutting me out of it."

Nick agreed. "We can get a feel for the place and maybe find a portal for him to come through."

"What does that mean?" I asked as we all walked out of the house.

"Demons can only enter or exit the earthly plane through specific areas. If we can't find a portal there, we'll have to find a different place." Alex explained.

"How will we know it's there?"

Nick answered as we entered the thick tree line that I had run through the other day. "You'll know. You will feel a pull, like it's beckoning you to cross over."

Dread filled me to the core. "Can I resist it?"

Nick jumped over a fallen branch with ease. "You can resist anything, if you really want to."

12

Alex led us through the forest; tracing the path he took to find me the day I had run away from him until finally, the dark, starlit sky was all we could see above us. Nick separated from us and slowly walked around the edges while Alex and I covered the clearing. Careful steps led us through the high grass. More than once I stepped into a shallow hole in the ground and cursed my twisted ankle before making a mental note of where not to step in the future.

"Here!" Nick called out from across the clearing. Alex jogged over to him, leaving me to limp toward them. By the time I covered the short distance, the pain in my ankle had disappeared.

"Are you sure?" Alex asked doubtfully. "I feel nothing."

Nick grinned. "This is Thann magic, I can feel it."

"I don't feel anything either," I added.

"I'd step through to prove it to you but there's a good chance I won't make it back out alive. Or you could just trust me."

It was clear that Alex didn't trust him, but I had no reason to question Nick. I had already been inside his mind and knew he wasn't nearly as malevolent as he thought he was. "I trust you," I said.

"Okay, so he will appear through there," Alex walked away from us toward the middle of the clearing. "We should be here. That will give me plenty of room to maneuver."

"He'll sense the sword. You'll have to find a way to mask it." Nick pointed out. He sat down on the grass and pulled a crumpled pack of cigarettes out of his pocket. Alex wrinkled his nose when Nick lit one and took a deep drag. "How about that fancy ring she's got on? It's just like the one you gave me, right?"

Alex shook his head. "I don't have any more of the stone."

"Don't I have to take it off in order for him to find us?" I stood next to Nick.

"Remember he isn't the only one who will be able to find you then," Alex forewarned.

Nick rolled his eyes. "I doubt we're gonna see some apocalyptic gathering of angels and demons. She can put it back on the minute he's dead."

I nodded, but Alex looked dubious. "Once he comes, then what?"

"Let's role play it," Nick suggested. "Just don't be too graphic." He winked at Alex as he stood up, crushing the cigarette butt under his boot. Leaving us, he went toward the area where he'd found the portal.

Alex stood closely next to me. "We will be here. I can place the sword in the tall grass." He spoke loud enough that Nick could hear him. "Where will you be?"

"Over here," Nick shouted from the other side of the clearing. "I can see the ground where you are standing. You'll have to hide it under something." He jogged back over to us. "You'd have to have a blanket anyway," he pointed out.

"Why?" I asked.

Nick cocked his head to the side toward me. "You really gonna give up your virtue in the grass? A real gentleman would have a nice blanket at least."

Alex reddened again. "Don't be so crass. The sword can be hidden under a blanket. After he comes in, Cadi, you run over there." He pointed to the area that Nick said he'd be waiting in. "I will take care of Zandros, weaken him. Nick, you will know when to bring Cadi back out?"

Nick nodded. "Of course." He turned to me again. "Alex and I will hold him down while you take his soul."

"How do I do that?" I didn't want to know, even though I had to.

"You have to pierce his heart, not that demons really have one." Alex was so cold the way he said the words.

Nick must've recognized the injured look on my face. "Really dude? Watch what you say," he reprimanded. "Now that we know the where, we need to start practicing on the how. How long do you think it will take to teach her how to use the sword?"

"It took me three decades." Alex replied stoically.

My heart sank yet again. I had twenty-three days, not thirty years.

Nick wrapped his arm around my shoulder and squeezed. "I can teach you in a day," he grinned.

"You've wielded a sword?" Alex was surprised.

"I've had my moments," Nick replied mysteriously. He tugged gently and pulled me back toward the tree line. "Let's get on that. I have a feeling we're going to need as much practice as possible."

"We have three weeks," I pointed out. I was tired and it looked like both of them were too. It had to be at least two in the morning by the time we'd left Alex's house in the first place.

"Twenty two days," Nick corrected, helping me over a bramble of thorny branches. "I'm sure he's expecting you to try something, especially since he knows about your little friendship with Alex. Knowing my uncle as I do, he'll think it's coming closer to your deadline."

"How can you be so sure?" Alex asked as he followed closely behind.

"He's arrogant, but not as arrogant as your people. He'll think you'll take as much time as possible to plot the perfect showdown." Nick was blunt with his answer.

"How about tomorrow then?" I suggested. We could all go home, get some rest, and then just be done with it.

"I need at least two full sun cycles to bless the sword properly. You should go to school and act like you normally would if nothing was going on."

Nick agreed. "Yes, I'd hate to miss out on the drama that is high school. Let's plan on Sunday evening at sunset." He stopped and looked back at Alex. "That gives you four days."

Alex nodded. "That will give you the chance to teach her how to use it."

Nick turned his attention back to me. "And that gives you a chance to graduate from high school and give that speech."

I agreed and silently walked back to the house. Mom and Dad would like to see that. As hard as I tried not to, I couldn't help but wonder what their lives would be like if I had never come into it. What would they do if something went wrong and I never came back? In the deepest part of my heart, I knew they would mourn my loss as much as they would if it were Sarah or Spencer.

Once we reached Alex's house again, Nick walked toward the Jeep instead of the porch. "My uncle will expect that we are still at my house. There's nothing to say he won't come back tonight."

"He was there?" Alex asked me and I nodded. "Then you should go back so he doesn't suspect anything. Just be careful."

I reluctantly got into the Jeep, watching Alex as we backed away down the driveway. A thick silence filled the car the entire ride home. Without words, we walked back into the rundown house and up the stairs.

When we reached the top of the stairs, he led me straight into a bedroom instead of turning to go to the library. It was sparsely furnished with a large four-poster bed, a small chest of drawers and an old rocking chair in front of the window.

Nick pointed at the stack of folded sheets that sat on the end of the bed. "This was my grandmother's room," he said with a faint nostalgic smile. "I can help you make the bed if you'd like."

I turned and faced him. His eyes seemed so deep I could swim in them. There was a small twig caught in his hair. I reached up and gently pulled it out. When I started to draw my hand away, he took it in his and pulled it against his chest.

"This will work, Cadi. I swear on my life it will."

"Why are you doing this? It's not just revenge for you, is it?" My heart jumped into my throat.

"There is a Native American legend that says a woman's highest calling is to lead a man to his soul and a man's highest calling is to protect woman so she is free to walk the earth unharmed." He kissed me on the top of the head, just as he'd done so many times in the past two weeks, before pulling away. "You remind me of the goodness my mother always promised was out there for me to find."

I stared at the door as he closed it behind him and sat down on the bed, too exhausted to think straight. How could my life have gotten so complicated in such a short time? Then again, it had been eight long years of chaos and obstacles, so why was I surprised?

At least it was almost over.

Morning came with a bright ray of sun warming my body. When I woke up, the blanket was spread across me and my shoes were on the floor next to the bed. Sitting up slowly, it took me a minute to remember where I was. I pulled on the tennis shoes and made my way to the bathroom. After brushing the tangles out of my hair, I squirted some toothpaste on my finger and ran it across my teeth. Satisfied that I was as ready for school as possible, I went to the library to see if Nick was awake yet.

He was sound asleep on the sofa, his head hanging off the edge and his leg draped over the back of it. Still dressed in the same clothes he'd worn last night, he hadn't even bothered to take his boots off. I quietly walked over to him and bent over to wake him up.

Before I had a chance to whisper his name, his hands grabbed my wrist and opened his eyes. His grip was strong, hurting my wrists. I froze where I was, bent over and prone. "I'm sorry," I said. "I didn't mean to scare you."

Released

"You don't scare me," he grinned, loosening his hold on me but not letting go completely. Sitting up, he leaned toward my face and gently kissed my lips. "Good morning."

I blushed and backed away from him. It wasn't like we hadn't kissed before, but it felt different this time, like things had moved in reverse at a fast speed. "We're going to be tardy if we don't hurry up."

Nick let go of me and stretched his arms. "You are probably the most goody two shoes demon in the world," he joked. "Let's not tarnish your perfect record."

I put my hands on my hips. "I'm not perfect, you know. I've broken rules."

"Like what?" Nick laughed as he stood up and grabbed his leather jacket. "I bet you even asked for permission to ditch on Senior Skip Day yesterday."

I had no defense. I did ask for permission. "I doubt my parents would be pleased to know I spent the night at a boy's house last night." I did my best to sound defiant.

"Come on, you deviant." He wrapped an arm around my shoulders and led me out of the room. "We'd better get to school before you become a real felon."

I didn't like him making fun of me even if it was true, so I spent most of the drive to school fuming out the window. When he pulled into the parking spot, students were still milling about waiting for the final moment before they had to go inside. He wrapped his arm around my waist as we walked toward the door. A cheesy grin spread over his face.

Released

I stopped mid-step, my entire body stiffening. Zandros was back, standing across the street just as he'd been the other day. Nick looked up, followed my gaze and winked at his uncle. With his free hand, he tilted my face toward his and roughly pressed his lips against mine, biting my bottom lip seductively.

I heard several wolf whistles call out from all around us. Nick pulled me toward the building, away from Zandros' prying eyes. "You enjoyed that a little too much," I whispered.

"I'd never deny that," he said with a knowing chuckle.

We walked through the building toward our lockers. In the hallway, students seemed to separate to let us pass as if we were the latest power couple. "This is weird," I said once we reached my locker.

"What?" Nick asked, absently twirling a strand of my hair around his fingertips.

"Everyone is looking at us." I couldn't help but notice that we were the focus of everyone's attention.

"I guarantee you that every girl is looking at you because they are jealous of your beauty. Every guy is looking at me because they are jealous that I'm with you." He gave me a light goodbye kiss before walking to his own locker.

The rest of the morning was filled with more awkward glances and several outright stares. No longer were people talking about the rumors that had spread about my party, or my brother's fight. Instead, they were talking about Nick Vikenti's triumph over the virginal captain of the dance team.

"Just because I didn't feel like dating any of them doesn't make me some frigid bitch," I complained at lunch when Nick came into the cafeteria and sat down next to me.

"Uh, trust me; I've got personal experience that you're no ice queen, even if we did get interrupted too early." He laughed until he noticed that I really was disturbed by the latest drama shift around me. "You really have to learn to let this crap go. They have nothing better to do with their lives than talk about other people."

"What are your friends saying?" I took small bites of my food. I couldn't even recall the last time I'd eaten and was famished. It took every ounce of self-control I had not to tear into the sub-par cafeteria food like an animal.

"My friends? You're my only friend, Cadi. I told you that already."

Sarah appeared out of nowhere and sat down across from us. She slid her cell phone across the table toward me.

I stopped it before it could fall onto the floor. A text message was open.

Your sister's got nudes posted on Facebook. WTH?

I looked up at my irate sister. "That's a lie," I said.

Nick looked over and rested his chin on my shoulder, reading the message. "She's right. It's only one picture, so nudes shouldn't be plural. And she's not naked anyway."

"I swear to God, I'm going to check when I get home and if this is even close to true, Mom and Dad will die of shame!" Sarah was so angry, she was practically spitting.

Nick pulled out his iPhone and opened the application. Clicking on his profile page, he set the phone in front of Sarah so that she could see the picture. "See? Not naked. Feel better?"

"Nick," I admonished. "You're really not helping."

Sarah grabbed the phone and scrolled down. She flipped it toward me dramatically and pointed at the status update he'd made last night. "Explain this then," she ordered.

Nick grabbed the iPhone from Sarah's hand and glared at her. "Cadi did nothing wrong. It's a private joke between us and I suggest you settle down. Your sister's purity is still intact."

"I bet no thanks to you," she spat.

I was shocked, turning to face my sister. "Sarah stop it. You really think that little of me?"

"Well when it's right there shoved in my face, what am I supposed to think?"

I stood up, anger boiling my blood. "You should think that I'm better than that." I left Nick glaring at my sister and ran out of the cafeteria.

Finding solace in an empty bathroom, I stood in front of the mirror and examined myself. Was I really so different now that my own sister, the best friend I'd ever had, would think so little of me? The door opened and Sarah came in. She looked as guilty as I felt.

"I'm sorry," my sister said. "I should've trusted you wouldn't do that."

"What if I had?" I watched Sarah through the mirror. "Would that make me a horrible person?"

Sarah thought about it for a minute. "If you love him that would be one thing. But you've only known him for two weeks, and I don't think anyone falls in love that quick."

I thought about that. I felt like there was no one in the world that would ever understand me. Love would never be a thing I'd have in my life. "Have you ever...?"

I let the question dangle in the air and watched her blush. "Yeah," Sarah admitted.

I turned around and leaned on the sink. "What was it like?"

"A mistake." Sarah replied immediately. "I thought it was right, but afterward, I just felt bad. And he never asked me out again, so I guess the joke was on me, right? What about you? How far have you gone?"

I was mortified at the thought of this conversation happening in a school bathroom. "Just kissing," I said.

"Yeah," Sarah laughed. "I heard all about that this morning. So there was just kissing, no serious make-out or anything?"

"Well," I considered. "There may have been a little making out."

Sarah's face lit up. All traces of anger were gone. It was gossip time. "I want all the dirt!"

I laughed uneasily. "You're serious?"

"Of course I am! What was he like? Like did he make you forget about the whole world around you?"

A nervous giggle came out when I thought about it. I clearly recalled the make-out session on the couch, but it was more like a dream than reality. "I don't really want to talk about this."

Sarah laughed and clapped her hands. Obviously, the scandal that enraged her not ten minutes ago had been replaced by teenaged excitement. "I can tell he's totally crazy about you. How do you feel about him?"

I couldn't answer that. I had too many feelings, so I just shrugged my shoulders. The bell rang at the perfect moment. "We're going to be late for class," I warned, heading toward the door without answering my sister's question.

Several students commented about Nick's online post throughout the day, but I managed to ignore them. After the final bell rang, I made my way to my locker. While I packed up my things, one of Spencer's friends approached me.

"Busy tonight?" he asked.

I couldn't even think of his name. He'd never expressed an ounce of interest in me before.

I could see Nick standing behind him, obviously amused by the exchange.

"Actually, yeah I'm busy." I straightened myself and closed the locker. My admirer leaned against the metal, pushing himself a little too close for comfort.

"Awe come on. I'm sure you can spare an hour or two," he insisted.

I tried to keep our exchange polite, but blunt. "Sorry, but I'm really not interested. I told you, I have things to do."

"I bet I could offer you better plans." The nameless boy had hot, foul breath that made me grimace. I didn't even realize what was happening when his meaty hand grabbed my butt.

Released

In an instant, the boy was shoved against the locker. Nick's hand was wrapped around his throat, squeezing just enough that the boy's face was turning purple. I was shocked to see the deep brown of Nick's eyes flash a crimson red.

"She. Said. No."

I pulled Nick's arm down, making him release the terrified kid. "Let's go home." He needed to calm down. His breathing was labored, as though he was trying to control his anger before he killed someone. Grabbing his hand, I led him away. He kept his eyes locked on the boy who remained pressed up against the locker, too frightened to move.

I fished his keys out of his pocket when we reached the Jeep. He was clearly too agitated to drive, so I climbed in behind the wheel. After shooting me a questioning look, Nick got in and I drove out of the parking lot. "Where to?" I asked.

"What do you normally do after school?"

"I go home and do my homework." How lame did that sound? Here I was, a demon-in-the-making that spent my spare time following rules. It sounded ridiculous the minute I said it.

"Then we go to your house. You don't really have homework, do you?"

There was only one day of school left, and that would be spent practicing their graduation ceremony. There were no assignments to do. "We have a little gym there. Can you teach me how to fight?"

"Deal," he said, settling back in the seat and closing his eyes against the sunlight.

"You okay?" I asked.

He nodded but said nothing. Letting it drop, I drove the country roads that led to my house. When I pulled in, I noticed that no one else was home yet. Climbing out of the Jeep, I waited for Nick to join me and went in the house.

He followed me up the stairs to my room but I stopped him in the doorway. "I have to change."

He grabbed my waist and pulled me into his body. "I could help you with that," he grinned, leaning down to kiss the side of my neck.

"Out," I muttered, pushing him away from me.

His smile never faded as he leaned up against the wall right outside of my door. Holding his hands up in surrender, he laughed when I shut the door. Quickly changing into yoga pants and a tank top, I opened the door while putting my hair in a ponytail.

He was wandering down the hallway, looking at the numerous framed photos that my mom had covered the wall with.

"You all look pretty happy." He pointed at the picture Mom had snapped of the family playing in the snow last winter.

I smiled. "We were. We are," I corrected.

"And you always will be," Nick added, heading for the stairs. "Where's this gymnasium of yours?"

I led him to the double stall garage that Dad had converted into a home gym. It had a treadmill, weight bench and a hanging bag. Other than that, there was nothing to say it was a gym rather than garage. "What do we do first?"

"Have you ever been in a fight that didn't involve rubber bands, nerf guns, or snowballs?"

I shook my head and bit my lower lip. "Dad taught me some self-defense, but that's about it."

He considered it for a minute. "Okay, show me what you got."

"Bring it on," I laughed.

Nick tried to grab me, but I spun away at the last moment, grabbing his arm and twisting it. He stopped and turned his wrist, grabbing my arm in one fluid movement. Now my arm was twisted painfully behind my back. Before it hurt me too much, he released his hold.

"First point goes to me."

I kicked my leg behind me, connecting with his knee. He cursed as he took an involuntary step backward.

"Is that a point for me?" I asked triumphantly with my hands on my hips.

He moved up behind me and wrapped his arm around my chest. Using his free hand to grab my upper arm, his fingers bite into my flesh. "Do it again," he dared.

I kicked again, connecting with his leg, but he didn't budge. "You'll have to do better than that," he sneered.

I tried bending over to flip him over, just like I'd done a million times to my sister. Sarah always went flying but Nick stayed with me. All I managed to do was double over to the ground with him on top of me. He released his hold in just enough time to reach out and slow our fall.

"If I was really trying to attack you, you would be dead right now," he whispered into my ear.

I took advantage of the fall's distraction and brought my elbow up to sharply crack against his cheekbone. He rolled off of me, hopping up to his feet with the reflexes of a cat.

I jumped up and braced myself for whatever he was going to try next.

"You obviously aren't going to win a bar brawl. Not unless you employ some different tricks." Nick rubbed the side of his face, the red mark disappearing quickly. He sat down and patted the floor next to him.

I joined him on the cold concrete and faced him. "I'm not planning on winning hand to hand combat. I just have to learn what to do with that sword."

Nick nodded in agreement. "Do you know where his heart is?"

My hand went instinctively to the area right below my left collarbone, right where I put my hand whenever I said the Pledge of Allegiance.

Nick chuckled. "No wonder you can't pass Biology." Leaning forward, he took my hand and placed it on his collarbone pushing my fingers against his chest. "Count the ribs. Go down six then move over toward the middle." He sat perfectly still while my fingers traced over the ridges of his ribs and guided my hand toward the center of his chest.

"The blade has to enter here and push up."

I nodded, memorizing the position of my fingertips. "What if I don't get the right spot?"

"Then you'll hit a rib and it won't hit his heart, which will do nothing more than piss him off." He dropped my hand. "We'll practice."

"On what?" I was horrified by the thought of stabbing someone.

Nick laughed. "There's a slaughterhouse at the edge of town. We'll get a pig carcass. You can't honestly expect to grab a sword that wants to kill you and be able to take down Zandros in your first attempt, do you?"

"It's a nice thought," I grinned. A car pulled up outside, drawing my attention to the door. "My mom's home," I said to him.

Nick rolled his eyes. "I'll get out of here then." He got up and held his hands out to help me stand up.

I shook my head. "Stay and meet my parents."

He sucked in a deep breath. "I don't know if you've noticed, but I'm not the kind of guy that you bring home for dinner."

"I think you might be wrong about that."

13

Mom was just putting away some groceries when we walked into the kitchen. I was still dragging a reluctant Nick behind me.

"Hi Mom." She turned and faced me, surprised to see the boy attached to my hand. "This is my friend Nick."

Her warm smile welcomed him. She held out her hand in greeting. "Nice to meet you Nick. Are you staying for dinner?"

"Uh..." His usual cocky arrogance was gone the instant he shook the woman's hand.

I answered for him. "Yes, if that's okay."

"Of course. I always cook too much anyway. I'm afraid it's nothing special tonight, just a Sheppards' pie." She began pulling ingredients out of the fridge.

"Need help?" I offered.

She smiled again. "You two go be kids. I'll handle this."

"We'll be in my room watching a movie," I pulled Nick behind me without waiting for her approval.

Once the door closed, Nick finally started breathing normally. I flopped on the bed and laughed at him. "I swear, you can look a demon in the eye but talking to a mom makes you melt?"

"Mothers are very intimidating," he admitted sitting on the bed next to me. "Fathers are worse."

"My dad's not that bad."

"I've met him, remember? All he had to say to me was something about wishing I was Alex." He grabbed the remote off the table and turned on the TV. "What do you want to watch?"

I climbed up onto the bed to sit next to him, leaning against the headboard. "I don't have cable, so you can pick a movie." I pointed at the slim selection of DVDs on the shelf.

"Do you have internet?"

I pulled my laptop onto the bed. He took it from me and clicked on a few websites before keying in a code that opened up an on demand movie site. Clicking through a few comedy titles, we settled in and started to watch a film that was filled with slapstick. Both of us were laughing at the insanity of it all. For a while, I was able to forget all about the threats that shadowed my life. I was a normal teenage girl, enjoying a movie with a friend.

The movie ended with both of us in tears from laughing so hard. I didn't hear the heavy footsteps on the stairs and jumped when Dad opened the door.

He stood there for a second, silently assessing the situation in front of him. His expression made it no secret that he wasn't happy that there was a boy in his daughter's bedroom. "Dinner's almost ready," he said finally.

"Okay," I whimpered, trying to collect my breath. "We were just watching a movie."

"Mmhmmm." He gave Nick a rather stern look then turned and walked out of the room, pulling the door shut behind him. As if he'd had a better thought, he pushed it open and left it that way before going back downstairs.

I stifled my laughter when I saw the distraught look on Nick's face.

Standing up, I grabbed his hands and pulled him to his feet. "It's just dinner. He's not going to kill you."

"Maybe not, but he wants to," Nick countered. "I could just go home and you could come over to my place when you're done."

I shook my head. "That would hurt Mom's feelings. You have to stay."

I really did want him to stay. He made me feel normal, regardless of the fact that neither of us could be farther from 'normal'.

He relented. "Fine, but after the table is cleared, I'm out of here."

"Chicken," I sashayed out of my room and Nick reluctantly followed.

Most of dinner was painless. Mom attempted to engage Nick in everyday conversation, asking him about his entire life's history and he deserved brownie points for answering each question quickly. Sarah explained that Nick was my tutor and Dad made a point to talk to everyone except Nick, acting like he wasn't even there. Spencer just glared through the entire meal. After the table was cleared, I made an excuse to leave.

"We made plans to hang out with Alex tonight. Is that okay, Dad?"

Dad's face brightened a bit at the mention of the boy's name. "You're friends with Alex?" he said to Nick, agreeing to let me go.

"Don't forget we have to go shopping tomorrow after school to get your graduation dress." Mom reminded me before we could leave.

I reassured her that I would be home right after school and was looking forward to it. By the time we were settled in the Jeep, Nick looked like he'd aged about ten years. "I hope you don't hold it against me when I refuse to do that ever again."

"You really are a chicken." I laughed and reached over to turn the music up while he drove down the dusty lane. I pulled out my cell phone and dialed Crevan's number.

"Allllloooooo?" The girl answered.

"Hey, we're headed over if that's okay?"

Crevan cleared her throat. "Um, we're not home. Probably won't be back until Saturday afternoon."

I sat forward and turned the music down. "Oh? Where are you?"

Nick looked over at me, apparently noticing the change in my tone.

"Well, my brother is occupied with a project for your graduation and I'm..." She hesitated. "I'm kind of at a party."

"It's going to last for two days?" I couldn't believe what I was hearing. Crevan was up to no good, I just knew it. "What is really going on?"

"Uh, nothing," the girl stammered into the phone. "I gotta go but I'll let you know when he gets back, okay? Okay, bye now." She didn't wait for a response before hanging up on me.

"What's wrong?" Nick asked as we neared Alex's driveway.

"Looks like Alex and Crevan are occupied for the next two days."

Nick sped back up and continued down the road. "Then where to ma'am?"

"Let's go to your house and practice some more." I knew I wouldn't ever be able to beat Zandros in hand to hand combat, but it wouldn't hurt to be a little better prepared so I didn't get my butt handed to me. After that kid grabbed me at school today, I wanted to know how to defend myself, even if it wasn't from a demon.

Nick nodded and went to his house, stopping at the local liquor store on his way. I gave him a curious look when he put the large paper sack in the backseat.

"How old are you?" I asked.

"I turned eighteen a few months ago. Why?"

I shrugged. "Just wondering how you were able to buy booze, that's all."

He grinned wickedly. "You'll soon learn that you're able to convince people to let you have your way when you want them to."

I'd already experienced that a few times.

"How old are you really?" I expected an answer like Alex had given me.

"Eighteen," he insisted. "As in, my mother gave birth to me eighteen years ago."

I doubted it. "So if I ask you the same question in ten years, what would you say?"

"Twenty eight." He glanced at me, humored. "Apparently, you're as lousy at Math as you are Biology."

"Very funny. I just figured you were older, like Alex is."

Nick shook his head. "Nope. What you see is what you get."

Released

For some reason, I was glad to know that he wasn't old enough to forget his own age. He carried in the bag and deposited it on the kitchen counter. I sat down on a rickety stool and watched while he poured a can of soup into a bowl. After heating it up, he took it, along with a fifth of vodka, into the living room.

From the doorway, I watched him try to wake his father up. The man was in the exact spot as when we'd left that morning. He muttered something to his son when Nick let him know dinner was ready, but I couldn't hear what he said. Nick dropped his shoulders and walked back toward me. Without a word, he grabbed my hand and led me to the back yard.

As the sun set, Nick was relentless, teaching me more self-defense tactics in those few hours than Dad had in the previous four years. By the time he was done, I was exhausted, bruised and able to escape most of the holds he put on me. I'd managed to get in several shots on him, all of which he claimed he allowed me to get. We were both hot and sweaty by the time we made it back inside.

Settling down in the library, I looked around more carefully. There was really nothing in here that seemed personal; nothing that indicated it was his personal space. "Is this really your bedroom?" she asked.

"Never said it was, why?" He pulled off his sweaty shirt and threw it at me.

I caught it and tossed it aside onto the couch. "Yeah you did. You said I was getting your bed dirty last night. And this is where you slept."

Released

He walked out of the room, beckoning me to follow. When he paused at a closed door at the end of the hallway, he stopped and turned to me. "I haven't been in here for years. But if you must know, this is my bedroom." He swung the door open and my breath caught in my throat. Every surface was covered in blackened dust.

I recognized the room from one of his memories. The gauze curtains hung limply on the windows, the bottom of the fabric still scorched from the fire. The bed was made, covered with a juvenile decoration. A baseball mitt sat holding a dirty old baseball on the dresser. In the corner was a pile of clothes small enough to fit a little boy. The smell of soot and sadness was overwhelming.

"You never came back in here?" I didn't want to turn around and look at him, but couldn't help it. His shoulders were drooped even more than when he'd walked away from his father's side.

He shook his head and turned to walk back out of the room. I stood frozen in place, wondering what it could possibly be like to live with this kind of pain. Closing the door behind me, I went back to the library.

Nick was on the sofa, his head in his hands. I was sure that if he had any tears left to spill, they would be pouring out. I sat next to him and wrapped my arms around him. "I'm sorry," I whispered into his head when he lay against me. There were no words, so I didn't bother trying. Instead, I just held onto him.

By the time he moved again, the clock on the wall read well past two in the morning. There was no way I could go home this late and not wake up my parents. "Let's get some sleep," I said softly, my hands rubbing his back gently.

He slowly moved off of me and I stood up. Holding my hand out to him, I led him into the room I'd used last night. I waited until he laid back on the bed before pulling his boots off his feet. After kicking off my own shoes, I climbed up next to him. Laying my head against his shoulder, I wrapped my body around his and pulled the blanket up over us.

He turned onto his side so that we were face to face and gently kissed me. "You keep changing my mind about everything."

Closing my eyes, I felt calmness come over me. For hours, we just laid there, content on being surrounded by the silence. By the time either of us fell asleep, the sun was nearly rising. Drifting off to sleep, I found peace in his arms.

When I woke up, the hot summer sun was on my skin and I was alone. I could hear Nick in the other room and got up, listening for him in the hallway. He wasn't in the library when I looked in. No matter what room I checked I couldn't find him, but I could still hear his footsteps. It sounded like he retreated farther away as soon as I got close to him. When I called out his name, my only reply was a hollow echo of my own voice.

Panicking, I ran out of the house into the backyard. In the orchard, I could see Nick's shadowed form disappearing into the grove of trees. I followed along, calling his name but getting no reaction. My muscles ached but I refused to stop. I had to run to get close enough to see his face.

He was standing underneath an apple tree, leaning against the rough bark. He smiled warmly, holding his hand out to me.

"Why did you run from me?" I asked.

He gathered me in his arms and nuzzled his face in my neck. "Because you've spent most of your life running from me."

There was something different about his voice. Looking up to his face, I saw that I was no longer looking into Nick's beautiful dark eyes. Zandros leered down at me hungrily.

I woke up screaming. Nick grabbed me, terror filling his own features.

I scrambled to get away from him but was tangled up in the sheets. Sweat poured from my body and I couldn't breathe. "You're not Nick," I gasped.

"What?" He grabbed at me again before sitting up and backing away slowly. "Cadi, please. What's wrong?"

"You're not Nick," I had the voice of a small child.

"Purple dinosaurs," he whispered dejectedly.

It took a few minutes to register what he'd said. Still, I couldn't slow my heart down. Pulling at my shirt, I tried to take a deep breath but failed. It felt like I was suffocating.

Slowly, Nick moved back to me. "It was just a dream, Cadi."

I wrapped my arms around him, feeling his touch, smelling his skin, knowing it really was him. Only then did I calm down at all.

Nick took my face in his hands and tilted it upward. "I'm right here, Cadi. For as long as you want me to be. Come on." He pulled me up out of bed. "We need to take a shower and get to school."

My eyes swept over his half-dressed body, hunger gnawing at my insides. School was the last thing on my mind, but I allowed him to guide me to the bathroom anyway.

Released

I groaned at the reflection in the mirror. My clothes were rumpled and sweaty from working out last night in the backyard. I looked like I hadn't bathed in a week. Glancing at the clock on my phone, I took a deep breath and dialed my sister's phone number.

"I need a huge favor," I said when Sarah answered.

"I've already done you a huge one." Sarah clicked her tongue. I could tell she was pissed.

"What?"

"Well, I told Dad you came in last night after he went to sleep. And then this morning when you were nowhere to be found, I lied and told Mom you went for a run before school."

I breathed a sigh of relief. "I love you," I said into the phone. Nick came up behind me and kissed the back of my neck. My whole body shivered in response to his touch. "Can you bring me some clean clothes?"

For some reason known only to the heavens, Sarah didn't ask for an explanation. "Where are you?"

"Nick's house."

"No, really?" Sarah's sarcasm came through loud and clear. "Do you think my GPS will know where to go if I just punch in the word Nick?"

She had a point, I thought. After giving Sarah directions, I hung up and turned around. "You need to stop that or we'll miss graduation practice."

"I can think of worse things to miss out on," he said, his voice dripping with seduction, pulling me closer. With nothing more than a quick kiss on the tip of my nose, he released me. "I have to go make breakfast anyway. Hungry?"

I was famished. Food was beginning to be on the top of my list of cravings. I didn't even care what it was. I just wanted to eat. A lot. I nodded and watched him walk out of the bathroom.

I consumed an entire box of cereal before I met Sarah at the door.

"Well at least you did something with your bedhead," Sarah scolded. "Are you okay?"

I smiled. "Yeah, of course. Thanks for bringing me clothes."

"Well hurry up. You can't be late and I have a final first hour."

I waved her off and went inside to change.

"Are you okay?" Nick asked from across the foyer.

"Yeah, it was just a bad dream." I flashed him a smile and headed for the stairs.

Nick grabbed my arm and stopped me. "Really?"

My gut came up into my throat. The terror and confusion I'd felt when Zandros walked into the library returned, but it was vanquished the moment I looked into Nick's eyes. "Should I not be?"

"I'm just checking," he said.

My throat was less tight and the smile returned. "Good. I promise I'm fine." I pulled away from his grasp and skipped up the stairs.

Looking at myself in the mirror again, I saw there was another subtle difference in my reflection. My skin was glowing, my eyes a little brighter. I smoothed the sundress over my belly. Everything was changing so quickly but I wasn't afraid anymore. All I could do was smile.

This is what hope looks like.

It was impossible to wipe the silly grin off of my face the entire morning at school.

By the time the principal finally decided we all knew what we were supposed to do, we'd run through the graduation ceremony five times. Nick sat in the row behind me and every time I snuck a glance back to him, he was watching me. Surely the entire world must know that I was different from everyone else, but I didn't care what people were saying anymore. They didn't live my life so their opinions didn't matter.

Sarah was completely non-judgmental even though I had expected her to be. The one time I saw her in the hallway, my sister just smiled.

The senior class was dismissed at lunchtime and Nick was waiting at my locker when I got there. He greeted me with a chaste kiss on the cheek.

"Well that was awfully polite," I joked.

"If I kissed you the way I wanted to, we'd both be arrested. Can I drive you home?"

"I hope so. It's a long walk." I let him take the bag that was stuffed full of my locker contents and walked out of the building for the last time as a student. The whole world was a little bit different today. I was done with high school and technically a grown up. It wasn't the end of anything though. Instead, it was a whole new beginning.

Released

Pulling up outside of my house, Nick parked right next to Mom's minivan. "Will you call me when you're done so I can come pick you up?"

I nodded and quickly kissed him goodbye before getting out.

It took longer than I'd hoped to decide on a dress. Between my mom's more formal opinions and my simpler tastes, we had to go to seven different stores to find the right outfit. When we were both satisfied, I was dressed in a simple white sleeveless chiffon summer beach strap long maxi dress. I paired it with simple white sandals and a pearl necklace.

When we finally arrived home, everyone was there waiting for dinner. We had thought ahead and grabbed takeout Chinese for supper. Strangely, I had no appetite while I sat at the table and watched everyone devour the sticky, spicy food. Finally, Sarah stood up to excuse herself.

"You ready Cadi?" she asked out of the blue.

I looked up at her, surprised.

Dad asked what our plans were for the night. "We're going to Amanda's for a slumber party," Sarah explained. "And we're going to miss out on all of the fun if we don't hurry up."

"Did you forget you're grounded young lady?" Leave it to Mom to remember her child's punishment.

Sarah's face fell so I picked up the rouse. "Come on, Mom. It's an end of the year bash. No boys will be there and I promise I won't let her get into any trouble." I batted my eyelashes and pouted.

"Fine, as long as Cadi's going." Mom relented. "Be home no later than noon Sarah."

Sarah wasted no time heading for the stairs. "Come on, we need to pack an overnight bag." She gave me a wink. Pulling me up the stairs, we went into my room first. She threw open the closet and started rummaging through all of my clothes. Pulling out a colorful maxi-dress, she held it against herself and gazed in the mirror.

I sat on the edge of the bed. "So I guess I owe you even more now?"

"Heck no!" Sarah laughed. "This is you paying me back. There really is a party I want to go to and you're the perfect babysitter. Besides, I'm keeping this dress." She giggled and went over to my dresser to rummage some more.

I didn't mind about the dress. It was too tight for me now anyway. The thing I did mind about was lying to my parents. "What are you doing?" I watched as my sister stared sorting through my underwear drawer.

"I'm finding the perfect thing for you to wear, duh."

I blushed and grabbed the garments out of my sister's hands, shoving them all back in the drawer. "Stop it. That's just wrong."

Sarah turned and gawked at me. "Well excuse me for trying to make sure you had something sexy to wear. Not that you really need anything with that push up bra working its magic." She poked her finger into my chest.

"Out!" I pointed to the door. "Now, or I'm taking back the dress and staying home tonight."

"Empty threat. You want to go out as much as I do!" Sarah skipped to her own room while I grabbed a spare pair of jeans and a sweater. As a second thought, I grabbed another old pair and a ratty t-shirt. Who knew when the pig-stabbing thing would happen? I didn't want to ruin anything nice with bloodstains. Shoving everything into my bag, I grabbed my toothbrush from the bathroom and headed down the stairs.

Dad met me at the back door. "Cadi," he said, stopping me before I could walk out.

I turned to look at him. Surely guilt was written all over my face, but I took a deep breath and tried to swallow it. "Yeah?"

"Are you really going to Amanda's?" He leaned against the counter, waiting for me to lie to him again.

I nodded slowly, the words refusing to leave my lips.

"Just promise me you aren't doing anything you'll regret and you're being safe about it."

Every inch of exposed skin turned scarlet red instantly. "Do we really want to have this conversation?"

"Do we need to?" He stared into my eyes like he was reading my mind.

"Mom delivers babies all day. We've talked before. Besides, it's not even an issue."

Sarah rescued me by honking the horn impatiently. "Go," he said. "Just... be smart."

I gave him a weak smile before going outside. As the door closed, I felt awful for lying to the one man whom I looked up to more in the world. Without a word, I slumped down in the passenger seat and remained silent the whole way to Nick's house.

Released

Sarah dropped me off at the front door and sped away with little more than a goodbye wave. Walking up the front door, I looked for a doorbell. Finding none, I raised my fist and knocked.

After a minute, the door swung open. A tall, dark haired man with a few days' worth of beard growth on his face was standing there. He was too skinny and his clothes hung on his body. Dark circles framed his deep brown eyes and there was a yellowish tint to his complexion. He stepped back out of the way to allow me to come in.

"He's in his room." His voice cracked when he spoke in little more than a mutter. "Tell him his dinner is ready."

I watched the man shuffle back to the living room.

Taking the stairs two at a time, I found Nick sitting on the balcony, strumming an acoustic guitar.

"Your dad is awake." I joined him on the terrace and looked out at the orchard. The scene reminded me of the nightmare so I turned around and leaned against the railing. "He says your supper is ready."

Nick nodded absently. "Yeah, he's decided to sober up and be a better example." A disgusted snarl came from his gut. "It's like I haven't heard that a hundred times before."

"Well, maybe this time he means it," I said hopefully. "You never know, one of these times he might do it."

"I'm sorry if I'm not interested." Nick angrily put the guitar down and went to the railing. "Want to go for a walk?"

"Sure."

Nick jumped over the edge before I realized what he was doing. For a second I panicked until I looked down and saw him standing there waiting for me with his arms held wide.

I screeched as I fell through the air, landing firmly in his arms. He put me on my feet and grabbed my hand, walking toward the orchard.

I hesitated. I didn't want to go there.

Nick tugged at my hand. "Can't beat your fears unless you face them," he said.

I planted my feet firmly on the ground and refused to follow. "Say the words."

Nick smiled sweetly. "Don't be silly. Come with me."

"Say the right words and I'll follow you to the ends of the earth."

He let go of my hand held the sides of my face softly. "I love you," he said, leaning in for a kiss.

I backed away quickly, shoving him away. The man in front of me shifted form. I screamed at the top of my lungs and ran toward the front of the house.

"Nick!"

14

Zandros appeared in front of me, grabbing my arms roughly. "Why must you always resist?"

I twisted my body around and kicked backwards, slamming my foot into his knee. Just like when I'd done it to Nick the first time, he didn't budge. Instead, his grip got tighter, his fingernails digging into my bare arms.

I fought through the pain, pulling my arm away from his grasp as hard as I could, ripping my skin in the process. My elbow found his eye socket and I felt a sickening pop. Only then did he let go and step back. I could hear Nick's footsteps running toward us from the back of the house.

"Uncle!" Nick roared as he neared us.

Zandros backed away, slowly clapping his hands together. "You surprise me Carina." He ignored his nephew. "I like that you have some fight left in you. Tell me, did Nikita teach you that little trick?"

Nick placed his hand on the small of my back and glared at him. "Are you here for a reason or is this a social call?"

Zandros held his hands out to either side of his body, as if he were demonstrating he was unarmed and innocent. "I just happened to be in the area and thought I'd check in on my dear brother. I hear he's been a little under the weather lately."

"He's fine so I guess you can leave now."

I stood frozen in place, waiting for Zandros to strike. Instead, he sneered at Nick and walked past us into the trees.

I watched him leave and became even more determined to get this weekend over with as soon as possible. I wished that Alex would get back tonight so that we could end this game with Zandros. "Why could I hit him if he isn't real?"

"Oh he is real," Nick answered. "You can be sure of that. Unfortunately, he comes here often."

"Why can't I just wish really hard that he was dead? Then we'd never have to deal with him again."

He chuckled and pushed my hair back away from my face. "If it was that easy, I would've made sure he died the day he killed my mother."

"Did you get the pig? I want to learn right now."

He led me back around to the back of the property to a small garden house. Inside, he flipped a switch and the fluorescent lights flickered to life. A huge, disgusting, and very dead pig laid on its side right in the middle of the room on top of a potting table. Flies swarmed around the stench that nearly overwhelmed my senses. Without hesitation, Nick went over to it and grabbed a long knife from the shelf next to the table. Motioning for me to come over, he held his finger on the creature's chest.

"Come on, it won't bite you."

I didn't want to get any closer. The foul odor made me gag. Steeling my will, I approached the table and took the knife from him.

"This is only going to give you a basic feel for how hard you have to push to get the knife to go far enough in." He guided the tip of the blade to the point he held his finger against. "Keep steady and go in as fast and hard as you can."

My hand shook as I poked at the pig. It took several attempts before I could even break the skin more than a scratch.

"No, that will never do. Imagine it's him. Pretend like you're really killing Zandros."

That was all the prompting I needed. Fury filled my heart as I plunged the knife into the animal's belly. When I pulled the knife out of the wound, blood sprayed across my face, staining my dress, dripping from my hair. I shook with anger; pulling the knife out and plunging it back in, over and over.

Nick grabbed my hands and stopped me in mid-strike. "Cadi, stop. He's dead."

I spun around, the anger eating at me from the deepest parts of my soul. I could hear his thoughts soothing my mind. He locked eyes with me and willed me to calm down.

"Ready for the hard part?" he asked.

Hard part?

"A pig has different bone structure than we do. You have to know exactly where to strike him. You'll only get one chance and if you don't do it, we're all dead. Where on my body is my heart?"

I pointed toward the general area of his chest.

"There's a rib blocking you there. What do you do?"

"I go a little lower and bend the blade up." I didn't like the direction this was going in.

"Show me."

"What? No!" There was no way I was going to stab him.

"It's just a kitchen knife. It won't kill me." He stood firmly with his hands to his side as if there wasn't an ounce of concern in his mind.

"I can't..." I stammered.

Nick shot me a stern look. "He's already proven that he can fool your eyes and make you think he is me. You have to trust me and be willing to do it no matter who he looks like. Now I want you to show me that you can do this or we'll call the whole thing off."

With a shaking hand, I placed the tip of the knife against Nick's chest. Squeezing my eyes shut tight, I pushed the blade against him.

"And... he just killed you," Nick slapped the knife away from his body.

I opened my eyes and saw the smallest drop of blood underneath the tiny hole I'd made in his shirt. He'd probably hurt himself worse shaving. I started over, placing the knife against his chest again. He grabbed my hand before I could push it in.

"Come on Cadi. You can't start with it against my skin. You need to build up force or it will never go in." He moved my hand back toward my own body. "Start there. You're the perfect height to thrust your hand straight out. Once it's in two inches, go up. Got it?"

I braced myself. Nick dropped his hands to his sides again, completely trusting me even though he knew what I was about to do.

Again, I imagined it was Zandros standing in front of me. Pulling my arm back against my torso, I shoved the knife forward as quickly as possible. Keeping my hand as steady as I could, I felt the steel sink into his flesh. I could feel the blade hit a rib and arched my hand just enough to go in farther.

His hand grabbed mine just before the tip of the blade managed to pierce his heart. His eyes bulged in pain as he withdrew the blade from his body sending a spray of crimson fluid across the shack. Blood poured from the wound. Stumbling backward, he dropped the knife and fell into the table, knocking the pig to the ground.

I rushed to his side, trying to catch him before he hit the floor. Slowly sinking to the floor with him cradled in my arms, I cried, apologizing over and over.

Nick held up a finger and spoke with a raspy voice. "I think you've got it."

"I hate you for making me do that." I sobbed, using the hem of my skirt to wipe the blood from his face.

"I'm not too thrilled either," he coughed. "I'll be fine, just give me a few minutes."

He closed his eyes and passed out in my arms. I held on tight, pressing my hand against the wound in his chest. The only comfort I had was the fact that I could feel his heart beating.

I wasn't sure how much time passed. The blood had stopped pouring out of his body some time ago but he remained unconscious.

A gentle knock on the door snapped me to attention. I didn't know who could possibly be out there. I watched in fright as the doorknob slowly turned. Relief washed over me when I saw Alex's face.

He looked shocked when he saw all of the blood. "Do I dare ask what happened?" He looked all around and saw the pig rotting on the floor next to us.

"He wanted to make sure I could do it." I leaned my head against the wall.

"Well I guess you can." He leaned over and pulled Nick's shirt up. After examining the wound he seemed satisfied and stood up. "He's already healing. Let's get him inside."

Alex pulled Nick up and threw him over his shoulders in a fireman's carry. I led the way to the library. After depositing him on the couch, Alex stood up and looked around. There was sadness on his face when he noticed the dilapidated condition of the few books that remained. He casually picked up Aiyana's diary and flipped it open. Scanning the pages quickly, he put it down and turned back toward me.

I was busy trying to make Nick as comfortable as possible, pulling off his boots and covering him with a blanket. When I finished being the nursemaid, he cleared his throat.

"I am ready whenever you are," he said.

I looked up at him. "You have the sword?"

He nodded. "Are we still planning on Sunday at sundown?"

I didn't want to wait that long. "Tomorrow," I said. "I want to get this over with as soon as he wakes up."

Alex agreed. "Fine then. Can I ask you for a truth?"

I cocked my head to the side. "I've always been honest with you."

"Do you love him?"

I wasn't sure how to answer Alex. Of course I felt a strong attachment to Nick, but love was such a broad term. What I felt for Nick was intimate, but so were my feelings for Alex. Even though it was different, having feeling for both of them left me confused. Regardless of the degree, I did love him, so I nodded.

"I have something for you." He reached into his jacket and withdrew a small book. "It's something I found a long time ago in an old library and only recently realized that you should have it."

He handed it to me. Opening the leather bound cover I found words written in a language I couldn't read. "I don't understand any of this."

"You will, when the time is right," he said mysteriously. Slowly walking to the door, he turned at the last minute. "Call me if you need anything. If he isn't better by the morning, I can help. Otherwise, be at my house tomorrow by five o'clock."

I thanked him and watched him leave, wishing he would've stayed. Holding the book in my hands, I sat at the end of the sofa and pulled Nick's feet into my lap.

By morning, the blood on Nick's shirt had dried to form a flaky brown crust. He sat up and gently kissed my cheek to wake me up. "You look like crap," he grinned when I opened my eyes. "I think you need a shower."

"You're okay?" My eyes flew open with realization. Grabbing the hem of his shirt, I pulled it up to see the wound. There was nothing but bloodstains on his skin. Running my fingers across his chest, I found it to be as perfect as it ever was. "Thank God," I sighed.

He stood up. "I'm going to take a shower. If you don't want to wait, there's another bathroom downstairs that you can use."

I got up and stretched my sore muscles. Grabbing my bag, I went to the other bathroom and took a shower. It took a while to get all of the blood out of my hair and when I was done, I threw my dress in the trash bin. Heading back up the stairs, I noticed Nick's father was passed out in the living room again, more bottles littering the floor as if he'd never moved. Shaking my head sadly, I went back upstairs and found Nick already dressed.

"We're doing this tonight," I announced. "I don't want to wait until tomorrow."

"What about graduation?"

I smiled. "That will be our victory celebration. Alex said to be at his house by five."

"What do you want to do until then?"

"This may be the last day of our lives." I looked at him solemnly. "What would you regret missing out on?"

He pulled my body close to his. "For the first time in my life I actually have hope for the future. The only regret I would have is not seeing your face tomorrow."

I blushed. "Well we have seven hours before we have to be at Alex's."

"Then we'll go pretend today is normal and do whatever it is that girls like to do."

The mall was filled with people; kids milling around lazily, parents shopping for the perfect last minute gift, senior citizens getting their daily exercise. Nick and I walked through the crowds hand in hand, stopping to window shop every now and then, lounging in the center court to share an iced coffee. After tossing the empty cup expertly into a bin, he pulled me back into the fray of things.

Pausing outside of an expensive jewelry store, he stood behind me. "Someday, I'm going to give you one of those," he said wistfully.

"I thought you didn't believe in marriage? In fact, I do believe you said you weren't even the dating type." I teased him when he pointed to the display of exquisite engagement rings.

"And I do believe I also said you've managed to change my mind about everything." He kissed the top of my head dreamily.

"Well first, we need to get through tonight." I took his hand and pulled him away from the store. "And then I think we should discuss the possibility of actually dating before you go planning out the next century for me."

He laughed and followed along, stopping in various stores to examine the merchandise. With a wicked grin, he dragged me into a lingerie shop. Grabbing a corseted bustier, he held it up with a grin. "You should totally wear this tonight."

My skin heated with embarrassment. "Stop it!"

Nick shook his head. "No really. It's sexy as hell, don't get me wrong, but it also will cover you up more than what you normally wear. Maybe give old-man Alexander a little less painful heart attack when he pretends to undress you."

I could see he was serious, and jealous. "It won't get that far. You have nothing to worry about."

He leaned over and kissed her. "Maybe I don't have to worry, but I don't like to share."

I took the hanger from him, too confused about his feelings for me to even make a smart comment. He went to the entrance of the store while I paid for it.

Released

As I walked out of the store, I saw my mom watching me. Her hand was covering her gaping mouth. Dad and Nick were caught in a rather heated debate.

"Mom? Dad?" I wanted to die of embarrassment. My own parents just witnessed me buying sexy lingerie.

Dad took the bag out of my hand and thrust it into Nick's chest. "Come on, Cadi. We're leaving."

"But..." I protested, begging Mom to intervene by some miracle. The woman stayed silent while the men stared each other down.

Nick tried to mediate for me. Very calmly, he stated the truth. "She is eighteen. And it's not like she's done anything wrong or sinful."

"We are leaving. Now," Dad repeated, ignoring Nick. "I'm sure you have plenty to do today. If not, there are chores to be done." He scolded me like a child, but I could tell he didn't say what he really wanted to.

"But I have plans to go see Alex today." I had no problem playing the Alex card since I knew how much Dad liked him. "Nick was just going to drop me off there."

"I'll take you myself," he barked.

Nick fell silent, glaring at the man as he forced me away.

"Was that really necessary?" I asked, climbing into his old pick up.

"I didn't know you kept secrets from me, Cadi." His voice was filled with disappointment.

I cowered down in the small backseat and fumed the entire way back toward our house. I was surprised when he actually pulled into Alex's driveway.

Stopping the truck near the house, he looked at me through the rear view mirror. "You said you had plans with him," Dad challenged, opening his door so that I could get out. "Is Alex aware of them?"

I stuck my chin out in defiance and climbed out of the truck. "As a matter of fact, Steven, he is." This was the first time in four years that I'd called him by name and could see the painful effect it had on him. Mom's tears were ignored as I stalked toward the house and walked in without knocking.

Leaning against the closed door, I waited until I heard the loud muffler leave the property before noticing that both Alex and Crevan were sitting at the table staring at me.

"I wasn't expecting you until later," Alex said. "Has Nikita decided against joining us tonight?"

I rolled my eyes and sat down with them. "No. My parents brought me here. I assume he'll be coming sometime soon."

Crevan grinned, the bubble popping on her lips. "I told you Bio-Boy was mad for you." She looked like she was about to break into an 'I told you so' dance. "Alex filled me in but I'm not clear on what I'm doing tonight."

I gave Alex a stern look. I didn't want Crevan there getting hurt. The less people involved the better.

"I need you to go home, distract Elric and make sure he doesn't try to interfere."

Her top lip jutted up. "Great. How so?"

"Take him to Melantha. That should keep him busy well into the night."

I cringed at the sound of my birth mother's name. If Elric went to her, she wouldn't be trapped anymore. Her name would appear in that God-awful book. I could think of worse things.

Crevan hopped up and skipped to the door when we heard the knock. With a huge grin, she let Nick in.

He was still fuming as he stormed over to the table and sat down.

"I'm sorry, I didn't know they were there," I apologized.

His anger seemed to disappear with a shrug of his shoulders. "Dads, what can you do?"

Crevan was about to explode. She loved drama. I noticed again how immature she seemed. Maybe she really was more like a thirteen-year-old girl than I'd thought.

"Go to Elric." Alex didn't give his sister time to start gushing.

"And tell him what? Where is she?"

Alex sat up a bit straighter, the puzzle solving mind at work again. "She's in a cemetery in Springfield."

Crevan pursed her lips. "That doesn't narrow it down."

Alex nodded. "Exactly. By the time you finally find her, this will all be over with, one way or another."

The blonde girl scowled and hugged me. "Good luck," she said. "I'll see you tomorrow, okay?"

I nodded, false confidence filling the air around all of us. "Are you okay?" I whispered into the hug. "You've been disappearing a lot."

Crevan just smiled and winked, mouthing "I'm fine" as she backed out of the room.

After she was gone, Alex turned toward me. "There are some details that need to be known before this happens; before it's too late to change your mind." He turned his attention to Nick. "What are Zandros' actual intentions for her?"

Nick stood up, hesitating to speak. Alex glared at him, not hiding his distrust of the young man for a moment. My hand reached out for Nick's but he moved to the other side of the room before he noticed. Alex saw it though, and he took a step that placed his body in front of mine as though he were shielding me from some invisible weapon that I couldn't detect.

"He said she had a special soul, one that would be a perfect mate." He took a deep breath, as if there was so much more to say about it that he didn't want to voice. Avoiding my gaze completely, he kept his eyes on Alex instead.

I could see every muscle in Alex's back tense under his shirt. His fingers tightened into two fists. Nick saw this and circled the room, placing the table between the two of them.

It was hard to breathe through the thick tension in the air when Alex cut through with the question I wasn't so sure I wanted answered.

"A perfect mate for who?" Alex asked?

"She isn't going to be his bride, she is meant to be mine."

15

Nick took a deep breath and continued when I didn't react. "He expects that our union will produce a child that would be able to overthrow the Dark Lord, which would give him ultimate power over the Shadow Kingdom."

Alex's instant glare shifted. "And how do you feel about such an arrangement?"

"I think it's stupid. First of all," Nick sat up straight and began ticking points off on his fingers. "You can't force someone into a marriage that they don't want. Secondly, you don't use a child as a pawn, no matter how vile their soul may be. And third, well, it's just stupid."

"What makes our souls so special?" I wasn't afraid to hear the answers anymore.

"Only one of our parents is demonic. The other is from Heaven."

This took Alex by surprise. He shook his head. "Neither of you have Veduny blood. I would have sensed it."

Nick gave him a lopsided grin. "I never said Veduny, I said Heavenly. One of our parents was an angel, sent for guidance, not vengeance. You would have been stricken down in awe if you'd ever seen my mother. I am assuming the same could be said about Cadi's father."

Alex acted as if he cautiously accepted Nick's word and turned his attention back to me. "When Zandros comes tonight, there is a good chance that one or all of us won't survive. Are you absolutely sure that you understand that and agree anyway?"

I nodded and watched Alex get up and start to pace.

"The Soul Seeker is a powerful weapon. It cannot be touched by a demon. Even if it doesn't take your life, it will cause you great pain just from coming into contact with it. When your fingers wrap around it, you're going to feel like your hands are on fire. When you strike his heart, you will wish you were dead."

I shuddered. Nick wrapped his fingers through mine.

"I don't have the healing abilities to fix your wounds, Cadi. You may be scarred forever, both your mind and your body," Alex warned ominously.

"I already said I would take her wounds," Nick interjected.

Alex stopped his pacing. "And who will heal yours? I cannot and I'm sure it will be equally painful for Cadi to see you suffer for an eternity."

My face fell.

Alex was right.

I couldn't bear it.

Nick shrugged. "Life is all about choices, right? I'm making this choice and as upset as you think she will be, it's better than her suffering the wounds. I won't let her."

All breath left my body at once. Just the thought of it made me want to back out immediately. Alex accepted Nick's determination and continued.

"Very well then, do you have any questions?"

Released

I was unable to form a solid thought, let alone think of a question. Even if we did survive this tonight, at least one of us would never be the same.

"Nick, please," I begged. "Don't hurt yourself for me."

"The woman shall be free to walk the earth unharmed." He kissed my hands softly. "It would be my highest honor, my reason for existing. Are you going to take that from me?"

I shook my head slowly, silently agonizing over the situation.

"It's time," Alex said quietly.

Nick handed me the shopping bag he'd dropped on the table. "Go get ready."

I nodded again and slowly went upstairs. I had to banish my negative thoughts, no matter what. In the next few hours, my fate would finally belong to me again.

I'd just pulled on my blouse and was quickly buttoning it when Alex knocked on the door. After receiving permission, he silently walked into the room.

"I'm very impressed with the both of you. Before I met you, I would've expected most of your kind to cower in a corner rather than stand up for what is right and moral."

"There you go again, assuming things about other people based on their DNA instead of their actions." I grinned playfully at him. "One of these days, you'll find that you've changed your way of thinking. Maybe we can all live in a peaceful world."

Alex nodded. "I've already reconsidered much. Once my obligations to my father are fulfilled I will be leaving the Veduny."

"What will you do then?"

He smiled wistfully. "Maybe find a wife, find out what a normal life feels like." His fingers found the top buttons on my blouse and nimbly attached them all of the way to the collar. "I have faith that you will live, but I must admit I fear for Nikita. When you take on the soul wounds of another, they are amplified tenfold. Only the oldest of our kind have the power to heal that, and even then it's near impossible."

I nodded in understanding. "I know you'll do your best."

I took his hand and started to walk toward the door when he stopped me. "What's wrong?"

Alex looked confused, as if he had something to say but couldn't find the right words. His mouth opened and closed a few times before sound finally came out.

"When we are in the clearing, out there waiting for him to come..." He paused, taking a deep breath, his cheeks warming with a deep blush. "I will kiss you, as a part of a charade. I know that you are involved with Nikita, but I care about you, a lot. I don't want the first time I kiss you to be a lie."

Butterflies danced in my stomach making my heart beat faster. I pulled him closer to me. He was tentative as he cupped my face with his free hand. The kiss he gave me was soft and gentle. Certainly, there was more than friendship behind the warmth of his lips, a promise of the possibility of more to come.

Someday.

Maybe.

He pulled back, the embarrassed blush still painting his face.

I smiled. "I read that the Veduny have no emotion and can't grasp the meaning of friendship. But you have been nothing short of the best friend a girl could ever ask for. I hope you don't disappear from my life as soon as this is all over."

"I will always be here for you Cadi. No matter how far my father sends me, I will never stop watching over you."

He squeezed my hand and headed out the front door, slinging a bag over his shoulder. Nick followed closely behind, stalking from a short distance.

Before we got too close to the clearing, Nick caught up to us and grabbed my hand. Pressing his lips to my forehead, he said nothing before releasing me. Neither of us wanted to say it out loud, but I knew it was his way of saying goodbye.

Once we reached the clearing and made sure Nick was waiting in the planned spot, I turned to Alex.

"I don't know if this is going to work." I was worried. Too many times Zandros had known my thoughts, my intentions. If he sensed this was a set up...

"Stop it." Alex grabbed my hand and squeezed it. "Stop thinking about it. Just remember what we planned and let it happen. I'll worry about the details."

"But what if it doesn't work?"

"Then it won't," he sighed. "But none of us will be around to care." He stopped and took my face gently in his hands. "Let's not think that way. Let's think of it as our big moment to defeat the hold he has on you."

"I'm scared."

He smiled warmly as my whole body shook in his embrace. "Good. Fear will keep the both of us on our toes."

With a deep breath and a winning resolve, I followed him into the field surrounded by a circle of trees. Once we reached the middle, Alex spread the blanket out on the ground. Pulling the sword out of the bag, he tucked it under the edge; out of sight but within quick reach.

"Remember, we just need to make him think this is really happening."

I nodded again and took another deep breath. Alex reached over to take the ring off of me but I stopped his hand. "What if I can't stop? What if the demon part of me takes over and I hurt you?" My voice shook.

Alex smiled, reassuring me. "Cadi, I have faith in you and I know my soul will be intact when this is over."

"No matter how this ends, I wouldn't feel safer with anyone else right now." I glanced over my shoulder to look for Nick. When I caught a glimpse of him, he was nodding encouragement to me.

Alex brushed his lips across my knuckles and agreed. "Me too," he said, breaking our connection and looking me in the eyes. "Ready?"

I nodded.

He took the ring off of my hand and slipped it onto the hilt of the sword.

Covering it back up with the blanket, he wrapped his arms around me in a tight hug. He slowly unbuttoned my shirt and pulled it open. I emptied my mind of all thoughts of anyone other than Alex and responded by pulling his t-shirt up over his head. I drew him closer to me, pressing my body against his.

We stood embraced for only a moment before the electricity in the air shifted. I could feel his heart beat faster, the adrenaline surging in both of us. Zandros was coming, and he was close.

"Just hold still," Alex whispered. "Relax."

Easier said than done.

How could I relax when I was about to die?

Zandros stepped out of a fissure of atmosphere in the field. Applauding, he stalked toward us slowly. "We finally meet, Veduny. I'm so delighted."

Alex stepped protectively between Zandros and me. "The pleasure is all mine," he replied sternly.

"I can sense that my lovely Carina has caught your eye, your heart even." He beamed with pride. "Very well done. It's not easy to turn the head of the chaste."

I cringed behind Alex. Please, just let this be done, I prayed.

"What makes her belong to you?" Alex demanded. "The word of a ten year old child? What exactly was the deal you made?"

Zandros looked thrilled to remember the moment. "Ahhh, that beautiful day when I was able to replace that pathetic disappointment with her perfect offspring. I guess Melantha wasn't a complete failure. After all, she gave me Carina."

Alex stiffened. "Melantha isn't dead, so how is it that you can transfer a soul debt from her to her child? Have your rules changed or are you just making up new ones as you desire? Why not tell Cadi Matthews the real reason you want her soul, because the lies you've fed her... Well she can't belong to you based on a lie now can she?"

His hand tightened around mine, signaling me to be ready.

Released

The challenge wasn't lost on the demon. He laughed an evil sneer. "I owe you no words, filth."

It was Alex's turn to laugh. He let go of my hand, taking a step away from me and toward Zandros. "I don't need to hear them to know that you've become the failure, not Melantha."

"I have failed nothing!" Rage filled Zandros' face as he charged at Alex. An unearthly growl emanated from his throat as he grabbed hold of him and threw him to the ground.

Alex landed with a thud but jumped to his feet immediately, grappling with his nemesis. The two fought in circles, tearing and scratching at each other.

Blood flew through the air, some splattering against my body. Horrified, I cried out. I was supposed to run to Nick, but I couldn't bear to see Alex being torn to shreds.

"No!" Running to the melee, I managed to get between the two men. "Please, stop!"

Zandros backed away a few steps, taking the opportunity to recover his composure a bit. Alex grabbed my arm, pulling me toward him, but I tore myself away from him.

"Promise me you won't touch him, or his soul, and I'll give myself to you now. Not just to your nephew, but to you too." This was stupid. I could just run away. I still had over two weeks left to live. Maybe I could run far enough away that he couldn't find me. One look into Alex's betrayed eyes said it wasn't going to work, but I had to try.

For Alex.

For Nick.

For my own conscious.

"Now you are beginning to finally make some sense," Zandros chided. Before I knew what happened, he was by my side, wrapping his disgusting arms around me.

Bile rose from the pit of my stomach, but I fought it back. Maybe it was just time to accept my fate so that my friends would be safe.

Cadi, no. What are you doing?

Hearing his thoughts, I looked Alex right in the eye and nodded slightly before turning my attention to Zandros. "Will you let him walk away right now? And you can have me right here, right now?"

Alex moved toward the blanket, but Zandros spun, watching his every move. There was no way he was going to be able to get to the sword in time.

Zandros ran his fingernail down the length of my throat, drawing beads of blood as he went. "You think I couldn't just take you any time I wanted? What makes you think I need to make a deal with you? It would be exquisite to eradicate more Veduny waste and top off the evening with a lovely moment with my new bride."

I cringed against the burning sting, but held as still as I could. The fingernail pressed in harder once it reached my collarbone. He was going to take my life, right now. My heart started to beat even faster, causing the blood to flow from the wound more freely.

I could hear the panic in Alex's mind, but couldn't decipher the foreign words. It only made my own fears worse. Closing my eyes, I braced myself for what was sure to be the end when I heard the strange cry.

"DRAW!"

Instantaneously flashing back to the times I'd teamed up with Steven against the twins, my body went limp and I dropped to the ground instinctively. At the same time, three circles of blood formed on Zandros' body. I saw the blood before I heard the gunshots that seemed to come from multiple directions.

One of the bullets went into the back of Zandros' skull and threw him forward. Stunned, he stumbled forward, trying to regain his balance.

Alex grabbed the sword without hesitation and, in one move, jumped to the fallen demon to slash his throat. The magic infused inside made the blade slide right through the flesh on Zandros' neck.

Nick reappeared from the tree line. The way the two men tore at Zandros' weakened body was like they'd rehearsed the moment a thousand times. Finally, Nick pulled the bloodied demon up and held him tightly from behind.

"For my mother, you can rot in Hell." His voice was different than I had ever heard before. It was clearer than ever, without a bit of anger. He nodded at me as Alex held the sword out.

Zandros' eyes bulged. For the first time in my life, he was the one who was filled with terror instead of me.

When I took the blade, it was nothing like Alex had described; it was worse. Crying out, it was all I could do to not drop the weapon and surrender to the pain. One look into Nick's eyes gave me the strength I needed.

Pulling my arm back just like he'd taught me, I let the agony and hatred that filled me drive the blade into the demon's chest. Sparks of electricity flew in all directions, filling my body with spasms.

Released

A strange red haze oozed from the wound, dancing in the air between us before finding my face.

Crawling into every orifice of my body, the smoke worked its way into my very being. Images flashed through my mind; memories of the thousands of terrors Zandros had been responsible for in his lifetime. I screamed in utter agony as the pain of the world filled my mind. Dropping to my knees, I clawed at the fiery blisters that were forming on my skin.

Nick tossed Zandros' limp body to the side and fell to the ground next to me. Wrapping his entire body around me and muttering a series of strange words, he somehow absorbed my pain, drawing the haze from my mind.

"I'm so sorry, Cadi Matthews," he muttered, falling to the ground beside me.

All agony was gone from my body, except for the excruciating pain in my heart. Nick was motionless on the ground, gruesome pustules covering his skin. "Help him, please!" I begged Alex.

The warrior stood over us, sadness filling the air. "I can't," he whispered.

I screamed into the nothingness that was filling my soul. Whatever Nick had done to take away the pain left me empty, terrified, miserable, and desperate.

"Please! Someone! Help him!" I begged the heavens.

Movement at the edge of the tree line caught my eye. At the edge of the field, I saw Steven with a Colt .45 lever action rifle resting on his shoulder. Sarah and Spencer flanked him on either side, each of them brandishing their own weapon. Their father spoke to them and the twins disappeared into the woods while he walked into the field toward me.

Alex went to my side and closely examined the wound on my neck that was already beginning to heal. Although the gash was still prominent, the bleeding had stopped. "It was what he wanted."

I held on tight to Nick, crying and wishing there was a way to heal his shivering, dying body.

"Sorry about shooting you," I heard Steven say calmly to Alex.

I hadn't noticed, but there was a round tear in the front of Alex's shirt, bloodstains running down his chest from the wound on his shoulder. "I'm fine," Alex said. He willed the bullet out of his body.

I was awestruck, watching the bloody metal fell from his body onto the ground at his feet.

Alex's entire form stiffened. He suddenly pulled me away from Nick and reached around my waist protectively. His mind called out to mine.

Everything is fine.

At first, I thought he was threatened by my father. Then I noticed another fissure forming in the air. The electricity shifted again. This time, a sweet smell permeated the field.

Elric walked toward us, amusement playing in his eyes. "Micah," he said, glaring at Steven. "We had wondered whatever had become of you."

"And now you know," Steven said, hitching the rifle back onto his shoulder casually.

"I see you've taken to the ways of the humans you so love. Guns are so barbaric." Elric said. "Tell me it's by accident that you're here, involved with these two half breeds?"

Steven shrugged, refusing to engage the pompous man in conversation.

Elric turned back to his son. "I've allowed you this one transgression. Now that you're finished, I expect you to fulfill your duties immediately."

I was torn between guilt over Nick and having to say goodbye to Alex so soon.

"Please," I begged Elric. "Don't take him away yet."

"We don't barter the way your kind does." He looked down at Nick's lifeless body. "And in the end, what did you really gain from this anyway?"

Steven stepped over to the wounded boy. Laying the gun on the ground next to him, he rested his hands on either side of his face. I watched carefully until I felt Alex take my hand.

"He will help Nick as much as possible."

I looked into his eyes. He was saying goodbye.

Right now.

If loneliness had a true definition, this was it. Nausea filled my entire being.

"Alexander!" Elric barked.

"I will always be near you," Alex said.

I could feel the cool metal sliding back onto my finger. Looking down, I could see the ring was back in its rightful place.

Released

As Alex and Elric disappeared into the ether realm, a sputtering cough caught my attention. Nick's chest was rising with each breath once again. The blisters on his face were nothing more than pink patches. Steven released his hold on the boy and stood up.

Offering a hand, he pulled Nick to his feet.

"Looks like I might have been wrong about you son," he said, helping him walk toward the trees. "Let's get you kids home. You've got a big day tomorrow."

***

Epilogue

From my position at the podium, I could see my family sitting in the crowd. One hundred of my classmates sat side by side, all dressed in the same black gown with mortarboard caps. Sadly, I looked at Nick's empty chair. Just as I was about to say the first word, I noticed two familiar faces standing at the back edge of the crowd.

Crevan waved and Alex just smiled.

I gave them a slight nod and took a deep breath before beginning the speech that I wasn't sure I'd be alive to give.

"Fear.

Other than the obvious excitement that today brings, that's the one thing many of us feel the most.

Fear of the future, the possibility of failure, fear of the unknown.

We've all worked hard in the past thirteen years.

Teachers, parents, friends and mentors have all helped shape us into the people we are today. But who will we be tomorrow?

We don't know yet, and that scares us.

If we all think back to our childhood, career choices were pretty limited. Nearly all of us wanted to be either a superhero or a princess. Now that we've grown and had a little taste of reality, we've learned those aren't really viable options. We can't sit around and wait for our Prince Charming; or hope that a radioactive spider will bite us.

Released

We have to go out there and figure out who we want to be.

Who we are meant to be.

It doesn't matter what world we were born into. Instead, all that matters is the choices we make for ourselves. We can be whatever we are determined to become, because that's what life is all about:

Making the right choices no matter how hard or scary they are.

Today marks a new beginning. It's up to us to decide what roles we play, in spite of our fears.

Once you've conquered that part, the rest is easy.

Congratulations and good luck!"

ACKNOWLEDGMENTS

For my ever so patient, kind, and sometimes absolutely dorky husband: You will never know how much I appreciate your kindness (even if I don't love you on Wednesdays). You never grumbled about a thing while I threw myself into this project, sometimes forgetting there was a real world out there even when you tried to remind me. You're such a great father to my children that it's no secret that 50% of Stephen is based on you.

For my amazingly beautiful children: I'm so glad you are the strong women this world needs. It's been an honor (and often an test) to watch you grow and I love you more than you will ever understand (especially on Wednesdays).

Extra special love to my "Handler":
Effie Applesluetzelbottomdude. You're my world Babe...

I couldn't have done this without the love, help, and encouragement of an amazing group of friends:

My sisters, Stephanie & Cassie: You are my rock, my light, and often the source of my insanity. I blame you both and now the whole world knows the truth.

My dear friends and Beta Readers: Rebecca Harvey, Steph Panou, Sonia Greeson, Mileena Phetsavanh VanTong, Laura Kolar, Erica Lucke Dean, Cheryl Murman, and Miranda Wagner. You ladies are the absolute best! Thank you for your careful eye, endless laughs, and occasional coffee breaks. You keep me sane when my sisters get too carried away (yes I just blamed them some more...)

Released

My Personal Paparazzi: Jennifer Slater, your lens captured my mental image of Cadi perfectly. Your talent stuns me more and more every day.

And last but so not in the least, my Social Media Angels and Demons (You know who you are), Thank you for all of your love and attention all over the internet. You have not gone unnoticed!

Jason Richbourg CEO and Lead Online PR Agent & Self-Appointed President of the International Sydney Raine Fan Club (It involves precipitation in Australia and his love for it),

The 550E Gang: Maggie Whittington, Marty McGraw, Derek & Bekka Fehr, Jamie & Mandi Horton, Rocky & Sheri Gray, Amy & Neil Hess, and honorary member Scott Gray

Tamara & Erin Morgan, Rebecca Harvey, Mileena VanTong, Cheryl Murman, Miranda Wagner, Kenny Turpin, and Janet Barker

My #1 Twitter Angel who's been my RT buddy since the beginning of time: @Emmie12750 Emmie (& Ollie & Toby)

@heidi124540 Heidi Butler, @SchmitzBeats Guego Schmitz, @13Godsend William "13" Morgan, and @hottotrot2002 Joann Cisell Hasch

And of course, I thank every one of you who took the time to read Cadi's story. I hope you enjoyed riding along! Come find me online, I'm always around somewhere...

www.ingramcontent.com/pod-product-compliance
Lightning Source LLC
Chambersburg PA
CBHW061551170626
46811CB00001B/161